The Art
of Escape

Linda Cross

First edition, October, 2013
Rising Hope Publishing, Wilmington, NC
ISBN-10:0615902448
ISBN-13: 978-0615902449

For David Charles Cross

—Twenty years and still cruising

1

Before the Sea

The invitations would be tricky. Marty sifted through mounded mail to find the form.

"Christine, the printer needs this by Wednesday. Let's get it done before you leave."

Christine had finished packing her purple Geo, impatient to start the three-hour drive back to school and her fiancé in State College, Pennsylvania. Smoothing the already perfect edge of a Nittany Lion sweatshirt around slim jeans, she sauntered into the dining area then flopped into a creamy leather chair across the table from her mother.

"April 27, 1999, St. Sebastian," she sing-songed to the ceiling, "followed by reception at The Oxford Room. What else do you need?"

Marty pressed the flat of her hand over her coffee. She let steam seep into the tender core of her palm until it became too hot to bear. Somehow, she'd gotten her daughter through the high grass of adolescence. Christine had gone off to college with the maturity to cut her own path, develop relationships, and plan a career. Now though, practically on the eve of her wedding, Marty noticed this childish response, her daughter's bitten nails, the nervous clothing adjustments, the hair twirling.

"Honey, you know what I need. The 'requests the honor of your presence' part."

"You're the host. You're paying for everything. Say 'Marty Arkus.'"

Ridiculous, a name like 'Marty,' in formal context. Why hadn't her parents settled on 'Mary Martha' or its reverse, instead of this jaunty compromise? Marty raised the coffee to her lips and inhaled its focus-sharpening aroma before sipping. She noticed Christine still avoiding her eyes.

"It doesn't matter who's paying. We can include your dad's name. I honestly don't mind."

She really did not mind. But should she? According to the psychologist, excusing Floyd's behavior was a more harmful example to Christine than appropriate rage would be. Still, Marty couldn't shake her own conviction. She thought her daughter was better off with a softer vision of the man whose genes she shared.

"Mom." Christine cleared her throat, pulled in her chair, and folded her hands on the table; a mature pose, ruined only when it unbalanced two stacks of sorted mail. "My paper's due this week. That's all I'm worried about right now." She swept in the fugitive ads and bills like the jacks player she'd been at age ten. "And I don't see why you would put Dad's name on the invitation when he can't even be invited."

"We've been through that."

"I didn't say we hadn't. That part's fine. But you can't make out like someone is this great host when he won't even be attending his own daughter's wedding." She picked up the guest list. "This whole thing is stupid. Half these people won't make it, and the ones we took off will be mad."

Potential guests had dwindled from over 200 to less than 70. Marty's co-workers at the paper, Christine's old high

2

school buddies, Christine and Sam's closest college friends, Sam's parents, and the few of his friends and relatives in California likely to make the trip to Pittsburgh.

Floyd and his extended family were off the list. Floyd had become far too erratic, and his parents and sister, who needed to believe this was all Marty's imagination, could hardly be invited without him.

Now, Marty's family was eliminated.

"When we started this thing," Christine said, looking at the scratched-off names, "it was mostly because of Grandma and Grandpa and Uncle Teddy coming from England. Now that they won't come, I don't even get the point. Do you?"

Marty covered her eyes, pushed caramel bangs off her forehead, resisted the impulse to twirl her own hair. Her parents and her brother Teddy had moved to London immediately after Marty married Floyd. She'd realized years later that her father's transfer had been his own arrangement, a civilized way to wash his hands of her as he'd wanted, as both her parents had surely wanted, since she was three years old.

"I didn't think Grandpa would expect you to schedule your wedding to coincide with one of their December visits."

Marty's father brought his wife and son back to Pittsburgh every year on December 17, and they returned to London every year on December 27. It never varied. Not even the year he'd had a searing case of shingles. Marty was now amazed she'd thought his only grandchild's wedding would merit an exception. She and Christine seldom saw aunts, uncles, or cousins unless her parents were in town.

When her father made it clear that the only wedding worthy of his attendance would be one held over Christmas week, the rest of these relatives were scratched from the list too. Let them wait for December. Then they could all flock to fuss and peck over Teddy, who was now, understandably, but unnecessarily and sadly, a 37-year-old child.

"I wasn't surprised about Grandpa," Christine said, building a little tepee of junk mail, "but I can't believe Grandma won't come herself."

"I'm sure he wouldn't let her."

Marty knew this was true, though she hated to admit it, but she didn't want Christine to feel that her grandmother wouldn't make the effort.

"What do you mean, 'let'?"

"Allow. You know Grandma. She'd never come without his permission."

"Grandpa's a chauvinistic dictator." Christine's wide eyes flashed, then narrowed. "How can he run her life that way?"

"He couldn't if she didn't let him. I consider it part of the deal she cut." What Marty also thought, when she could bear to think about it, was that her mother had endured a perpetual childhood. But there was no reason Christine should ever have to worry about that.

"Some deal."

"It's her life. Her decision. Most women in that generation made the same contract. You support us; I'll have your babies and run the house the way I want until you get home at night. Then we do everything your way."

–
4

"What do you mean, 'that generation'? You and Daddy were like that too."

"Not quite so much."

It was true. The breast-pumps-in-briefcases era had just gotten into full swing. Marty had worked from home, and only part time, when Christine was little. She'd fought for and feared for the surf and turf lifestyle her daughter was likely embarking on.

Christine rested her elbows on the table and her chin on her hands. "I always figured Grandma deferred to Grandpa because she felt guilty about Uncle Teddy."

"I did that, not Grandma."

"Mom, you were a baby yourself. Grandma should have been watching you."

"It was early. She was sleeping. It wasn't the least bit her fault. But you're probably right. I'm sure she felt guilty anyway. Mothers do."

Marty shook her head abruptly and picked up a cruise advertisement from the mail stack as it toppled again. She handed it to Christine. "Look at this. You and Sam should plan a honeymoon cruise."

Christine took the ad from her mother's hand.

"Yeah, if we could afford it."

She paged through the brochure, then, without looking up: "Is that what always made you defer to Daddy? Some kind of guilt?"

"I sure don't know what I'd feel guilty for."

"Maybe getting pregnant with me?"

"Honey, that's ludicrous. Having you was the best thing I ever did. Besides, he *was* involved." Marty tried to adopt a lighthearted tone. "Or did we skip that little talk?"

"Did he want to marry you, Mom?"

"Well, he did, didn't he?" Marty could almost feel the psychologist poking the back of her thick cardigan. She crossed her wrists and fingered both its unraveling cuffs.

"But he never seemed happy. I think he resented both of us."

"Don't be silly. Your father loves you. He has big problems. You know that. I can't fix them, and I couldn't live with him anymore. It had nothing to do with you."

Poke. She sat straighter, pushed up her sleeves.

"Mom, I know there were good times, but I barely remember them. I mainly remember my eighteenth birthday when he said the worst day of his life was the day I was born."

"That was the illness talking. He told you later he didn't mean it."

Some things in life are just too ugly; Marty excused herself, no matter how you tint your glasses. So we squint halfway to bearable, tell ourselves it's only a movie, a sickness. Besides, the psychologist's concern was that Christine would end up with a man like her father. She hadn't. She'd found Sam.

Marty reached across the table and took back the cruise brochure. "If you're serious about wanting a honeymoon cruise, I'd love to get it for you as a wedding gift."

"Sam would never let you do that. *We* wouldn't. Besides, the wedding is already too expensive."

"I don't think money is a problem anymore." That was true. After nearly three years of relative poverty during the separation, what lawyers called "equitable distribution" had occurred with finalization of the divorce last week. She would get the details tomorrow. She hoped she'd also get some solutions to Floyd's worsening harassment. Marty didn't want Christine to know any more about that than was necessary. She had witnessed enough to understand why her dad couldn't come to the wedding, but had no idea it continued, or had escalated.

"Speaking of weddings…" Marty picked up her pen and returned to the stationer's fill-in-the-blank form.

"Definitely just put 'Marty Arkus.'"

Marty heard sadness seep through the certainty. She put the pen down.

"Christine, how set are you on this wedding?"

"What do you mean?" Her daughter looked nervous.

"Not the wedding. The *church* wedding, the *reception*."

"I still don't know what you mean. It's all decided. The dates. Helen and Liz ordered their gowns yesterday."

"Okay. I guess that's what we'll do."

"What did you mean, how 'set' am I?"

"Well, I was just thinking. Look at this." Marty opened the cruise brochure to a page about cruise weddings. "If we changed it, and you got married on a cruise, you and Sam could have your wedding and honeymoon for no more than the cost of the wedding as it is now."

7

Christine studied the page. "But who would come?"

"I don't know. Maybe Sam's family. Maybe just me."

"So we could honeymoon with our parents"? Christine smiled through the sarcasm.

"Talk to Sam when you get back tonight, and think about it. Maybe Sam's parents and I could get off the ship after the wedding. Or maybe we could just cruise to an island where you'd like to honeymoon, and you could get married there and stay for a week. Something like that."

"What about Helen and Liz?"

"I could reimburse them for their dresses if it's too late to cancel. Do you think they'd be upset?"

"I doubt it. Liz was complaining last week about having to study for finals and plan my shower at the same time."

"Hell with 'em then."

"That's pretty much what I told her. Almost every bridesmaid I've known has turned on the bride before it was over anyway." Christine looked down at the stationer's form. "I think I like this idea. It would be less, I don't know... sad."

Marty felt a clutch in her heart. She nodded. "And this whole St. Sebastian, Oxford Room thing is probably more for me than for you anyway."

She waited, but Christine didn't deny it. The thought came unbidden: *Or for your Grandma.* "Talk to Sam. Let me know."

To the Sea

"Face it, Mar, you married an asshole. You had no way of knowing he'd become a psychotic asshole. It's not your fault."

Marty stared across the desk at her old neighbor Mike Pattern. She sipped the bourbon he'd foisted on her the minute she'd entered his downtown law office.

Plain and powerful, truth and whisky. Neither good.

Her gut still responded defensively to this judgment of her ex-husband. Floyd's descent had been so gradual, so inconsistent. She feared she'd caused it, and her vanity had often convinced her that she could control it.

"I saw his face at the settlement hearing," Mike added. "You should still consider a PFA."

"All a protection from abuse order will do is make it illegal for Floyd to come within a hundred yards of me or something. It don't think he cares if it's a crime."

"You still think it would piss him off more?"

"I know it. It would infuriate him. No telling what he'd do then. I wish they could just lock him up."

"He'd have to hurt you first," Mike said. "And you are right about the PFA. He can hurt you with or without it.

I'll trust your judgment that serving him with the order could make things worse."

Marty cringed. These were straight words, without sugar or mint leaves. This time there was no tinge of doubt in Mike's voice, no tone that implied "if what you've told me is true..." like she'd heard from so many before. Surely, she hadn't preferred that doubt? She cradled the Waterford tumbler in both hands like a child drinking milk. So, she was right. Paper wasn't bulletproof and the answer was that there was no answer. The cost would be her life, one way or another.

"The wedding is the least of it. I'm sorry. He shouldn't know where you live, where you work. From what you've told me and what I've seen, this isn't just harassment. He's stalking you."

Mike paused and Marty chewed her lip.

"And you're no safer because the divorce is final. It might get worse. Probably will. If you start in a new city," Mike said, "and give it all up, and I know, this means your home, your friends, credentials... That would be rough. I know."

He rounded his desk and reached for her now empty glass. "Here, let me fill this, or get you a soda or something."

Marty handed it up and blinked. "Just ice, please."

"Just ice?"

"Yes. Thank you. That's all I want."

"I know what I'm saying here," Mike spaded cubes from the bucket on his credenza, "but at least you'd have a chance. If you don't, the best that will happen is this terror will continue, and the worst, well," he paused to catch her gaze and held it, "you might not get another chance."

"I'm sorry," he said again, passing back the glass and taking the leather chair beside her. He leaned forward and turned to fix on her face even more intently, hands gripped between his knees. "I can't see another choice. If you were my sister, I couldn't see one."

Mike waited. Marty crunched ice. There was nothing to say.

"There is a woman," Mike said finally, "who helps people disappear. She used to be a skip tracer, someone who tracks down bail jumpers. So she knows their tricks."

Marty was confused. "Bail jumpers?"

"Never mind. I think she can help you. Her fees are high, but she can give you some good suggestions if you decide to take my advice." Mike took a business card from his pocket and handed it to Marty.

She read the card. Just a name, 'Katherine O'Malley,' and phone number.

Mike stood. "Give Katherine a call. You can afford her now. At least the settlement was fair. It should be a pretty decent stake for a new life. If that's your decision."

His words echoed off the bourbon in her brain as she trudged through Pittsburgh slush. "Your decision."

What decision? It's not fair. No justice.

Stunned by the awful reality, she eschewed the elevator and climbed five flights in the dank garage to clear her head. She stopped three steps from the top and rested her shoulder against the filthy concrete wall; considered plunking down on the gritty stair, simply waiting for someone to come and get her. *To kill me or to rescue me?*

Other people's words played back.

Her best friend, learning that Floyd had slapped her during their first month of marriage: "Get away from him. Put the baby up for adoption, or go to your parents." Then, when he'd straddled her chest, knelt on both her arms, and repeatedly punched her face four years later: "What the hell is wrong with you?"

The family counselor, ten years after that: "Why won't you protect your daughter?"

Floyd's psychologist: "Possible borderline personality disorder. Manic-depressive illness."

The priest at St. Sebastian's: "You can apply for annulment, but there is a child to consider."

The Baltimore Catechism had been Marty's manual for life. Marriage was a sacrament. "In sickness and in health...till death us do part," were vows for which she'd never been able to rationalize an alternative translation. And she could see herself through the eyes of her father. She'd dreaded having him learn she'd failed at marriage as well as sisterhood and daughterhood, and had once again failed to live up to her potential. God Himself had probably had it in for her since Teddy. She might have been only three, but it was no accident. She'd always remembered that sense of relief.

Heavy footsteps clomped on the lower garage steps. There wasn't a soul in sight, but the clomping put her on edge. He was getting closer. Marty tried to will herself forward, but her grip felt welded to the rail. When he lunged around the landing, she closed her eyes. He stopped. Labored breathing. Hers or the man's? She dared a peek. It was neither Floyd nor the hit man he'd once claimed to know and threatened to hire, but a scraggly string-mop of a teenage boy, surely no more than fifteen. A fat chain drooped from his pocket; one hand in a fingerless glove clutched the same rail that supported her. He lifted a grimy, lace-less sneaker to the next step and looked at Marty's shoulder bag.

"Got a buck you can loan me?"

When she didn't respond immediately, he added: "I need food."

Marty dismissed the idea of asking why he wasn't in school and considered the $20 bill in her wallet. He looked like he might buy drugs. Still, she couldn't let him go hungry. She reached into her bag and brought out the brown-sacked cheese sandwich and banana intended for her own lunch.

"Here's something."

The boy stared at her offering for a second. Then he climbed the remaining three steps, took the bag, and bowed elaborately.

"Thank you, Ma'am."

He walked a few steps beyond her to a trash receptacle near the elevator, raised the bag high over the metal drum, and dropped it in with a flourish. Then he strutted on toward the center of the garage, thumping cars with his fist as he passed them.

Marty took out her keys and clutched them like a weapon as she scurried to her old blue Buick in the first row.

A boiling sensation rose in her throat. She didn't recognize her own voice in the growl that spit through her mouth:

"You…lousy…little…creep."

She turned the ignition, screeched the car backward out of the stall, then forward and around the last car, nearly on two wheels, aiming for the boy. He saw her coming and raced for another set of stairs. Snapping back, Marty slammed on her brakes, but the Buick slid sideways into a parked Toyota. Air left her lungs in ragged sobs, her forehead rested on the steering wheel. Several minutes passed. Nobody came. She began to control her breathing.

"Get a grip," she whispered to herself.

She pulled away from the car she'd hit and got out to assess the damage: just a scrape on hers and a broken taillight on the innocent Toyota, *meaningless*, considering what she might have done. God, she couldn't let herself *become* this. Trembling, Marty opened her wallet, copied her insurance agent's name and number onto the back of a business card, added "Sorry I bumped your car," and signed her name. She slid the card under the Toyota's wiper blade, but as she walked back toward her own car, she changed her mind. Retrieving the business card, she jotted the Toyota's license number on it. She looked around the garage. Nobody else seemed to be on that level. She put the card back into her purse.

Then she drove straight past her newspaper office and went home.

Her room was dark when Marty came awake, aware despite the comforter against her ear, of heavy bootfalls below her bedroom window. She pushed the comforter down and pinned its muffling softness with her chin, concentrating. The furnace fan kicked off. Nothing. No, something. Just a car slush-patting down the main street, a block away from the second-floor rented condo where she had existed since the separation. She peered beyond her pillow to the clock radio: digital 4:52. Maybe a neighbor leaving early or coming home late, maybe a dream? No...it was beyond her open bedroom door, the hall, the living room...someone downstairs out front now, at the private entry. Trying the dead-bolt.

She brought the comforter around her shoulders, sat, and crossed its plumpness with clenched fists against her heart.

The doorbell, twice; then several minutes' pounding. Marty's pulse throbbed in her ears. She reached for the phone. She had neglected her past practice of setting the redial to a direct number for the local police before bed, and sat frozen, unable to remember it. Would this justify 911? The pounding stopped. A minute of silence, then the boots clomped again, a car door opened and slammed, and the familiar purr of Floyd's green Jaguar left the parking lot behind the building.

Even when she called, the police never came. "Without a restraining order, unless there is physical evidence," they told her, there was nothing they could do.

On Mike's advice though, she usually did call. The dispatcher knew her voice by now, and he would take down the information "for the log." The idea was to keep a record of threats, like the one just before she moved out of the house, "Nobody leaves here outside a body bag," and build some kind of a case. It seemed to Marty that she was merely helping them with their paperwork. If, or when, he did kill her, their evidence would be nicely organized.

There was no enforceable law against stalking in Pennsylvania; terrorizing someone, at least someone with whom you'd had an intimate relationship, was not usually a provable crime. In the months after the separation, there had been numerous incidents. They'd slacked off when Floyd started dating a woman with whom he'd been selling computers. Although he was supposedly living with her now, the threats had resumed several months ago, just before the divorce was finalized. She'd hoped the final papers would make a difference.

But Mike was right. It just wasn't going to end.

Marty made a conscious decision to breathe when the Jaguar pulled away, sank back into her satiny nest of covers and pillows, and paced each breath while she lay motionless for the next hour.

With daylight, she locked herself in the bathroom for a long shower. He usually spaced these a few weeks apart. The night's anxiety should, at the very least, have purchased a period of peace. St. Sebastian's chimed seven o'clock mass—a daily reminder of her failure—as she clicked off the hairdryer. She went down to the door in her robe for the newspaper.

The red roses on her front stoop assured her there would be no sabbatical. She lifted them by thorny stems and carried them to the kitchen trash almost tenderly, then squashed the love-turned-hate token down with all her might. Wracking sobs seemed to come from somewhere else as she felt thorns lacerate her fingers. Minutes later, she found herself sitting cross-legged on the cold vinyl floor, contemplating the blood on her hands, right index finger poised over a big drop on her left knuckle; a tiny red balloon. She touched it curiously, and drew its stain delicately down her ring finger. The blood paint faded by the time her finger brushed the old-lady vein she had noticed on the back of her hand this year, but she continued the motion toward her wrist, then around to its underside. Then she got up and washed her hands.

The detachment stayed with her throughout a routine day. Like driving through heavy fog, she made calls, conversed, and sorted notes, her to-do list the faint beacon of taillights ahead. Finally, she took the card from her wallet and dialed Katherine O'Malley's number.

Yes, Ms. O'Malley could see her at six.

Daylight was gone when she got home.

In the downstairs entry, Marty locked the door behind her, tossed the mail and her purse on the stairs. I'll have to get a console table in here someday, she thought, then remembered her meeting with Katherine. 'Someday' would be somewhere else. She needed time to consider it all. She turned to hang her trench coat and paused. The closet door was standing open. Odd. She attributed her trepidation to nerves, and hung the coat. It hadn't been a typical morning. Probably, she'd been so anxious to get out that she just forgot to shut the closet.

She picked up her purse and sorted through the mail, starting up the stairs. A Federal Express packet contained an inner envelope decorated with a bright green scallop, like a child's drawing of an ocean wave. Marty smiled as more cheerful anticipation edged her tension aside. The cruise documents had arrived.

She opened the envelope and kicked off her high heels. What a relief it would be to get out of this place. Out of town, maybe out of the country, for God's sake. She glanced through the papers—a Caribbean confetti of detail about island weddings and shore excursions—trying to stave off the edge of anxiety—paranoia, she told herself—that seemed to be pressing back in. She set the papers aside to check for bills. Junk. She dropped the ads on the dining room table. She sniffed. Tobacco?

Marty had started to wean herself from cigarettes a few months after the separation, when she realized she'd been using Floyd as an excuse for everything wrong with her life. She was down to one a day now, weekdays in the car on her way to work, and weekends at home with her morning coffee. It was Tuesday. If the odor lingered this long, she should switch to outdoor smoking now that spring was coming.

God, she could use one. She considered it, opened her purse as she parked it on a dining room chair, and took out the cigarette case. The old thing was filthy, but still rather elegant, Marty thought, fingering the tapestry-covered square that had belonged to Grandma Mary. It opened like a large powder compact and could hold twenty cigarettes. Marty had started using it when she decided to cut back, packing it daily with one less cigarette each week. Now she filled it once every twenty days and did not intend to stop. The process reminded her of the self-piercing earrings she'd once endured. It had seemed better than submitting to the quick sharpness of a needle punch. They'd felt like regular earrings screwed on too tight, and it had taken thirty-odd hours of torture before she couldn't stand it anymore and pushed them the rest of the way through her lobes. Glancing again at the cruise documents, craving nicotine, she considered the foolishness of her obsessive methods and ran her thumb to the edge of the slim case in her hand. The metallic click of its opening clasp snapped her resolve back, and she slapped it shut and headed down the hall toward the bedroom, already unbuttoning her skirt.

What she saw on her bed from the doorway froze her fingers to the button at her side.

Feathery red clumps desecrated the yellow matelassé coverlet. Marty gasped, then blinked to focus. Each broken, bloodied rose had been retrieved from the trash and placed in a symmetrical pattern across the bed.

Shaking, she stepped into the bedroom and pressed her back to the wall as she reached for the telephone. Their legal terms flitted through her brain as she dialed 911. "Physical evidence, breaking and entering…"

"Nine-one-one operator. What is your name?"

Marty whispered it.

"What's your emergency?"

Marty's throat closed. Was he here in the room? In her closet? Would he hear her? Did it matter?

She whispered. "Someone… my ex-husband… someone who's been stalking me…"

"Ma'am, you'll have to speak up."

"Broke into my house…" She still whispered. "He left physical evidence."

"Ma'am," the operator's voice was loud, and Marty pressed the phone hard against her ear, "I have you at thirty-seven Mockingbird Lane. Is this correct?"

"Yes."

"Is someone in the house with you now?"

"No. Yes. I don't…"

"If you think an intruder might be in your house now, leave the premises. Officers are on the way. You can wait for them outside. Ma'am?"

Marty slipped the phone back onto its cradle, then slid down the wall until her bottom hit the floor beside the nightstand. What if he was still here? He'd never let her get out.

She leaned forward to raise the dust ruffle, peering under the bedframe, then sliding out her weapon. She rose to her knees, then her feet, with the black aluminum ball-bat in hand. Outside traffic hummed nor-mal, nor-mal, nor-mal in the distance as she turned and looked toward her bedroom closet. God, God, give me courage. She gripped the cold bat tighter, then jerked the door open and attacked the closet's contents with vicious stabs. Nobody.

Marty twirled through the bedroom doorway and into Christine's room. The bedspread was off the floor by inches, so a quick bend cleared that area as a possible hiding place.

Christine's nearly empty closet stood open. No legs were visible beneath the few old skirts and slacks and blouses. Marty still clenched her bat, and she jabbed into the longer hanging dresses just in case. Relieved, she slid a clammy hand along the bat's gold lettering, took a deep breath, and then stepped back into the hallway beside the bathroom. She felt the pulse in her temple throb as she moved toward the door and peered in. The faucet dripped, a damp hand towel lay on the floor, the toilet seat was up. She gripped the bat with both hands and stepped forward. A cigarette butt floated in the bowl. The shower curtain was closed. She tightened her hands around the bat and could no longer breathe. The yelp she heard was her own as she swung her weapon through the curtain and blasted it aside.

She lowered the bat and breathed.

Okay, he's been here, and he wants me to know that, but there's no other place big enough to hide, so he's not here now.

She ran for the stairs, but at the landing, remembered the entry closet she'd have to pass. With a scream, she charged it, poked her bat into the coats for extra measure, opened the front door, and ran outside.

The cruiser pulled up.

After a preliminary explanation, the two policemen went in. Marty waited in stocking feet on the damp front lawn, shivering. Less than ten minutes had passed when one policeman returned to the door, "It's all clear."

She noticed an angry rash on the backs of his hands when he handed her the shoes he brought from the dining room. He steadied her balance as she slid them onto her wet feet, then Marty followed him back inside. They had checked all the windows and found one unlocked in the spare room, Christine's room. The screen was gone. Marty looked down to see it at the edge of the lot, beside a neighbor's van beneath the window. Floyd must have climbed from the van's roof to the ornamental brick ledge that wrapped the building's second-story base. The policeman flipped the casement's lever.

"You should keep these locked."

Was his tone accusing?

The other policeman was writing in a notebook. They *weren't taking fingerprints*. They were *touching the crime scene*.

"Shouldn't we leave things the way they are, uh, so that…" she tried.

"These locks are useless if someone really wants to get in," the first policeman said. "You need a track bar."

"Did you see this?" Her voice cracked.

The two policemen crowded into the bathroom doorway behind her.

"Yep," the one with the notebook said. We got it."

The first policeman took her elbow, and she pulled away, noticing his rash again, but he gently took the bat still clenched in her hands, set it aside, and put his arm around her. They returned to Marty's bedroom, and looked at the roses. He picked one up. Marty pointed out the smear of blood on the coverlet.

"Looks like he jabbed himself," he said.

"That's probably my blood." She held out her scratched hands. "When the roses were out front this morning and I put them in the trash, they jagged my hands."

The notebook policeman came into the bedroom and the two cops exchanged a look.

"Will you be able to arrest him?"

The notetaker evaded her question. "We'll go over and have a talk with him right now."

"But this is physical evidence. That's what they told me you needed."

They exchanged another look and moved to leave.

"But don't you need the evidence?"

It was apparent they did not intend to pick the roses up with plastic gloves and seal them in an evidence bag.

"Don't worry. We've seen it." The notetaker flipped through his pad. "Roses on the bed. Your blood. Cigarette butt in the toilet. You smoke?"

"Only one a day, that's not mine, I haven't smoked one in here for two days."

"What's your brand?"

"Winston."

"Looks like what's in there."

"Well, yes. But that's what he smokes, too."

"I see." He made another note, then started down the stairs.

He spoke into his radio, and Marty made out the word "domestic," in a tone that implied "squabble" more than "assault."

Now the other policeman followed him, and Marty brought up the rear.

"Should I stay here?"

"Well," the rashy policeman turned to face her as his partner went out the door, "you might want to go to a friend or relative for tonight and calm down. But you want your lawyer to file an order of protection, and you should keep this place locked. And put a track bar in those windows."

"But, when will I hear…"

"Don't worry. We'll call you if there's anything else. You call us if he comes back." He started across the lawn, then turned once more. "Don't forget those track bars."

Track bars. Marty couldn't conceive of making a trip to the hardware store and returning to a possibly-not-empty condo.

She estimated the length of Christine's window track to be a little over a foot, thought of cutting her broom handle to jam it, but didn't own a saw.

She rummaged through the tools she did have, kept in a pillowcase at the bottom of her linen closet. Maybe she could break the broom with this hammer. No, the hammer itself could serve as a jam! It slipped neatly into the window track. When she tested, it worked. The window would not slide open more than four inches. Satisfied, she started to search for something to block the track on the other back window, then realized that a hand could slip through the four-inch space, and maybe reach around to remove the hammer.

Back to the broom. Marty laid it on the kitchen floor. She kicked off her shoes, placed one foot about fourteen inches from the handle's tip, and tried to break the wood dowel by yanking up its ends. Impossible. She couldn't even slide her fingers under to get a grip. She positioned the broom across two chairs and tried cracking it with the hammer. Nothing. She tried starting a breakpoint by sawing with a kitchen knife. A scratch. Finally, she wedged it in the bathroom door by the edge of the vanity and, holding the door, crowbarred her full weight against the broom handle. The handle splintered. The piece was a bit long, but she managed to jam it into the track. Then she repeated the process—this time, breaking a door hinge and ruining her pantyhose—to split a length for the other back window.

This was crazy! What the hell did they expect her to do? If they didn't arrest Floyd, and it sure hadn't sounded like they would, was she supposed to board the place up and lock herself inside? She left the splintery mess behind, went to the dining room; got her cigarette case, a lighter, and an ashtray; and took them with her to the computer desk behind the table.

Twenty hours later, she was able to sleep, ensconced with essentials and a large amount of cash in a bed and breakfast in Lewistown, close to State College, where Christine and Sam were about to graduate from Penn State University. There was a "Stop mail- no forwarding," at her post office, a closed account at her bank, and an apologetic letter of resignation—alluding to her mother's health and an immediate opportunity in London—on her editor's fax machine. The evidence roses were in the dumpster behind her building, along with the food—no time for guilt about hungry homeless when you're rushed to *get* homeless yourself—that had been in her cabinets and refrigerator. Nearly everything she owned was in a rented storage locker at a nearby "Hold It." The locker rent was paid in advance with cash and under Katherine O'Malley's name. Marty had paid her $800 fee for an hour's worth of advice, but had balked at buying or using a fake ID, so Katherine had offered the use of her own name for this purpose only.

Under her own name, Marty had purchased a one-way plane ticket to London—first class—and submitted a rental application for an apartment in London. She would use neither of these, but the investment would create a paper trail that should mislead anyone Floyd might hire to follow her. All were charged to her credit card, and full payment would be mailed with the new London apartment as change of address, postmark "U.K.," with her mother's innocent assistance. Marty prepared two sealed envelopes to be enclosed with a letter reminding her mother to forward the mail on her behalf. One envelope was her credit card payment; the other was addressed to a London bank, and it contained a travelers' check pounds deposit and all necessary documentation to open an account. Her mother would believe this was just a housekeeping chore that Marty wouldn't have time for on the cruise.

Utilities were paid and scheduled to cancel. The landlord had the key to Marty's condo, her notice of intent to vacate, and two months' final rent. She would spend six weeks until the cruise in this tiny room of a big Victorian, less than an hour from the apartment Sam and Christine shared during their last semester.

Marty woke just before dawn and placed an overseas call collect from the telephone beside the B&B's canopied bed.

"Mom?"

"Marty, is something wrong?"

"No. I'm sorry I'm making you pay for the call. I'm not at home now, but I wanted to let you know about Christine's wedding."

"Don't be silly. I'm glad to pay. I just thought something might be wrong."

"No. Nothing's... Well, about the wedding..."

"Marty, I'm so sorry we can't make it. You know I wish…"

"I know. That's okay. We aren't having it now."

"Christine broke off her engagement?"

"No, no. We're having the wedding on a cruise." Marty twisted the phone cord around her wrist.

"Oh! Well, that should be nice." Her mother's tone said anything but. "Do cruise ships have priests?"

"The ceremony won't be on the ship. I guess the captain would have to do that. This will be on the island of St. Croix."

Apparently "St." in the name of the island had enough religious nuance to satisfy her mother, because she now said it sounded wonderful. Didn't ask the date or anything else, but did say "wonderful."

Marty cleared her throat. "Well, the thing is…"

"Do you need money? Is it much more expensive?"

"No. Not at all. In fact…"

"Because I'm sure your father would be happy to…"

"No, Mom. I don't need money. The divorce is final now, and I got my share of the money. What I need is for you to mail some bills. We'll be gone a couple weeks, and I don't want to pay these too much ahead. I'll just send you the envelopes and you can pop them in the mail."

"Your father has automatic banking. You should try that."

"I know, Mom. I plan to. But just for now, will you mail the bills I send?"

"Of course I will. And I'll mail Christine's gift too. How do I mail it to St. Croix?"

"You don't, Mom. Just send it to their new place in Raleigh. Sam's starting his job down there. He's already rented a place. Christine and I will board the cruise ship in Florida, and Sam will move down to Raleigh first, and join us on one of the islands. Do you have the Raleigh address?"

"Let me get a pen. No, let me call you back. I promised Teddy his cheese and pickle sandwich right before you called."

"That's okay, Mom. I'll send it to you. Don't forget to mail my bills."

"Love you, honey. Bye."

"Mom, wait! One more thing. You know Floyd isn't invited to the wedding, don't you?"

"Of course he isn't. You didn't want him bringing his girlfriend, and I don't blame you."

Marty gritted her teeth. The girlfriend had actually been a relief, but that story had been an excuse her parents would accept easily.

"Right. Well, we aren't telling him about the cruise because we're afraid he'll try to bring her, so if he would happen to call you, don't mention it, okay?"

"Marty, he never called here. I don't think he would now. But that's fine. I won't mention it if he does. You know, Teddy is waiting…"

"Okay, Mom."

They disconnected and Marty blinked a few times as she unwound the phone cord from her wrist. Poor Teddy. Poor Mom.

Marty had no inkling where she would go after the cruise, but she knew for certain she would not be going home or to London. In the Limbo of waiting to decide *when* to decide, she drove to the Harrisburg mall each day and shopped with cash. She shopped for cruisewear and Christine's wedding gifts, and she dined in the food court. Some days she sat beside the beautiful Susquehanna River and pretended she lived on one of its tiny islands. Her extra week on the cruise, after Christine and Sam disembarked for their island honeymoon, would be time enough to plan the future. For now, her only daughter's wedding would be the focus.

3

Night Three, At Sea

The elevator doors slid together, their embossed pattern forming an ancient ship. A whimsy in pressed tin, the vessel plunged from a frothy crest toward a lute-playing nymph. Marty stared at the design, registered the descending hum that would deliver her daughter to Baja Deck, and considered her options. The prospect of fitful hours in her own stateroom held no appeal, so she strolled back toward the edge of the lively Lido Deck crowd.

Christine had just hugged her 25th new friend and headed for her mini-suite, explaining that she needed the early night. Ten was early compared to their first nights onboard. So much activity, so many friendly strangers, and so like Christine to fit it all in. Marty considered the improbability of joy in a future without her only child close by.

She smiled at the honeymooners who faced each other on bar stools, likely toasting their future. Christine had photographed them together five minutes ago, when she'd noticed them taking each other's pictures by turn and offered to help. Marty had noticed them first and considered making the offer. Then she'd remembered the kid in the garage who'd thrown away her lunch.

Over the years, she'd often felt like a skittish mare raising a self-assured colt. "A pre-lib woman in a post-lib world," Christine called her once. Marty had argued her journalism career as proof to the contrary, but they both knew better. Marty's lifework, the purpose of her existence, had been raising Christine and making a happy home. She'd failed miserably at the latter, but it wasn't her fault. Supposedly.

At least her return to school and eventual job had been an example for Christine, who rocketed through college with honors, and would be starting a career, simultaneously with a marriage, of her own. A rather pre-lib career, teaching. Marty smiled. She'd have to mention that.

Physically as well, it could be said, mother and daughter contrasted even as they paralleled—light and dark, soft and hard, short and tall—yet with sapphire almond eyes under startled brows so identical that teachers could recognize Marty the first time she walked into any of Christine's classrooms.

After the wedding and honeymoon a few days from now, Christine would move to join her husband 600 miles from home and would take her place in some unfamiliar classroom—this time at the front—one that her mother would probably never enter.

The sadness shamed Marty. Christine's wedding was a happy occasion. She wasn't preparing for grief here, standing some kind of deathwatch. No. The problem was not Christine's growing up, leaving home, getting married. The problem was Marty herself. She couldn't envision a future at all beyond the next weeks. Couldn't imagine where she might live, or how she could be safe once this ship returned her.

Marty took a step back toward the elevator, but the band kicked up and changed her mind. She lingered with the night rhythm and even let a smile stretch her lips. Calypso. Appropriate. Calypso, who delayed Odysseus on the island of Ogygia for seven years in Homer's *Odyssey*, must be the nymph on the elevator doors. Turning to face the moonless Atlantic, she inhaled its magical healing salt. If she could stay on this spot long enough, she'd forget all of it. She could easily imagine staying for seven years. They were still at sea, but St. Thomas twinkled in the distance.

His voice startled her.

"Fifty-five thousand people on that rock."

An owl-bespectacled blond man moved in beside Marty at the ship's rail. Together, they looked toward the distant shimmer that was St. Thomas.

"Fifty-seven by morning," she said, rocking her shoulders with the calypso rhythm of the Sundowners band behind them.

He didn't respond at first but withdrew a piece of cardboard, stuck with metallic stars, from his tuxedo jacket. "Blue for those who know the passenger count," he said, "but gold if you know how much that island population will really change by tomorrow."

Marty laughed at herself, realizing she wanted the foil star. "How about a hint?"

He offered his arm and exaggerated his tone to one of grand formality.

"For that you will have to accompany me."

Apparently noting her confusion, almost alarm, he added: "Don't worry. I can't spirit you off to the hills before we dock. And we won't leave the deck."

Marty considered, and feeling silly for her nervousness, strode aft along Lido Deck with her instant escort. His name was Garrett Maxin, she learned, but when she probed for more, her rather odd-looking companion reminded her that they must concentrate on her shot at the gold.

They made half a lap, peering down to Riviera Deck through a large cutout in Lido's center.

"Three bars, one under water." He narrated, as though quoting the brochure. "Two swimming pools, and four hot tubs to the inside."

Marty paused to look down at the pools, one empty of swimmers now, and still. Even by night, it was impossible to imagine the tranquil decks along those blue, blue pools as anything less than inviting. Garrett took her arm and urged her toward the outside rail. He could not have been taller than five-six. In three-inch heels, she was shoulder to shoulder with him. Marty liked that, but could not think why.

"I never get tired of ocean nights," he said.

She stared into inky skies then down to the Atlantic-now-turning-Caribbean Sea. Barely perceptible phosphorescence skittered along the comforting vastness. Several tiny lines of light glimmered among distant waves. Other cruise ships. *Mare Majestic*, with her 2,000 stargazing, gourmet-dining, ballroom-dancing passengers, was just a line of light to all of them.

Garrett released Marty's arm and turned to face her, smiling open-mouthed anticipation. Marty took a step back.

His teeth were not entirely straight, but gleamed white. Quirky looking, but attractive. And those shoulders. His green eyes sparkled behind the little round spectacles, and he seemed to follow her gaze.

"Still thinking," she said, and started to walk again.

But they had passed the elevators and were back at their starting point before she managed to remember the question.

"All of these ships are headed for St. Thomas," Marty recited like a TV quiz show contestant, "and more are probably coming from other sides of the island. Okay, then I guess the population of St. Thomas will double by tomorrow. No. Wait. Technically, we won't become part of the population." She laughed now, warming to the inanity. "No, that's silly, wait again. There are other cruise ships leaving the island tomorrow, and we're just replacing them. It's the same. The population of St. Thomas will be the same tomorrow as it is today."

Garrett peeled a star from its backing. "Do not think for one minute," he warned in exaggerated playboy speak, "that you won this award just because it matches the color of your hair exactly."

He paused, then held the golden star where her cape of cream cashmere had fallen away from her shoulder. She laughed, more nervous.

"But also do not think," he said quietly, pressing it gently to her gown, "that I don't know pure gold when I see it."

Flirtation was a forgotten experience for Marty, married since adolescence. Compliments had not been part of Floyd's repertoire. She gasped, then felt her face go pink as she realized he must have noticed.

She looked out to sea. "My daughter..." she began, with no idea what else to say.

Garrett interrupted. "Your daughter is probably dreaming bride dreams by now."

Marty squinted and almost felt the memory shuffle into consciousness.

"Oh, the blood test!"

Garrett, previously introduced as the ship's Dr. Maxin, had come to their rescue in the first day's panic when bride Christine and her mother realized paperwork for the marriage license must have been shipped to Christine's new home. Dr. Maxin did Christine's required blood test, and groom-to-be Sam faxed his own results so the license could be issued. Marty hadn't recalled Garrett's face. She wasn't sure she had even looked beyond his nametag that day, but the deep voice was familiar.

"I never did make a strong first impression," he said, then offered to buy her a drink.

"On the condition that it not be in the underwater bar," she said.

He agreed, "On condition that it not have one of those little umbrellas."

He led her up to Tower Deck, where a small lounge provided privacy and a panorama of the night outside. Garrett handed the table's dish of garlicky cheddar snacks to the waiter and ordered champagne and slices of apricot-almond cake. Then he took a rose from the centerpiece vase and presented it to Marty. She shrank from his offering, pressing her back into the chair and folding her hands tightly on her lap.

"Allergic?" He moved it away from her, puzzled.

She knew it was rude, she felt downright mean, but she couldn't help it.

"No. Sorry. I just—"

"What? Hate flowers?"

"No. Just roses."

"That's okay. No problem. Here."

He returned the bud to its vase and moved the vase to the table behind them like someone locking a Golden Retriever in the basement to placate a nervous guest. This was not going well.

The waiter brought their order. Garrett toasted "new friendships," and the awkward moment passed. He inquired about her cruise so far, and when Christine's fiancé was expected. Marty explained that Sam Joly was scheduled to board the ship at Sint Maarten, which would be Day Five of the Eastern Caribbean leg of the cruise. The wedding would take place at St. Croix on Day Six, and Christine and Sam would disembark at Eleuthera Island in the Bahamas on Day Eight to continue their honeymoon. They would fly home a week later to Raleigh, North Carolina, and begin married life.

"I like your Day Five, Day Eight," Garrett said. "You speak cruise."

Marty smiled. "She'll only have three months to find a teaching position, but she isn't worried. There's a real shortage of math instructors, especially in the South."

"When do they usually hire teachers?" Garrett seemed interested, but he refilled her glass as he spoke.

"August. You might want to give her some of those stars you carry around," Marty said, fishing for an explanation of what might simply be his woman-sticking props, "to encourage her students."

Garret laughed and patted his pocket. "Took these from Little Majesties, our kids' program. I stopped by to introduce myself, let them try out a stethoscope."

"Oh, so they won't be afraid if they need a doctor on the cruise."

Garrett nodded.

"That's a nice policy."

"Not really a policy. Just a thing I did today. There aren't many kids on this cruise, a few young ones. We get more mid-summer and Christmas."

Marty told him she would remain onboard for *Mare Majestic's* next cruise, using the time to rest, check out the *Western* Caribbean...and make some plans.

"What sort of plans?"

She shrugged, nibbling cake.

"Now you're being mysterious."

She did not respond.

"What?" He smiled and waited.

"Well, my divorce was finalized recently, and I might be looking for a new job soon." She paused, then added: "Maybe a new field."

Garrett probed, and she told him about her work at the newspaper.

"Officially, I'm a news reporter, and there's getting to be some pressure to do more of that. I prefer features. Living. Style. You know. What they used to call 'women's pages.'"

"Don't women still read?"

She laughed. "It's not P.C. to imply that it's all we read."

"What's your favorite section?"

"Science, actually, after the front page and advice columns. I'm just not sure journalism's right for me anymore. I was really looking for flexibility when Christine was young. I started writing freelance articles for a local paper so I could work from home."

"Was journalism your major?"

"Yes, but only because I was already doing it for the convenience."

Was this true? As she said it aloud, Marty realized that it probably was.

"I didn't go to college until Christine started school. I like to write, but I've never enjoyed reporting. Not the hard news. Things people don't want to have written about them."

"Guess I can understand that, but it is important work."

"It used to be, when integrity was a reporter's stock in trade."

The quick set of his jaw registered shock. She hastened to prevent a bad impression.

"I guess that's not fair. Recent disappointments. Or maybe I'm just less assertive than most of my colleagues."

And maybe by-lines are pretty fair indicators of a person's whereabouts, she thought.

"I should introduce you to Congressman Brasheer," Garrett said. "He'll get a kick out of meeting a reporter who doesn't like to report."

"Richard Brasheer? From Florida?" Marty recognized the name, and Garrett nodded.

"Isn't he the one who just proposed some kind of anti-stalking legislation?"

She wondered if Garrett knew something. No, probably just a coincidence. She'd have to watch this creeping paranoia.

"That's him. Thinks we should make it a federal crime for people to terrorize ex-bosses and jilting lovers because state laws vary so much."

He poured more champagne into her glass and met her eyes.

"Frankly, I need a date. He's cruising with his new wife, and I'm slated to have dinner with them tomorrow at the captain's table."

Marty sipped the elegant fizz, then rubbed her nose.

"Would you join us? I think you'd find him interesting."

She took a breath. "I'm not sure. Federal anti-stalking laws are a good idea, but I don't have a special reason. I mean, I'm not planning to write about the legislation."

Marty concentrated on her glass, rolled the stem between her palms.

"Somebody should. It's not just a good idea, it's long overdue. Laws vary too much from state to state. If a guy just makes a threat, it may or may not be grounds for arrest. Depends on where he lives. If it is grounds there, he might move and continue inside the law."

Marty nodded and looked toward the wall of glass, feigning disinterest.

Garrett leaned across the table as he spoke. "Some follow through. Even if they don't, their victim's lives are wrecked. They're afraid to go to the store. To work."

Marty hunched into the cashmere on her shoulders.

"You cold?"

She shook her head.

"They have security systems installed," Garrett went on. "Can't sit on their porches. They buy guns for self-protection and then can't sleep because they're afraid to have a gun in the house. Or in their purses."

Marty hadn't bought a gun.

"What got Congressman Brasheer going on this?" she asked.

"Don't know."

"He's been divorced?"

41

Garrett laughed. "I know what you're thinking, but I've met his first wife, and both his sons. They've taken at least two of my cruises. Richard came by himself last year, spent time with a woman onboard. I wondered if they'd show up together this year, but the new Mrs. Brasheer is not her. Seems a lot like his first wife in temperament. Not the stalking type. Intelligent, pretty social, I'd say. And of course," he added, "my first impressions are always golden."

Marty wanted a cigarette. She'd worked back up to five a day in the weeks following her decision to leave her life behind, and had resolved to quit entirely, or, at least, get back to smoking no more than one each morning. The pack she'd brought on the cruise, just in case, was still in her stateroom. It hadn't even been difficult. Why she'd want one now, and at night? Well, she wasn't used to drinking much, certainly not champagne.

She smiled. "It's been fun, but I'd better be getting back."

He was behind her, adjusting her cape, ready to pull out her chair, before she could begin to stand. "I'll walk you."

Not sure whether it would sound more foolish to protest or to accept, she said nothing, but she took the cruise key card from her bag and clutched it as they boarded the elevator. Marty started to say goodnight after he bowed her through the doors at Caribe Deck, but he followed. Their footsteps on thin carpet were the solitary sound in the narrow hallway. Her grip on the key card tightened as they approached her cabin. She stopped outside the door.

"Well, what do you think?" he asked.

Did he expect to be invited in? Is that what people do?

"I really need some sleep. Christine will…," Marty paused, the card slid against the dampness of her palm. She was way beyond her element, a baby bird, proud to have made it two branches from the nest, but without a clue how to go farther or get back.

"I mean about tomorrow night. Dinner?"

Marty was confused. "Dinner?"

"With the captain and Congressman Brasheer? No reporting. Just a date. You shouldn't have to work on vacation."

She noticed his eyes sparkling again, avoided looking at his shoulders. *I'm such a fool. Is he laughing at me?*

"Of course. I mean, that will be fine. I'd like that."

"Pre-lib woman okay," Marty muttered, recalling Christine's gentle taunt.

She dropped her bag on the twin bed just inside the door and sat on the one nearest the balcony to rummage through the nightstand drawer. The cigarette case was where she'd tucked it the first day of the cruise. *What the hell am I going to do?*

She slid off her shoes and pushed the phone for room service to order coffee, then decided she might be better off knocked out than woken up. When Paras, the cabin steward, answered, she requested a bottle of chardonnay. He tapped on the door just after she'd finished changing into shorts and her Victoria's Secret "Country" sleepshirt. Yes, he'd be happy to bring her an ashtray as well. When he did, she took it with the wine and one of the two glasses he'd brought—apparently that *is* what people do—to the balcony, and settled on a chaise to await the arrival of St. Thomas and a plan.

She pondered the decisions and the stupid indecision that had resulted in this ludicrous crisis of identity.

Face it, Mar, you married an asshole. You had no way of knowing he'd become a psychotic asshole. It's not your fault.

Marty stood. She placed her wine glass on the table and looked out to sea over her balcony rail. She stretched, reached her arms out over the abyss then jerked back in near panic. The rail was armpit high; water never frightened her, and certainly, she was in no danger of plunging the 50 or so feet down to the waves below. But neither was she actually in danger during all of the nightmares that woke her these nights. The dream locations varied: a cliff, a rooftop, a Ferris wheel, the open door of an airplane; but the anxiety was enough to wake her in heart-pounding sweat just as her balance gave way. She realized it was all due to her perception that she lacked control. Well, she had taken control now.

This will be fine, Marty told herself. Chin on hands, she finally relaxed against the rail. Christine was having a great time on the cruise, showing no sign of mourning the big church wedding plans. When Sam arrived, she'd be even more excited. Besides, didn't lots of people, people who weren't fugitives for God's sake, go off to have their weddings on exotic islands?

This safe plan for Christine's wedding would also be the launch point for Marty's new life. She had two weeks to figure out what that might be, or at least where it might start.

St. Thomas appeared to be sailing toward her, rather than the other way around, even picking up speed, and Marty lost her nerve again and backed away. She settled into the deck chair beside her chaise, slid the table with the wine bottle over to use as a footrest, and stared over the balcony rail from this safe distance, up into the endless night.

When St. Thomas finally arrived, it was not in the company of a plan. Marty counted the ten cigarettes left in her case, corked the half-full wine bottle, and went inside. *I'll just sleep on it*, she thought. Then, remembering Calypso rhythms and sparkling green eyes, smiled as a Meatloaf song ran through her head. "Baby, baby let me sleep on it…"

———

He smudged a tear from his cheek with the heel of his hand and sat stone still, staring up through the transom until the sky darkened. Then he rubbed the back of his neck and adjusted the high intensity lamp again. Better than good enough, and good enough was all the new lettering would have to be for as quick as they'd glance at a license or passport. Just in case though—his fingers jittered over the keyboard—let's check out the university brag board on grad placements. Ah. A decision was in order now.

"One if by land, three if by sea," he recited aloud, "but I on your little ass *will be*!"

Home to Mummy, or Super-Mummy? He thought a while. Decided he knew how she'd think. He hated to waste his artistic achievement, but it might come in handy, even this way.

———

4

Morning Four, St. Thomas

The rickety jitney lurched onto a precipice for the photo stop. Marty released her grip on the seat and bailed out with Christine and ten other passengers, all eager for a respite in this wild ride north from St. Thomas's port of Charlotte Amalie. Cameras ready, most approached the overlook. Marty stood tiptoe behind Christine and reached around to cover her eyes. She nudged her to within a yard of the edge, and spread her arms, staying poised to snatch her daughter back if she should stumble.

"Magens Bay!"

Truce and Leon, from Marty and Christine's regular dinner table, were with the shore excursion group. They both clapped, and Truce cheered:

"Worth the bucks!"

Christine leaned back against her mom as they watched the sea nestle into its sandy cove like liquid turquoise spilling onto a sugar-drifted plate.

Marty had noticed the same Caribbean blue lapping the southern side of St. Thomas, back down the mountain, where *Mare Majestic* had docked at Charlotte Amalie. From the window of the ship's Regency Dining Room, the seedy port town had been pretty. Tiny buildings sprinkled its dark hills with a Froot-Loopy vibrancy. Christine reminded her mother that she had never seen an island before, and wasn't sure what she'd expected. Now, with the bay spread beneath them, she tried to explain.

"Maybe flat sand, a few palm trees, thatched huts? Like the island in my old turtle bowl?" She laughed at herself. "Oh, what a sophisticated world traveler am I."

Marty shook her head slowly and smiled. Sweet, sweet little girl. Hard to believe it's all gone so fast.

"Remember when Myrtle the Turtle died," Christine asked, "and we weren't sure, so we kept her a few days to see if she'd move?"

A horn tooted, and the protracted final hours of Christine's childhood turtle were trumped by the problem at hand. The group shifted uncertainly. Marty dreaded the prospect of climbing back into the jitney for the ride down the switchbacks to the cove. The others seemed to share her concern. She took a cautious look at their pot-smoking driver, who swung his head like a metronome set for adagio, brushing each bejeweled ear against a raised shoulder.

Another dreadlocked fellow, this one leading a gardenia-hatted donkey, ambled up. He hailed the gathering with a grin that split half his face and introduced them all to his donkey "Princessa." Marty heard a few soft clicks as Truce and another tourist snapped the donkey's photograph.

"Two dollah," he said, still smiling broadly.

"What, darlin'?" Truce asked.

Marty heard a few more clicks.

"Two dollah!" The smile was gone.

During the lecture that ensued about how he had to feed and care for the donkey and had walked all the way up here just for their picture-taking, Marty watched Leon videotape him. When the donkey owner noticed this, he demanded $10. Leon laughed.

Donkey man reached into his saddlebag for God-knew-what, and choosing the lesser of two terrors, Marty shoved Christine toward the jitney and grasped the rusty metal to pull herself up behind her daughter. Most of the tourists, including Truce, joined the scramble. Marijuana man took off down the switchback, and Marty saw Leon and several others—finally getting the picture—running behind the wagon, fumbling in pockets for donkey man money. She watched Christine pull a $5 bill from her fanny pack and wave it, calling to donkey man, who ran alongside to grab it, then bowed his thanks.

Marty grabbed a camera for a fat girl who was barely able to hoist herself onto the wagon as it jerked around the first sharp curve. In the process, her own bag dropped onto the dirt road. Marijuana man lost a wheel to the edge and regained it just in time, sending her on a slide across the seat, then slamming her back into Christine before she could grasp the splintery slats. She heard one passenger murmur prayers and another, not so lucky, mumble about lawsuits.

It wasn't until they reached the cove that Marty considered the import of losing her bag.

Cruise ships were a cashless society, with each passenger issued a "cruise card" to use as cash. The cards were convenient for the passengers who could charge shore excursions like this one to Magens Bay, pina coladas and casino chips, beauty treatments, paintings at art auctions, and boutique items such as the Llardo Madonna and Child sculpture that tempted Marty. They were a great idea for the cruise line, because passengers adjusted quickly to indulgence, and few bothered to total up their purchases. The programmed plastic also functioned as a stateroom keycard, and served as passport for disembarking or re-boarding the ship.

Marty's cruise card was in her bag. Her bag was at the top of the mountain, between the beach and donkey man.

She plunked herself down on the sand to wait for Christine, now basking in kudos across the road for her heroics during the donkey-man incident, and tried to decide what to do.

Marty caught her daughter's happy glance, then watched it dissolve as Christine spotted her and left the group. Guilty, Marty rose and forced a smile. She was about to make a joke of the lost-bag situation for Christine when a Jeep roared down to the sand, horn-honking, from behind them. A large safari-clad passenger rode its running board, waving a bright blue bag over his head.

"We got it!"

Marty approached the Jeep as it pulled in.

"Thanks so much. That's great."

She reached up for the bag. Then reached inside for money to offer a tip.

The powerful looking man waved off Marty's gesture.

"No problem, as they say in these parts. We were right behind you. Figured you could only be headed one place."

A silent woman with waist-length hair the color of rich red teak was in the driver's seat, and a lovely teenager rode in the back, wedged in behind a large, flat package that protruded a bit from each of the Jeep's open sides. The girl also had very long hair, auburn.

"Well, I really appreciate it. We're on a cruise—"

"Figured as much. Which ship?" He had stepped from the Jeep's board to shake Marty's hand.

"Mare Majestic."

"How about that, me too. I'm Richard Brasheer."

"I'm Marty Arkus. Are you Congressman Brasheer?"

"Sure am. Are you Floridian?"

Marty told him she was not, but had been invited to join him with Dr. Garrett Maxin at the captain's table that night. She smiled at the Jeep driver, who hadn't moved, and now looked away. The girl behind the woman wrapped her arms around her chest as if to ward off a chill in the 95-degree breeze. With a tight smile, but not another word, Brasheer reboarded, and his Jeep sped down the beach.

Christine had approached during the introduction.

"What's up with that?" she asked.

Marty shrugged, staring after the Jeep.

"He was pretty rude, Mom. What's going on?"

"Don't have a clue. Maybe he only wants important people at his dinner."

"What does it have to do with Dr. Maxin? Wasn't he the doctor who did my blood test?"

Marty laughed at Christine's questions, and admitted she had accepted Garrett's invitation.

"Why didn't you tell me you had a date?"

"Well, it's not exactly a date," Marty tried to explain. "That's only what he called it."

"Uh huh. And what do you call it?"

"I don't know. A dinner seating? A captain meeting?" Marty slipped the terry romper off her swimsuit, dropped it with her bag where she could watch them, and sprinted through the sugary sand toward water.

"Last one in's a peppercorn!"

A few yards in, she turned to keep an eye on the bag. Christine peeled her dress up and flung it over her head.

"Don't change the subject!" Christine tossed her fanny pack toward Marty's bag as she followed her into the water.

But her mother pretended not to hear.

Refreshed by the swim, Marty drifted into thought and Christine into sleep as they baked dry on coarse towels provided by the cruise line.

Was it a date? If so, it would be her first in more than twenty years. No wonder she felt so silly. Actually, now that she calmed down a bit and thought about it, he had acted pretty silly. Of course, she had, too. No doubt about that. She blushed just remembering.

Smoothing sun block, Marty reached over to dab some on her snoozing daughter's nose. Christine tanned easily, had never needed lotion even in her swim team years, but on a day like this it was best not to take chances. The sun glittered her daughter's brown hair into a confetti of reds and golds that conveyed their sparkle to her peachy complexion. Her teeth were perfect in her perennial smile, showing even now as she dozed.

Christine's personality was coming back up full volume, like the Sundowners' steel guitars last night, when Marty had breathed a prayer of gratitude for that. Was there any hope that she could return to her self too? And who was that, anyway? Not Floyd's wife now, certainly. Still Christine's mother? Certainly a screw up.

Marty flipped to her stomach and rocked elbow ruts into the sand through the towel. While a few of her daughter's friends had dropped by or called for advice during the years Christine was in State College, Marty's role and reputation, which had earned her the nickname Lemonade Mom, and, as Christine and her friends grew up, Doctor Mom, faded out.

Christine had closed like a little clam around the time she left for college. Marty assumed that was due to her new independence, and had been surprised, okay, jealous, when Christine developed a close relationship with her roommate's mother. She'd made one shameless stab at regaining her status: a sheet cake with a dozen paper fortunes inserted, sent to Christine's dorm. It was the sort of thing Christine and her friends would have loved a year before. Their lukewarm response had left Marty feeling outgrown. But she hadn't dwelled on it much. She was desperate to save her nightmare of a marriage, and there hadn't been time.

She'd finally left Floyd the summer after Christine's freshman year. He had been more irrational than ever, and when Christine came home that spring, had been especially hard on her.

She had deserved Christine's desertion. The truth was—and Marty hated to face it, but she had to—that her own life, her own problems, eclipsed her daughter's during Christine's college years. It was too late to get those years back now. She could only pray the reverse had been true for Christine, that she had been too involved with her own life to notice her mother's detachment.

Perspiring, Marty sat back up and picked at her rose-painted toenails. She inhaled the salt breeze. Amazing, how it cleared your head. She remembered doing the same thing last night. She remembered every detail that led up to what was, apparently, a real date.

Her recent encounter with the congressman had certainly not made a golden impression. She didn't know what to make of his rudeness. She must have offended him. No, she'd only said she'd be joining him for dinner. Maybe that was it. Maybe he didn't want intruders at his dinner with the captain. The Jeep driver must be his new wife. "Not the stalking type," Garret had said.

The woman's hair was about the length of Marty's years ago. That hair was what first attracted Floyd. It had joined their widening graveyard of contention bones when she cut it short on Christine's first day of school. She'd never had more than a trim since. Now she pushed it up from where it was sticking to her back, probably dried to a frizz. Garrett hadn't mentioned that the congressman's new wife had a daughter, but that must be the case. That hair.

Marty shook her head, and decided to let Magens Bay bring on the new and toast off the old. She nudged

Christine, who squirmed awake, and suggested a walk to the far end of the cove.

"Okay, if we don't die of heat exhaustion."

"Well, it is a subtropical climate," Marty chided, tucking her sandals into the blue bag. "Anyway, the average temperature here is seventy-eight."

"You couldn't prove it today," Christine wiped her forehead as she walked. "It feels like a hundred and seventy-eight."

"I'd love to see St. John," Marty continued, ignoring her daughter. "They say it's the unspoiled Virgin Island, because it's mostly a national park. But we don't dock there."

"I can't wait for St. Croix."

"No kidding, bride girl." Marty patted Christine's arm. "That should be pretty, too. Not as commercial as the harbor here. And the botanical park for your wedding will be more gorgeous than you can imagine. A storybook."

"Speaking of storybooks," Christine turned to her mother, "Sam picked up an application packet for me in Raleigh. He said some students—high school kids!—were sitting in a circle around a teacher outside, and she was reading them a story."

Marty heard the excitement in her daughter's voice, and she smiled. "Sounds like an apple tree."

Mother and daughter walked silently. Marty remembered how the "apple tree" had started. They'd been walking to school one morning, when Christine, about seven, noticed how low the branches of an apple tree were compared to a nearby oak. Marty had explained that the apple tree was "considerate," keeping its first forks within easy reach of children who might want to climb to get some fruit. Between them, "be an apple tree" evolved as mother-daughter code for "explain that more clearly," and later became a metaphor for teachers who made their lessons easy to understand.

Half a mile east, they found themselves alone. The turn of the cove shielded them from the wind, but not from the sun's broil. A shady path beckoned between nearby trees at the mountain's base, and they took it. It widened about 20 steps in. The women spread their towels under the canopy of foliage.

"You know, Mom, sometimes I worry about Sam."

Please, please God, don't let this be bad. "How so?"

"We never argue. I mean, we argue issues, politics, stuff like that. But we don't have personal arguments. We don't fight."

"Christine, that's a good thing."

"But sometimes I feel like I'm waiting for the other shoe to drop. Like he's too good to be true."

They sat on their towels, and Marty looked up into sun-spattered leaves. "Honey, you've just had a poor example of a marriage."

"You mean a poor example of a man."

Marty considered her words before speaking. Another shoe *could* drop. And she didn't want Christine to endure it too long if things went bad.

"Let me ask you this. Are you kind and fair to Sam?"

"Well, yeah. I think so."

"Doesn't it make sense then, if he is a good person, he'd treat you the same?"

"I guess."

"Christine, do you sometimes wonder if you deserve a man as good as Sam?"

"Maybe."

"Then who does? I mean, what qualities would a woman who deserves a husband this good have?"

"Qualities?"

"Yes. Name the five most important ones."

Marty tried to focus, but she was distracted by a surrounding silence so pure it felt dangerous. Silly. She brought her full attention to catch up with Christine's words.

"Okay. I guess considerate, honest, smart, interesting, and well, maybe attractive."

"Sounds like a woman who'd make a good wife for Sam. Now, which of those do you lack?"

Marty knew her daughter couldn't deny a single quality on her list. She watched her smile in the recognition.

"So stop worrying. You deserve the best. And if Sam ever turns out not to be the best, he won't deserve you."

"Well, I'm not blonde."

"And does Sam prefer blondes?" Marty pretended to fluff her hair.

"Not now. But that could change."

"That's when you put in a call to Miss Clairol."

"Like I'd change my hair color for a man!"

"See? Spunky, too. You can add that to your list."

They could still see the bay through a leafy tunnel as they watched a brown pelican bob along the waves. Another pelican appeared overhead, took aim, bent his enormous throat pouch, folded his wings back, and pitched himself into the water. Then he floated alongside his companion, the tail of a fish wriggling frantically to escape his gray bill. Marty knelt to focus on the scene through her camera. She snapped the shutter just as Christine screamed.

Marty spun toward her daughter, misgivings about their seclusion ratcheting up toward terror. The cause of Christine's scream, though, was not the rapist or robber Marty feared. It wasn't Floyd, or even donkey man come down from the hills to charge for a photo. It was an extraordinarily ugly lizard. The tiny creature had jumped from a branch to investigate the intruders.

"Well, that's it," Marty laughed, gathering their things and running to catch up with her daughter who was already halfway to the water and flapping her arms in a squeamish fit. "Does Sam realize he's about to marry a wimp?"

"Hey," Christine said. "If God wanted me to interact with nature, He wouldn't have invented aluminum siding."

A man in a business suit rammed his rented Mustang into fourth gear, keeping just one North Carolina highway lane over, and two car-lengths behind his subject. This was easy. Who did they think they were dealing with? When you can't find the bitch, you just follow the bone to her puppy.

5

Afternoon Four, St. Thomas

"Okay, so what's the real deal with Doctor Maxin?" Christine asked her mother as they power-walked back toward civilization.

"I don't know. He's probably some stereotypical, cruise ship playboy. But then, I'm probably a stereotypical divorcé, about to be empty-nester, so why not?"

Her daughter was getting ahead, and she sprinted to keep up with the young woman's longer stride.

"It's not as though I'm moving into his cabin. It's only dinner. And with a ship's captain and a United States Congressman to chaperone at that! Wait, Christine."

Marty huffed and Christine stopped. "Does it really bother you?"

Christine looked at her mother and resumed walking, now at a slower pace.

"I guess not. I mean not the part about you having a date." She shook her head. "Actually, it's about time. Should be good for you."

Marty tried not to smile.

"Just don't take it seriously, okay Mom?"

Marty did smile.

"I mean," Christine placed an insistent hand on her mother's arm, "I actually have more experience with all this than you do. He seems nice enough, at least he had a nice bedside manner when he did my blood test, but he's probably pretty casual about women."

Now Christine grasped Marty's hand and swung it.

"And remember, he took bedside manner lessons at medical school."

"What I remember is that I used to be on the other side of this conversation. But okay," Marty turned to her daughter. "I do understand. Besides, I just thought! You could join us. We'll say we need to review plans for the wedding with the captain. Actually, we do need to do that."

"So I'll be chaperoning you on your first date. Cool."

"Weird. We better have a shower before this sand is permanently glued between our toes."

Marty pointed to a sign touting hot water at the dressing cabana.

"Too late for my toes," Christine called from one of the uncurtained dressing rooms.

Marty pushed her own still-gritty feet back into sandals to get them off the damp concrete and fished in her blue bag for clean underwear, trying to breathe through her mouth to avoid the musty odor. She caught a whiff though, as she smiled at her daughter's complaints from two doors away. She hustled to dress and escape her dank cubical. She headed toward sinks and mirrors clustered near the cabana's doorway. Christine was already there, showing off her diamond to another new friend, this one a girl pulling long reddish hair up into a fabric-covered elastic.

Marty didn't want to intrude, so she busied herself at a mirror around the corner, dragging a brush through her own tangle.

The girl was talking. "Congratulations. I guess," she said. "I can't imagine being sure enough to get married to anyone. Are you from one of the cruise ships?"

"For now."

Marty could hear the smile in her daughter's voice.

"My fiancé will meet my mom and me tomorrow at St. Martin and we're getting married on St. Croix the next day. We'll go back to the ship for two nights, then get off at Eleuthera for our honeymoon."

"That's romantic, I guess," the girl said, sounding very serious.

"Are you from one of the ships too?" Christine asked.

"No. We just flew over for today. We're staying on St. Martin."

"Our next port," Christine said, then returned to what she apparently considered the subject. "Wait till you have your first boyfriend. You'll think everything's romantic. You'll want to marry him. The same with the next one, maybe even the next. Then suddenly, you really *are* sure." She laughed. "I think."

Was Christine having serious doubts? Marty moved one sink closer.

"I did have a boyfriend," the girl said. "Pete. But that was a big mistake. He was kind of weird, and when I stopped liking him, he turned out to be awful. He tried to run me over with his parents' car."

"Oh no!" Christine said.

Marty was stunned that the girl would reveal this to a stranger. She wondered if it were true.

"What happened?" Christine asked, and Marty cocked her head to hear better.

"His parents put him in a mental hospital. But then he came back to school and started leaving notes and things in my locker. Love notes and a necklace, things like that. But they weren't really."

"What's 'weren't really'?"

"You know. Notes that said we did things we never did. So I'd be afraid to show my mother. And then saying he didn't leave them when I did tell my mother and the school shrink called him in."

Marty peeked quickly around the corner. Even drawn up, the girl's hair reached halfway down her slender back. What rang a bell here?

"The necklace had a silver gun charm on it," the girl continued. "He said I put it there myself. The shrink told my mother maybe I did. She said Pete was doing well in his classes and all, and maybe I was exaggerating. I wasn't though."

Marty peeked over again; the girl was still facing Christine.

"Did your mom believe you?" Christine had been searching through the jumble in her case, probably for a lipstick. Now she turned toward the girl, who turned to face the mirror. Marty recognized her.

"Yeah. That's why we're here. We left Virginia for a while to stay with one of Joseph's friends on St. Martin. We're on the French side."

"Who's Joseph?" Christine asked.

"My mother's husband. Like a father. I don't have one. A father."

"Me neither, pretty much."

Christine ran the zipper back and forth on her makeup case. "Well, I hope Joseph helps too."

The girl made a fake sounding laugh and wrapped her thin arms around her body. "I don't think so."

Another woman tried to squeeze in at the mirror, and to make room, Christine and the girl moved outside. Marty followed, but didn't approach. She waited under an awning just outside the cabana's door when the girls stopped five or six steps beyond it. She heard that the girl's name was Olivia, and watched as Christine got her Virginia and St. Martin addresses so she could send her a postcard later to tell her about the wedding.

Just after this exchange, Marty stepped from the awning's shadow and greeted them both. Christine introduced her new acquaintance, and Marty said she looked familiar.

"I know," she added, as though she'd just now remembered. "You were in the Jeep with Congressman Brasheer. The one who rescued my bag."

"No," Olivia said. "I don't know a congressman. I better go." And she disappeared immediately into the crowd.

"Well, that was strange," Marty said. "I'm positive that was her."

But the congressman's name isn't Joseph, she thought.

"I can't believe I'm this hungry after a three-course breakfast four hours ago. All I eat at home is half an English muffin."

The elegant middle-aged woman voiced her complaint in a soft drawl. She was a fellow tourist who had offered to share a taxi back to Charlotte Amalie with Marty and Christine. Who knew if their jitney driver would return for them, or for that matter, whether they'd ever reach the Virgin Islands' capital in one piece if he did? Marty recognized her from the crazy ride to Magens Bay. She was the only one who hadn't left the vehicle when they stopped for photos.

Christine said she was suddenly starving too, which amused her mother. That morning, just after mentioning her size-six wedding gown, Christine had ordered tomato juice, papaya, eggs Benedict "with a sausage patty instead of Canadian bacon," and sheepishly, "a vanilla Coke." Marty had eaten only plain wheat toast, causing Christine to raise an eyebrow.

Marty was merely thirsty now. She purchased bottled water from the cabby for $3, checked the seal, then drank the entire liter before they crested the mountain and dipped back toward town.

Christine started to tell her mother more about Olivia, but Marty admitted she'd heard the conversation. Christine said she'd really asked for the addresses because she thought Marty would help the girl. She pulled out the slip of paper with Olivia's number and asked her to call.

"Honey, I can't get involved in that. It's none of our business."

"I'm really worried about her, Mom. Nobody believes her. You know what that's like."

Marty played with the empty water bottle, screwing the cap off and on.

"Sounds like her mother's on her side."

"Yes, but you saw her. She's a nervous wreck. And you think she's lying about the congressman."

"Well, maybe she's lying about the rest of it."

"No. She was so open. So vulnerable, you know?"

Marty sighed. The last thing she wanted to think about now was stalking and stalkers. But she did know what it felt like to be doubted, to have people think maybe you were the one who was crazy. And to have that happen when you're only fifteen?

"We'll see. Tonight we'll have dinner with the congressman. Maybe we can bring it up then."

"Congressman Brasheer?" The woman in the cab spoke.

Marty nodded. The woman reached her braceleted hand across Christine toward Marty. "I'm the congressman's wife, Nan Brasheer."

The cab pulled up to the dock.

"Well, I guess we'll see you tonight," Marty responded, shaking her hand. She didn't know what else to say. This was not the woman who had been driving the Jeep.

She turned to Christine as the taxi stopped. "I'll see you before dinner. I have a hair appointment on the ship at four."

"Are you wearing different foundation, Mom?" Christine asked, as her mother and their companion paid the driver.

Marty said she was only wearing mascara and lipstick.

"Well, something's different," Christine responded suspiciously. "You're pink and glittering."

"You're nuts," Marty said, even as she felt herself pinken more.

She considered returning to the ship immediately with Christine, who was bent on a five-course lunch and a nap until dinnertime and was now walking toward the dock with Nan Brasheer. How embarrassing. Marty tried to remember exactly what they'd said in the cab about the congressman, wondered if there was any chance at all that Mrs. Brasheer hadn't been listening to the entire conversation. She really should rescue Christine, she thought, turning away, but this was her chance for a secret shopping expedition in Charlotte Amalie, and she was looking for something special.

She found the gift in a little shop at the end of Drake's Passage, a busy arcade presumably named after Sir Francis Drake, whose fleet, they'd been told at a port lecture, used to launch from Magens Bay.

The delicate pendant was ideal. Tiny pearls that shaped the graceful heart would symbolize Christine's purity, diamond chips that shaped an even smaller heart within it would symbolize her strength, and the heart of gold center would mean just that. Perfect. And well worth its $2,500 price tag to Marty.

She was ready to pay that; had forgotten the port lecture about bargaining, when an elbow jabbed her arm, and she recognized Truce's shrill voice in the jeweler's shop.

"That is gorgeous. Absolutely stunning! I would offer seven-fifty. I just bought this ring!"

A purple tanzanite ring flashed too close to Marty's nose when she turned.

"They wanted over two thousand dollars, but I got them down to nine-hundred."

Disconcerted, but appreciative, Marty offered the jeweler $1,000, and was grateful to Truce when he came back at $1,200. Truce, still at her side, pressed her to "stick with a thousand," when Marty suddenly realized that she had no means of paying even $100. She explained to the jeweler that she did have funds to cover her purchase on deposit with the ship's purser, but would need to go there for the cash. No problem. The jeweler would dial up the purser for her, and she could make arrangements. No need to leave the shop. Of course not.

An hour later, Marty tipped her head back onto the cushioned edge of the hairdresser's sink, and let warm spray relax her scalp and soften the bustle of the crowded shipboard salon. Blessed hot oil was massaged into her hair, which had become brittle from the combination of dye and sun. She'd maintained her streaked natural golden blonde with not-so-natural help for several years, since the streaks faded and the first wisps of gray started adding character she didn't appreciate.

She thought of the color card kept by "Mr. Charles" at the Adoria Salon in back home, and wondered if women in witness protection programs got to take their color cards along to their new lives. Charles, who had become a friend to some degree, hairdressers having the knack of inspiring confidences, would probably wonder what had become of her when a month or two had passed, when she hadn't taken her customary, third Tuesday seat. But then, so would a lot of people wonder, she realized. It was all starting to sink in.

When she got back to Harrisburg, she would call some of them—but then what? She couldn't stay at the inn permanently. She'd have to find a place. Why in Harrisburg? Christine would be gone. Better to locate in one of those little Pennsylvania towns that she had traveled to last year as part of a special series on small-towns.

Each of the paper's four feature writers had been dispatched for two weeks. The magazine section editor had assigned them to spend time in at least five small towns each.

Nanty Glo, for instance. An old coal mining town where folks still lived in houses that had been company-owned and where addresses were "patches" rather than streets with names. What kind of life would that be? What could she possibly do there other than hide?

Maybe Coudersport, in the far north center of the state, whose claim to fame was its ice mine. She could be the ice mine tour guide. No, that was probably a plum job reserved for members of old families—or veterans of something more important than marriage to an asshole.

Maybe teach school somewhere? No. If she knew anything about herself, Marty knew this. She drew her energy from the tiny space between the ink and the paper and used that energy to face the world. Not the other way around. She had to keep writing. Well, not to worry about all that now. The luxury of being blown dry with her arms resting comfortably made it easy to simply bask in the present.

Present. She reached into her blue bag on the floor beside her chair and removed the little treasure. She slid the cover from the Diamond Importers box and lifted Christine's bridal gift by its fine gold chain. The hairdresser switched off the dryer to admire the necklace, and Marty explained its meaning and purpose.

"Your daughter is a lucky girl."

"Well, I hope she'll like it. She doesn't wear much jewelry."

"No, I mean lucky to have a mother who's so proud of her."

Marty felt something approaching good. Each problem seemed a thousand miles behind or a thousand miles ahead. Fluffed and happy, she ducked into the dressing room to remove her smock and fix her makeup, retrieved her bag from the hairdresser's station, and waited at the desk outside the salon to pay. She unzipped her bag and smiled once more at the jewelry box, holding it as she fished out her cruise card.

"Hope you plan to declare that, golden lady."

The familiar voice caused an involuntary thrill.

Garrett Maxin fell in step beside her. Marty related the general highlights of her day on St. Thomas, omitting mention of Nan Brasheer and the congressman and his association with the beach bag so as not to reveal her clumsiness, physical or social. She described her symbolic gift for Christine, and he said that was great, but he didn't ask to see the necklace, so she didn't bother showing him. Men were different about these things, no matter how sensitive they seemed. Garrett termed his own day "a light one," since the few passengers afflicted with seasickness had been first in line for port when they docked. One man refused to return at all, he said, and had made arrangements to fly back to New York directly from the island.

They paused at the elevator.

"What happens in a case like that? Does he get his money back?"

"Not from us." Garrett laughed. "Majestic doesn't lose money. His travel insurance might pay, but we'll not only keep his money, we'll offer a cut rate for his stateroom, and maybe pick up a new passenger at one of the ports."

"Lovely. Well, so far so good for Christine and me. We haven't been sick at all."

"It's not that common these days, with better stabilizers on big cruise ships. With two thousand passengers though, there will always be a handful. Some people get sick just watching waves on TV."

"Why don't they take pills?"

"Well, that's a tough decision. Hey, how about a drink?"

Marty said she'd have tea, but he led her into temptation by trays of beautiful hors d'ouevres at La Patisserie.

"To get results with seasickness medication, you have to take the stuff early, before you know whether you'll need it," Garrett continued after they were seated. "And it does put you out. When you're spending a hundred dollars a day for a great vacation, you don't want to sleep through it."

A piano's soft lilt joined the ship's gentle ambiance. Marty ordered a glass of pinot noir and selected a crab puff, one that was misshapen and slightly burned.

Marty learned that Garrett had worked at sea since shortly after his divorce nine years ago, and loved it.

"At first, it was just escape. I was a plastic surgeon in Boston. The pace, and the attitudes of some patients, I guess it was getting to me."

He eased farther into the armchair and crossed his legs, explained that he and his wife had once taken a cruise with some friends and met a young doctor from England who worked for the Cunard Line.

"I was a ham-radio buff in those days, and we stayed in touch that way for a few years before e-mail got to be the thing. When I reached a drop-out point, after the divorce, a temporary job like practice on a cruise ship just seemed logical. My friend was back in London then, but he knew Majestic was looking, and I gave it a shot. One six-month contract led to the next, and here I am." He spread his arms.

"So, you've been here ever since?"

"Not quite true."

Marty hung on every word while he admitted meeting a special woman onboard once.

"A few years ago. She was from Charleston, South Carolina, where I grew up. I fell in love, well, in like." He made silly finger quotes. "Decided to spend some time back in the old hometown and see what developed. My dad had a general practice there and was gradually retiring. I was welcome to come in and take up the slack."

"And haven't you missed plastic surgery?"

"No. That was a mistake from the get-go. Greed — not interest. No, Charleston, or someplace like it, is where it's at. Small city, family doctor, that's me."

"Why didn't you stay?" Marty was deeply interested.

"Dad was the problem. Not his fault."

"Used to being in charge?"

"You got that right." Garrett smiled and nodded slowly. "Besides, this ship is like a small city, and what I do onboard here is family practice stuff. I'm family doctor to the crew."

"What about the woman? The one you were 'in like' with?"

Garrett laughed. "You know how you meet someone, have a few Saturday night dinners, go dancing, maybe see a play? Then it's breakfast some Sunday, then sailing or antiquing? Then everybody starts to expect things?"

He uncrossed his legs and leaned forward.

"Her co-workers have a party and you're included, you're assumed, and you think whoa, what's happening here?

I barely know this person. You realize that's as good as it gets. You know?" He tapped a finger on the cocktail table for emphasis.

With absolutely no idea what he was talking about, Marty nodded.

"Well, after six months, it seemed time to make a move, so I made mine back to the ship. Seemed like that or marriage. Then. When I think about it now, she probably would have laughed at the very idea."

Now Garrett laughed.

"Still get cards from her now and again. She's dated at least two guys since. How about you? Dated much?"

"I've been separated three years, but the divorce was only final a few months ago," Marty said carefully.

"Well, if you want your dinner companion well rested," she changed the subject, "I think I'd better nap a bit." She rose to go.

Garrett stood to take her elbow, and walked her out of the lounge.

"I'll come for you at eight-fifteen."

"For Christine *and* me," she said, remembering. "If that's okay? There are some wedding things she'll need to discuss with the captain."

"An honor." Garrett mock-bowed, and appeared to be watching her legs when she looked back on her way across the Grand Plaza.

Alone in the elevator, she made faces at the mirrored wall and silently mimicked herself. Oh sure. I know how it is... you meet someone, have a few Saturday night dinners, breakfast some Sunday... Sure. I'm cool.

Marty was smiling by the time she reached Caribe Deck. I've dated, she thought. School dances and drive-ins a hundred years ago. Was Garrett a dangerous playboy? He just seemed too kind. But then, didn't they always? The playboy types? He had definitely been looking at her legs.

Well, so what? Floyd had liked her legs. Construction workers still whistled occasionally. He hadn't missed a beat when she told him Christine would be along on their date. Wouldn't a playboy be disappointed? Ah, but a *clever* playboy would hide it, wouldn't he? She was almost laughing aloud by the time she reached her stateroom and decided that the only dangerous thing about Dr. Maxin was her reaction to him. She loved that he had been looking at her legs. Just acknowledging that to herself made her face feel hot.

———

Very nice indeed, having such a stupid son-in-law-to-be. Stupid enough to discuss tomorrow's flight from Ft. Lauderdale to St. Martin with the clerk at Raleigh-Durham. Time enough to board the Ft. Lauderdale late in first class and beat him off the plane to connect tonight.

———

6

Night Four, At Sea

Refreshed by her nap, Marty shifted back into Mom-gear and rang Christine's suite. No answer. Sam would be onboard in that suite tomorrow, and Christine would move in with her mother for one last night before the wedding. Sam should be in Ft. Lauderdale by now, and flying to St. Martin tomorrow, Marty thought, and she wondered if Christine had talked to him yet.

Her daughter was getting married in two days, and here she was, worrying about whether Christine had coordinated their meeting place with Sam. She pulled the second leg of her pantyhose over her knee and watched the nylon split. Damn. Oh well. It hardly mattered with an ankle-length skirt. Christine had a degree in mathematics, for God's sake. She was certainly capable of scheduling a meeting. Marty blinked back a tear that surprised her.

Christine still didn't answer at eight, so Marty, now in formal attire for the captain's dinner—ripped-hose-hiding skirt, gun-metal gray, with a wide bustle bow and a scooped silver bodice—walked up to Baja Deck to knock on her daughter's door. No response. Darn her. She knew what the plan was. How could she be this inconsiderate? Marty decided to return to her own cabin and wait for Garrett. She was done raising a child and it was time to start living for herself. She thought this all the way back down the corridor to the staircase, but when she reached it, she couldn't go down. Instead, she hurried up to Riviera Deck to check the pool, Christine's usual hangout. Christine had, after all, been left to re-board alone at Charlotte Amalie, really an iffy place once you were up close. Well, not exactly alone. She'd been with Nan Brasheer. Probably worse. And now they had to get through dinner with that poor woman.

Marty's formal outfit, amid the swimmers and golf-jerseyed bar patrons on Riviera, drew attention. From the spa area she heard whistles, then a male voice:

"Hey Mom! Come and join us! The water's fine."

Christine giggled in the hot tub with a group of other young people too numerous to *fit* in one eight-foot circle.

"It's my bachelorette party!" she cried, waving a wine glass. Christine's new friends performed a toast to the bride-to-be, and one of the young men again invited Marty to join them. She laughed, relieved to see Christine so happy, and beamed at the flattery.

Then, reverting to a more comfortable role: "Just be sure you don't break a glass and get cut in there."

"We can't break a glass!" a twenty-something blond guy shouted. "And you know why we can't break a glass?"

The group hooted back: "Because they're plastic!"

Marty raised one eyebrow at her daughter.

"Oh no! It's The Look!" Christine teased.

"I know The Look!" yelled another young woman. The kids covered their eyes and made hex signs pretending to ward off The Look, as Marty waved good-bye.

"You, I will see after dinner," she called to Christine, who responded to the effect that her mom should have fun on her date. This set off a chorus of remarks about The Date, and Marty was still chuckling when she reached Caribe and met Garrett just outside the elevator.

"Ah ha! Caught ya! Nobody stands up a low country boy!"

"Apparently," she welcomed him, "you got that right."

When she explained that Christine would not be joining them after all, he did not seem disappointed. He looked fabulous in a white jacket. And still those sparkling eyes.

Nan informed the captain that the congressman was not feeling well and would dine in their cabin. Garrett told him the extra guest, Christine, couldn't come either. So, the gracious Commodore Anthony Mascellino invited Leon, from Marty's usual table, to join them with a guest. Leon brought Truce, and the captain's table was treated to the tale of her heroic bargaining on Marty's behalf at the jewelers. The ship's head chef arrived to advise the captain of the evening's specialty, but had to wait while Truce continued her story.

Finally, with a haughty look in Truce's direction, the chef fluttered his fingers and effused about the soup. "A rich beef broth with vegetable strips, Petite Marmite Henry IV." He forced each word through a thick Italian accent and addressed himself only to the captain, who, beard bobbing, agreed that it sounded delightful.

The chef left, and Truce resumed her monologue. When she started quoting prices for each of the too-many pieces of jewelry on her person, Leon changed the subject.

"So, day after tomorrow's the big day?"

Talk of Christine's wedding ensued and Marty invited all present. All accepted. Just as Truce questioned the whereabouts of the father of the bride, the waiter flourished a napkin onto Nan's lap and distributed the evening's menus.

Marty ignored Truce's question, and focused on the menu.

"Marty. I said, where is Christine's dad? He's not on the cruise, is he? Is he coming for the wedding?"

Marty smiled across the table.

"No." Then, immediately, "Look at this! Any of these appetizers alone would make a meal."

At Garrett's urging, she started with Caspian Sevruga caviar, then the broth recommended by the chef. While others enjoyed the pasta course, Ravioli with Porcini Mushroom Sauce, she settled back to observe.

The captain, like Garrett, sported dress whites, but while his ruddy complexion—at least what was visible above his full beard—would have been better served by navy, Garrett's tan, his silver-rimmed glasses, and his bright smile were well showcased. He was not classically handsome, but he had an unusually interesting face, Marty decided again.

His eyes, she thought, trying, but unable, to look away from them. Greener than any she'd ever seen, in the same way the Caribbean Sea was bluer than she expected. She lowered her own eyes when he met her gaze, but then couldn't help noticing the breadth of his shoulders. Deliberately, she turned to Leon on her right. He wore the rented tuxedo typical of male passengers on formal nights. Marty wondered if his cummerbund was wrong-ways when an upward facing pleat rescued a crumb from his roll. Handy, she thought, and smiled at him brightly.

Nan, about fifty and from Maryland, had that flamboyant but still-this-side-of-classy look common to wives of politicians everywhere. Fairly slim, she wore a beaded black jacket over a silvery shell with a high neck. Her dark hair, in a blunt page style, was pulled back on one side to show a large, silver hoop that matched the charms on her bracelet. Already seated at the captain's right when Marty and Garrett arrived, her bottom half remained a mystery. Marty guessed black chiffon and silver shoes.

Apparently, Nan was choosing not to acknowledge their awkward first meeting. Marty knew she should be relieved, but the social correctness irritated her. She wondered again how Christine had fared on her walk back to the ship with this woman.

Truce wore sequined turquoise, cocktail length, and tight, especially over the tummy. Marty, whose own hands were bare, counted six rings in addition to her other jewelry. Truce noticed the appraising glance and complimented Marty on her earrings—tiny diamonds, chosen for the outfit since they were the only non-gold pieces she owned and gold hadn't seemed right with the gray skirt.

After ohhs and ahhs over the entree, "Roast Royal Pheasant Flambe," Nan's conversation with the captain captured the attention of the table. She said she was a new bride herself, having married "Congressman Brasheer," as she referred to her husband, only three months ago. Her immediate task had been to organize the art collection at his home in Florida, she explained, and commute to his Watergate apartment in Washington, D.C., where he stayed throughout the session. So this cruise was their delayed honeymoon, and also the first time they had spent more than two consecutive nights together since their wedding.

"The congressman has worked tirelessly," she drawled, accent a mite south of Maryland, "on behalf of those poor women who are victims of stalkers."

Warming to her campaign rehearsal, she added: "Now, no woman will *ever* have to endure fear. No policeman will have his hands tied and have to wait until it's too *late* to respond."

Marty caught a whiff of sarcasm. She wondered if this little speech was for her benefit, if Nan was related to Olivia somehow. She tried again, and failed, to remember exactly what she and Christine had said in the taxi. Possibly, the congressman's being with Olivia and that woman in the Jeep had to do with Olivia's being stalked. Maybe he was working on her behalf.

Her piece said, Nan seemed to retire from the conversation. A curious mixture of shyness and bravado, Marty thought, and though eager to know the exact changes in the law, she was afraid that questioning Nan further would demonstrate too much interest in the subject. She was surprised when Garrett reached over and patted her hand at just that moment.

Over coffee and liqueurs, Nan spoke up again, this time to invite the table to visit "the congressman's home" in Ft. Lauderdale when they reached that port. All but Leon, whose cruise would end at Ft. Lauderdale, accepted.

"We'll have a lovely tea," Nan smiled, apparently satisfied that a proper congressman's wife's duty had been accomplished. "Let's say three o'clock." She took vellum cards from a tiny satin clutch and passed them to the group. Truce reached over Nan's shoulder to grab one as she and Leon said their goodnights and headed for the casino.

"I gotta see that art," Truce whispered, leaning to pat Marty's shoulder on her way out.

Later, strolling Promenade Deck with Garrett in a gathering night breeze, "to digest the chocolate soufflé," Marty worried that he might bring up the congressman's law again. After two glasses of Piper Heidsieck and a Grand Marnier, she might reveal too much. Instead, he discussed her name.

"Fits you. Strong and unusual. Is it short for anything? Your father's name Martin?"

Strong and unusual? Marty liked that. She preferred to think he saw qualities in her that she hadn't recognized herself, rather than that he was a smooth talker. Well, he did seem perceptive. She explained that her grandmothers' names had been Martha and Mary. Her parents, wanting to honor both their mothers, had debated the virtues of Martha Mary and Mary Martha for a week before reaching the compromise of Marty.

Marty told Garrett that she could barely remember Grandma Martha, who was said to have died young from wearing herself out waiting on her husband and 'doing for' relatives and neighbors.

"And I didn't really spend much time with my father's mother, Grandma Mary," Marty said, adding that Grandma Mary had been an early member of American Mensa, part of the organization for people with high IQs, and had belonged to some kind of futurist club.

"She was always traveling here and there for meetings and events. She died recently."

Marty recalled family members speaking of Mary's husband having to "do his own cooking" as though that were proof of the woman's eternal damnation. Even during her father's childhood, Marty knew, his mother participated in various organizations and didn't stay home much.

"They sound like the Martha and Mary in the Bible," Garrett said.

"Exactly. One does all the work and one joins the conversation."

"If you had to choose one of those names now," he asked, "which would it be?"

Marty smiled, looked at her hands.

"The dilemma of my life and times."

Garrett took both of her hands in his. She couldn't look up to meet his eyes. Unaccountably, she thought of the runner in her pantyhose.

"I'd better get back."

"I'll walk you," he said, and put an arm around her shoulder.

"No, no. That's okay. I have to stop somewhere. I need to go."

He took his arm away and cocked his head as he stared at her. She looked at him now. Was he amused, or only curious? He spread his arms, palms up.

"Your call."

"Thanks for the dinner, it was fun." Marty was halfway to the elevator before she'd finished the sentence, and she didn't look back.

———

The man who would be handsome without the snarl and the crease it pressed between his eyebrows flipped his seatbelt and prepared to exit as the sixteen seater taxied to the gate at Aerodrome de Esperance. He'd find a place to stay tonight and would be rested and waiting, ready to follow the bone at 10 a.m. The bone would go to the puppy and the puppy would be with the bitch.

"Stupid bone."

The flight attendant turned to watch, more bewildered than insulted, as Floyd stalked across the tarmac.

———

7

Morning Five, Sint Maarten/St. Martin

Marty rolled a crumbly, nut-studded dough ball in powdered sugar to make a Mexican teacake. She put the tiny cookie in the center of a baking sheet, then looked around the kitchen for the dozens of others she must surely have prepared. Nothing! Her daughter was getting married, and nothing was ready! She woke in a panic. As reality dawned, the dream panic became a crushing daylight anxiety.

How had it come to this? Dear, lovely Christine should be walking down the aisle of St. Sebastian's. The white runner should be spread between rows of carved-oak pews filled with friends and relatives. Christine should be gliding toward Father Paul and Sam, pretty friends in flowery gowns behind her. Hundreds of beautiful cookies, baked by her mother and her great aunts should be waiting at the reception hall.

Marty lay in bed and continued the vision, escorting her baby to the future. Drifting off again, she imagined a sudden disturbance from the back of the church. Floyd, throwing darts everywhere! The people his targets. Dear God! Everyone! Even his own child.

"No!" Marty screamed inside, hearing the rap on her stateroom door. She clutched the sheet to cover her mouth, and breathed carefully. "Okay, okay. Get a grip."

She opened the door to the incongruity of Christine's sunny smile. The bride-to-be babbled incessantly—about the people she'd met the night before, Sam's impending arrival on St. Martin, and what she should wear, buy, eat, and plan for the evening—enabling Marty to recover from her dream without Christine's noticing her distress. She kept nodding agreement until Christine, remembering that coffee was prerequisite to conversation for her mother, went to get it. Marty shuffled toward the shower, realizing how much it helped, that just one day before her wedding, Christine radiated bliss without pining for tradition and home-baked cookies.

Marty let the hot water pound the top of her head. Surely Floyd would not hurt Christine. But he was unstable. *Unless, of course, I'm the one who's crazy.* Hadn't she been crazy to assume his suspected diagnosis—Borderline Personality Disorder—was a mild one? No, damn it, the mental health community had let them both down. Any lay person would assume "borderline" meant "on the edge of." And "personality disorder" certainly hadn't been a surprise. They should have explained it better, provided pamphlets. The psychologist should have referred Floyd to a psychiatrist, and he probably should have been hospitalized, even against his will. That might have helped him. At least it would have protected Marty. It wasn't until she could use the Internet for research that she learned what a serious mental illness her husband was thought to have.

She remembered the night, during their marriage, when she tried to have him committed for observation after he charged the bedroom wall in a rage, actually ramming his head through the plasterboard. Certain he was seriously injured, Marty rushed forward to help him, arms open. Floyd spun, frenzied, and reached for her throat. Then, just as he

86

got his hands around her neck, he stopped and laughed. It was an ugly laugh that slid into a sob as his hands left her neck and caressed her shoulders. Marty stood frozen in horror. Then he released her and stumbled to their bed. He sat there weeping while she held his hand and made the call.

"It's a great life if you don't weaken," he said, after she hung up the phone.

When the police and the ambulance arrived, Floyd stopped crying and adopted a sardonic attitude. At the hospital, he changed again. He was downright affable, convincing the resident psychiatrist and the social worker that he had accidentally damaged the wallboard while trying to repair some wiring. His wife, he explained, was particular about her home, and hated his trying to be a handyman because he usually messed things up. By the time Floyd recounted several colorful tales of botched attempts to repair appliances and plumbing, the social worker was laughing with him. He couldn't blame Marty, Floyd told them kindly, she probably did think he was crazy.

They released him with the suggestion that she go to her mother's "and calm down."

Marty prepared to unlock her car in the psychiatric hospital's parking lot, and Floyd swept the keys from her hand with a grin. She had forgotten her purse when she followed the ambulance, and her choices were two: ride home with her certified sane husband, or call a friend or relative to come pick her up at four a.m. And explain. Explain what? That her husband, Christine's father, was crazy, but only *she* knew it? That psychiatrists didn't know as much as she?

And maybe he wasn't crazy. Maybe he only pretended to be. But wasn't that insane? It had occurred to Marty more than once.

He started the engine and shoved the passenger door open. Marty considered for a moment, then climbed in. They hadn't gone four miles when Floyd stopped the car in the middle of a deserted highway. He took a razor knife from his pocket.

"That's how thorough your professionals are," he laughed.

Assuming he would cut her throat or slit his own wrists, Marty, beyond confusion, didn't even try to stop him. She wasn't certain it was really happening. Pressing back against the headrest, she closed her eyes. Abruptly, Floyd shifted gears. He finished the drive home as though they were returning from an evening out.

Maybe I am the crazy one, Marty had thought then, but she moved out and filed for divorce within the week.

Christine returned with grilled pecan rolls, pineapple juice, and coffee from the Lido Deck buffet. She placed the offering on her mother's vanity, apologized for standing her up at the captain's dinner and teased her about her date. Sipping, then blow-drying her hair, Marty said little. She brightened considerably by the time they set out to meet Sam.

According to Christine, Sam was fine with his family's decision to skip the cruise wedding. They had decided instead to host a reception during Sam and Christine's visit to California over Christmas week.

Orient Beach was "clothing optional." Marty discovered this tidbit through the chatter of tour mates during the bus ride. They were traveling from Philipsburg on the dingy Dutch side of the island called "Sint Maarten" to the French "St. Martin" side, where Sam was to meet them. It wouldn't take long. According to brochures, the entire island was only half the size of Washington, D.C.

A chorus of "Viva la France" broke out on the bus when a "Bienvenue Francaise" sign appeared on the bumpy roadside. Marty couldn't tell if the crowd was applauding the relaxed French attitude about nudity or the improved road as they crossed the boundary. She gave a singing Christine The Look, and her daughter laughed it off.

"Well, what did you expect? Anyway, 'optional' means optional. You can keep your swimsuit on."

"I expect you will too. And Sam had better not be naked."

"Mom, you are no *fun*," Christine kidded. "Now that you're dating, you should check out the guys."

This time The Look brooked no argument from Christine, but Marty herself relaxed into a chuckle.

"God, when I think how awful it is just trying on bathing suits without a tan...I can't even imagine!"

"Mom, you have a great figure for your age."

"For my age. Exactly."

Marty had never been to a nude anything, but on her own, would have found it interesting at least. This would be about as much fun as watching an R-rated movie with your kid, she thought. She could remember keeping her eyes fixed on the screen as her face flamed, not daring to glance at

Christine on her right. Only later did she realize that her daughter felt just as embarrassed, and had missed an entire movie, miserably feigning preoccupation with her bracelet.

Far from the orgy Marty half anticipated, the beach's natural beauty overwhelmed her senses first. Translucent turquoise beckoned from across an expanse of hot white sand. Here and there, people played volleyball and Frisbee or generally milled about—a couple of women topless, but all in shorts or at least swimsuit bottoms. Well, nearly all. As they approached the waterline, Marty noticed a few totally nude beach strollers. Looking quickly away, she found an entire lower-layer population—folks sunbathing on chaise lounges and beach towels, in various stages of undress. Most of the women were at least topless, and about a third of the men were completely naked.

Having been focused on diapers during the sexual revolution, Marty had never actually seen a grown, naked man other than Floyd. Certainly she'd seen pictures and movies, but never anything this up-close and impersonal. The people were all shapes and sizes, the effect more National Geographic than Hustler.

Two men—probably a 60ish father and 30ish son, Marty thought—strolled past. The older man had a pronounced paunch. The younger man looked like a basketball player—nearly seven feet tall—and had a long, thin penis that flapped against his thighs as he walked. It appeared to be pierced by a pewter ring. Their lineless, tanned bodies tattled that they normally wore nothing but their Birkenstocks for sunbathing. A slim young woman, ten yards behind them, gathered shells. She had a thong bikini bottom, very white breasts, and a deeply tanned tummy.

"Well, when in Rome..."

Marty broke her stare and spun toward her daughter before she realized Christine was joking. She couldn't say anything, because almost within arms' reach, a chubby, grandmotherly type, naked as a trout, doled out sandwiches and chips to also-naked children on towels beside her beach chair. Beyond the grandmother, another family group was similarly occupied, and next to them, a swimsuited young couple slept or stared comfortably behind sunglasses. A rustic hut, declaring itself "Chez Mare" in bamboo letters, beckoned as their Sam-assigned, high noon meeting place. It was only 11 o'clock, and the place looked like a bar, but Marty suggested an iced tea.

She marshaled her daughter past the sunbathers. Relieved by the shade of Chez Mare's thatched roof, she closed her eyes for a few seconds to adjust to the dimness. Christine led her to a flowery padded chair at a bamboo and glass table. Soft calypso music vibrated, palm-frond fans spun overhead, and with few patrons, the restaurant was an oasis of quiet cotton. Waitress, bartender, drinkers and diners were clothed. In fact, Marty, in a two-piece-but-midriff-covering swimsuit, felt that she, and Christine, in her modest bikini, were underdressed.

Marty recognized Nan, the congressman's wife, drinking a frozen concoction at the bar. She sat alone. In olive sundress and mid-heeled sandals, and with a Gucci bag and sun hat on the stool beside her, she looked more the West Palm Beach shopper than the honeymooning sunbather. Marty considered inviting her to join them, but remembered the Sam-Christine reunion and decided against it. She wanted to talk with Nan alone at some point, though, and this would have been perfect.

Before she could mention Nan to Christine, who chatted with the waitress about exotic rum drinks, the fat, 60ish man who had been walking nude on the beach with his son twenty minutes ago, approached Nan at the bar. Now clad in swim trunks and a loose shirt, his face was familiar. Probably another passenger, Marty thought. Nan moved to a table with him immediately, and they were just out of Marty's sight when the man pulled in his seat. The congressman was nowhere around, and come to think of it, had not been on their bus, though Marty did remember spotting Nan in line for the tour.

"Strange," she said, bringing Christine up to speed, "for a newlywed couple so anxious to spend 'more than two consecutive nights together.' Yesterday, Richard Brasheer's at Magens Bay with that woman and the girl you met, and Nan's on the tour, but not with them. Then she's at the captain's dinner while he stays in their room to eat. Now, here she is, here. With a naked fat man."

Christine leaned to peer around the corner. "Nobody's naked in here, Mom. There's a sign on the entrance that says diners are required to dress—maybe it's a health department rule."

"Well, he was naked on the beach. In fact, look! There's his son."

Christine turned to see the extremely tall, now casually dressed, blond man with a baby mouth step up to the bar. "How do you know it's his son? I thought they were probably a gay couple."

Marty considered, and agreed to the possibility. "Or maybe they're just friends. Golfing buddies."

Christine laughed at her.

"But then I wonder why the guy who's not his father is over there with Nan. Apparently they arranged to meet here."

"You know what I wonder, Mom?"

"What?"

"Why you care."

They both laughed, and the waitress brought rum drinks and menus.

"When in Rome," Marty toasted her daughter. Christine took a sip.

"Whoa. When they say rum, they mean it."

"Be careful, Christine."

"Oh, Mom. Will you please loosen up?"

Christine sat silent for a minute. Then she changed the subject. "You know, Olivia said she didn't know any congressman. But you're sure that was her in the Jeep with Richard Brasheer, aren't you?"

Marty nodded.

"Then I really wonder if she's okay. I mean, why would she lie?"

"Maybe she didn't know he was a congressman. Maybe her mother knows him and she doesn't. I'm assuming that must have been her mother in the Jeep."

"Maybe neither of them know him, and they just gave him a ride?"

Marty shook her head. "No. I think her mother knows him for sure. Hey, by the way, what did Nan Brasheer say after the cab ride? I felt so bad sticking you with that."

"Yeah, right. Thanks a lot. I was a wreck, but she didn't say a word. She probably didn't even hear us. She wasn't paying attention."

"I doubt that."

"Drinking and carousing again!" Sam's familiar voice carried across the room, and Christine jumped up to kiss her intended. After quiet hugs and "missed you's" they sat to rejoin Marty. Sam looked great. His wide smile boasted perfect orthodontia and his bushy black eyebrows didn't detract from his green eyes. At thirty-one, he was in a physical prime, and a woman in the bar turned to stare unabashedly.

"You girls!" he laughed. "Can't leave you alone for a minute without finding you on a nude beach, swilling rum with the natives."

Confronted with a mother-daughter version of The Look, he corrected: "You *women*! Swilling rum and nudity..."

"Quite all right sir," a voice interrupted.

The tall blonde man from the bar approached.

"They have been under my watchful eye since I entered this fine establishment," he continued, obviously joking, but maybe a little drunk, "and I can assure you—they have only swilled—not nuded."

"May I present the man who is not the son of the other man," Christine said regally, joining the fun, "and to you sir, may I introduce my fiancé, Sam. And, of course, my mother, Marty."

Everyone smiled and looked puzzled.

"Well, I guess you had to be there," Christine added, blushing a bit.

The tall man put out his hand. "I'm Joseph," he said. "Olivia's stepfather."

Only then did Christine and Marty notice the beautiful teenager standing behind him. Olivia had tied her auburn hair back again, and wore navy shorts and a high-necked, short-sleeved white jersey. No makeup. She smiled shyly, and Christine made the introductions and invited them to join the group. Olivia indicated a tall woman in a white sombrero and blue silk pants outfit who stood near the door. She explained that she and her mother had only come for Joseph, but when she saw Christine, had to stop by to wish her a wonderful wedding.

Joseph said he had come to the beach early to collect shells, and that Bethany and Olivia were collecting *him* to lunch in Marigot. He described the town as "a bit of real France" and urged them to see it during their visit.

"According to legend," Joseph said, "a gin-drinking Dutchman and a wine-drinking Frenchman walked the 37-square-miles of this island to see how much land each could claim for his country in a day. The Frenchman walked faster."

Olivia fidgeted while Joseph waxed eloquent about La Brasserie de Marigot, the restaurant where they intended to lunch, and where he said he had once worked as chef's assistant. He was so caught up in his monologue that, when the waitress came to take their orders, Marty feared that Joseph would order for himself and ignore his waiting wife. Obviously irritated, Olivia said good-bye and walked toward her mother while Joseph continued, now directing his praise of "authentic French" dishes to Sam. Marty peered around the high back of Christine's chair to get a better look at the woman in blue, whose face was a bit less shaded by her hat at this angle. This absolutely was the woman who had been in the Jeep with Congressman Brasheer.

"What's wrong Mom? You looked like you saw a naked ghost!"

Joseph had finally left, and they had ordered lunch.

"Well, besides all the Nan and Richard Brasheer not being together and being with other people on their honeymoon business, we now know Olivia's mother is the woman in the Jeep for sure. That was *her*. She was waiting by the door for Olivia and Joseph. She was staring over there," Marty flipped her thumb toward the far side of the restaurant, "probably at Nan and the guy who's not Joseph's father."

"Whoa," Christine exclaimed.

"What?" Sam looked like he had just disembarked from one of those roller coasters that twists riders upside down. Both women laughed, and gave each other "go figure" looks for his benefit.

"I guess we better catch him up," Marty said, and started to do so.

"It really is strange," Christine interrupted. Then she told Sam the whole story about Olivia—the birthmark, the stalking boyfriend, the necklace. "Now that she's lied about being with the congressman though, I probably shouldn't believe her. But somehow I do."

She turned to Marty.

"I really think you could help her Mom."

Sam looked at Marty with sympathy. He probably knew as much as Christine did about what she'd been through, and that was most of it. Marty had tried to protect her daughter, had spent years denying and excusing Floyd's behavior—until that gateway moment just before the separation, when the family counselor had given her the key.

"Don't you realize," the psychologist had asked, "that in her eyes you know *everything*? If you act like it's okay, for her it *is* okay? She's grown up thinking that rage is normal. Will she marry a man who rages? Think she *deserves* it?"

Marty's mind had snapped-to. And while she had not been able to change Floyd with her new confidence, she had tried to start setting an example of stronger substance for her daughter. Christine was a very intelligent young woman, already away at college then, but home most weekends. Marty had watched her daughter's heart break. And she had watched Christine gradually pull what she felt in her heart together with what she knew in her head. Marty knew the process; knew it couldn't be rushed. Knew that Christine's marrying this nine-years-older man was part of it, but that Sam seemed to be a great, maybe even God-sent, choice.

"I think ole Marty-Mom here has enough to do right now," Sam said. "Mother-of-the-bride-ing can be a full-time job."

"Speaking of full-time jobs," Marty said casually, "I wonder what it's like to work on a cruise ship?"

"Why don't you ask your boyfriend?" Christine teased. That required another detailed explanation for Sam, who expressed delight.

"It's about time. I was ready to fix you up with someone from work. I didn't know if you'd want a toy boy or a ready-to-retire executive who might kick the bucket and leave you his pension."

"As enchanting as they sound, wasn't there someone in the middle?" Marty asked her son-in-law-to-be.

"Nope. If the forties and fifties aren't married, they're divorced and dating women younger than Christine. Some even if they *are* married. That's what women tell me."

"Aren't men lovely?" Christine asked her mother, who smiled and nodded in resignation.

Lunch done, it was decided that Sam and Christine would head for the ship since Sam had forgotten to fish out his swimsuit when he arranged to taxi his bags from the Aerodrome de Esperance. Christine and Marty had forbidden him to swim au natural. He was also eager to make certain that his "trousseau" had arrived safely in Christine's suite, and, Marty was sure, to spend some time alone with Christine. Marty said she'd take the later bus and catch up with them at dinner.

She waved from the road as Christine and Sam boarded a bus for Philipsburg in Sint Maarten, back on the Dutch side, where *Mare Majestic* was docked.

Floyd Arkus had been rested and waiting when the stupid bone arrived. He'd followed the luggage the idiot sent ahead to the Sint Maarten dock.

The swarthy man removed his wool blazer in the sweltering Philipsburg heat, yanked silver links from his

French cuffs, and rolled his damp sleeves. Finally, the clerk returned to the harbor office window with papers.

"I'm afraid the only vacancy is an inside stateroom, Mr. Arkus."

"Fine. Fine. When can I board?"

"No rush. She won't hoist anchor for another six hours. There might still be time for an island tour…ahem…if you're interested, we have the brochures."

The clerk handed him a clipboard and some literature. Floyd swept the brochures off the counter to the ground, threw his jacket on a bench and sat beside it with the clipboard.

"Oh, well, I guess you're anxious to change."

Floyd didn't look up. Started filling out the papers.

"I mean, we can take your bags from here if you don't need them. You can go straight to your cabin when you board. Or, they have lockers at the beaches."

"Fine."

"The last bus to Orient Beach leaves in five minutes. Most of our passengers have gone there for the day. You won't even need a swim suit there." The clerk smirked. "It's thirty dollars."

"Fine."

———

8

Afternoon Five, St. Martin

Marty stood by the road and watched Sam and Christine's bus disappear up a hill and into a tapestry of greens, then walked back to the beach. She was still intimidated by the nudity and not sure where to look. Her eyes were naturally drawn to the unusual, the bodies around her, but it embarrassed her to think that people would think she was looking. Every time she turned her head, though, she found herself face-to-butt...or breast or penis. Wishing for a pair of those obnoxious mirrored sunglasses to hide behind, she settled back on a chaise lounge and gazed in the safe direction of the sky.

A parasailer glided by, far above the sun-glinted waves. Christine had wanted to try that. She'd been reading the shore excursion brochures and making choices among the adventures available at each port. Marty had talked her out of parasailing by saying it was too expensive and they wouldn't have time, but her real concern was Christine's safety.

Friends had often called her an over-protective mother, but that hadn't seemed to harm Christine who had grown up with neither phobias nor broken bones. So what if she didn't ride her bike on the street quite as early as the other neighborhood kids, or date before sixteen? Marty had kept her daughter safe. Safe from everything except the ever-escalating hell of home.

While Marty's own fears were many, and always had been, they did not extend to water sports. She could power up speedboats with the best of them, and had once surprised her family by diving from a platform at 10 meters, three stories above a bubbling diving pool. On the other hand, flying—except over water, even though she realized the absurdity of that—riding in cars she wasn't driving, standing near low windows in high buildings, and even crossing streets, often generated what she suspected was more than a normal level of anxiety.

Her fear of heights, especially, had worsened over the years, and it became disabling at times. She had once written a feature on Pittsburgh's Incline, regular transportation for some and always a tourist's must-do, and sworn she'd never repeat the experience. As the little car lurched up the track to Mt. Washington, Marty had inadvertently glanced below to Station Square and was gripped by such panic that only her inability to draw breath prevented her screaming. By the time she'd finished the torturous climb and stepped out on Grandview Avenue, upper lip drenched in perspiration, she had started to hyperventilate. She hadn't even been able to interview the incline operator.

Being at great height over water, though, that just might be a possibility. She watched the parasailer reel in smoothly to a little boat below. She imagined *having done it*— telling Christine at dinner, telling Garrett!—but she could not imagine *doing* it. The boat anchored offshore, just down the beach. Marty found herself walking in its direction.

Remembering to bargain, she tried at the little beach shack where a French boy sold the tickets. He told her haughtily that the $50 price was not negotiable and that he wasn't even sure they would take the boat out for "a single." Didn't she have a friend? But just as she started to hope that having tried would be as good as having done, the boy tore off a ticket and said "forty dollars."

She paid, and he pointed to the boat, still fairly far out in the water. Marty realized she was expected to board it there. She waded in stiffly, her blue nylon beach bag held waist-high, then overhead, as the cool water lapped through her swimsuit against her goose-bumped chest. She shifted the bag to her head as she got deeper. This wouldn't work. Waving one finger to the crew, to indicate that she'd return in one minute, she made her way back to the beach and tossed her bag. Not a good idea, but everyone else seemed to be leaving possessions strewn about the sand. She doubted the boat would wait if she ran back to the lockers near the beach entrance, and if she missed this one, she would surely change her mind.

The water was chin deep by the time she reached the boat, ticket in mouth. Two beachboy-brown Frenchmen, the parasail boat crew, were settled back with beers. They looked at her languidly, expecting, she thought, that she would hop right into the craft now bobbing a foot above her head. It must be possible, she reasoned, or they wouldn't expect you to do it. She jumped to grasp the edge. Pull-ups had never been her forte, but she made a mighty effort. Nothing. She tossed her ticket into the boat and plunged beneath the surface, cooling her embarrassment and soaking the top part of her hair to match the rest of what had become a dampened moppy mane, then pushed off hard from the sandy bottom. Catching the boat edge as she popped out of the water, she heaved herself even with its height. Both men stared, but neither moved as she struggled to straighten her elbows and raise herself over the side. Finally, just as she prepared to succeed anyway, one of them gripped her thigh and waistband and flopped her onto the boat floor like a marlin.

"Thank you very much." Marty glared at them.

She felt foolish, but these guys were jerks, she decided, as they spoke to one another in rapid French that even her four years of study didn't render comprehensible. No way to treat a paying customer, she thought, now an irate consumer. In this defiant mood, she followed the boatman's heavily accented instructions, refused the life vest, and climbed without fear into the harness set-up on a platform astern. The pilot sped them farther out to sea. When the boatman tried to fasten the buckle across her chest, she yanked it from his hands and took over.

A moment of panic seized Marty as her parasail caught the wind and the boat line attached to the harness started to feed out. Had she done the buckle properly? She reminded herself that she was obviously safer in her own hands than in those of this snotty kid, and adopted a fatalistic attitude as she rose rapidly above the water.

Suddenly, it was fun. Glorious fun! Speeding along, bathing in the coolness of the wind beneath the toasty sun, ascending like a proud gull over the sea. Relaxing into the harness seat, Marty released the rope handholds, leaned her neck back, and let her arms spread in the breeze. Delicious. Flying and unafraid! She even waved to the nasty boatmen, who were watching but didn't wave back. Gazing down at the beach and still rising—eighty feet, maybe a hundred— she had a crazy idea. She reached carefully around her back and undid the bow, and then the short zipper, of her green gingham bathing suit top. Shifting her position—very carefully, getting higher now—to make space under the harness that crossed her chest, she slipped the top from her body and felt the wind against her breasts. Never looking down, she heard the boatmen cheer, and she waved her little green-checkered flag of liberation.

She was giddy with freedom. She had not been outdoors in the open without a top on since childhood. She had certainly not sailed through the sky hanging by a little strap before. Never had she been so daring, so physically courageous. If she could do this, she could... Do anything.

Marty looked down from her proud perch to survey the old world and was stunned to realize that, in a kind of quick retribution, it had all but disappeared. Instantly, she gripped the ropes at her elbows, the wind snatched her top in the process, and her euphoria vanished.

———

A man in rolled-up shirtsleeves stood on the beach beside Marty's bag. He wished she could see him watching her through rented binoculars, could hear him call her "slut, mother-of-the-bride slut." A nude woman standing nearby walked away quickly when she heard him mutter that.

———

From Marty's perspective, the boat had become a peapod and the Frenchmen brown peas, lounging more than 300 feet beneath her dangling legs. The panic began to overtake her as she tightened her grip on the three-quarter-inch ropes.

'Breathe. Breathe. Okay. Okay now. Get a grip.'

Her physical grip tightened and her fingertips pressed into her palms. Forcing herself to loosen slowly, she finally released the rope in her right hand just long enough to give a thumbs-down signal even as she realized it couldn't possibly be seen. She reminded herself that she was not holding herself up, that she could safely let go of the ropes, and tried to relax into the harness again. Remembering to breathe deliberately. Slowly. Evenly.

Finally, she did it. The boiling panic subsided to a simmer. Relinquishing rope again, she used her right hand to pry her left hand from its own grip, and folded them carefully and calmly on her lap. She opened her eyes and looked up at the parasail, and from side to side at nothing. She felt some internal lift, like on a Ferris wheel, and realized they were starting to reel her down.

Maybe she could do this. Wait, she *had* done it. She couldn't let it go to waste by ending in anxiety. She had already been as high and as scared as she would get. It was all downhill from here. Okay. Easy. The task at hand was to enjoy the ride. She reveled in the last sixty or so feet. When the guys slowed the boat to dip her, then sped up again to raise her briefly, they were all having a great time.

Not until she was back on the platform unbuckling her harness, did Marty remember she was naked from the waist up. Not a problem for the boatmen, now much more solicitous—arranging a seat cushion, asking in English whether she had enjoyed her "sky ride"—and she felt oddly at ease with them. And she loved the sensation of fresh air on her skin. They were approaching shore, though. Her bag on the beach contained a towel, a comb, a camera, Christine's necklace, her cruise card—and the key to the beach locker that held her clothes. The locker was nearly a quarter-mile down, and all the way across the beach.

He watched from the side of the souvenir shack, where he had returned the binoculars. He enjoyed her obvious embarrassment as she waited in line to buy a tee-shirt. He was close enough to read the message on the shirt as she hastened to pull it on. "Women Fly While Men Are Sleeping."

"Oh baby, you just think I'm sleeping. Baby, you are flying now. But you're about to crash and burn."

9

Night Five, Sint Maarten

The maître d' gushed Korbella into the Regency Dining Room on Emerald Deck. He lifted her hand to his lips for a spongy kiss, then held it high and swept her toward the table. Marty wiped the back of her hand against the slinky green dress that signified her reign as "Korbella, Goddess of Champagne," for this Mardi Gras costume night. Before she could join their seated tablemates, Christine, "Bordella, Goddess of Mother's Disapproval," hastened to head her off.

"Mom," she whispered, shoving Marty toward the ladies' room, "Donna just told everyone you were topless at the beach. What's up with that?"

Marty looked straight into her daughter's eyes. She never lied to Christine.

"Donna must be nuts."

Christine laughed. "I didn't think so. That would have been too cool."

Marty adjusted the nylon net "champagne" around the chef's hat that corked her.

During the first dinner at sea, each table group had been challenged to come up with a costume theme for this Majestic-designated Mardi Gras. Pointing to Marty's champagne, Christine had suggested her mother's costume. Truce had urged Christine to spend her last single night as "a wild child." Over, and because of, Marty's objections, the "Goddess of Mother's Disapproval," as well as the gods and goddesses theme, was born. Noting her daughter's fishnet stockings and red-plastic-tablecloth mini-skirt now, Marty still shook her head.

Marty ignored Truce's daughter Donna, who grinned in her direction as they sat, and started a chatter about everybody's creative efforts. Truce and Donna were twins in response to Leon and Charlie's comments on their striking resemblance. Truce inferred that they meant she and Donna looked the same age. Her attempt to accentuate this with sea nymph outfits had the opposite effect, and Marty felt sorry for her.

Lots of women crossed that line. It was almost as if mid-life crises conveyed with daughters' puberty. Marty had seen it among her own friends, and had worried it could happen to her. It never had. Partly, she supposed, because she had so much else on her mind during these last few years, but also because she had somehow escaped envy of her daughter's youth. Young adulthood had not been much fun for Marty, and had passed quickly. She was enormously grateful that Christine enjoyed it, that she seemed to be making such a success of it against all odds. The hardest part for Marty now was learning to take her daughter seriously as an adult. When she considered her own early twenties, she thought of Floyd and Christine and the attendant load of worry and household responsibilities.

Truce's daughter, Donna, couldn't be much older than Christine, but she was a frumpy little thing. Her usual attire was somewhere between old lady and street urchin, and her usual attitude was insolent adolescent. Donna's getup tonight was even less flattering to her plump figure than it was to her mother's. Now Truce reached over to adjust Donna's veils.

"Hold your stomach in," Truce said, a stage whisper that could be heard around the table.

Truce appeared to suck in her own stomach, at least she thrust out her chest, and smiled in Leon's direction. Donna moved a crab cake from her mother's plate to her own.

Leon and Charlie, both divorced midlife, referred to themselves as bachelors and were usually replete with gold neckchains. Male examples of Truce's style. Leon, "Maltus, God of Good Beer," stood and reattached his cumbersome beer-barrel belly, including an obscenely-placed tap, for latecomer Marty's benefit. She applauded limply. Charlie was "Thermadore, God of the Sea-Gar," indicated more by the clever business cards he passed around than by his gold leotard and strung cigar necklace. Sam, having just arrived today, had no choice but to assume the "Digerati, God of Computers" persona designed by Christine on his behalf. The purple silk shirt she borrowed from Charlie, and bright green shorts purchased in the ship's boutique, brought him in line with the color theme. The pen-filled pocket protector, flipped-back Dilberty necktie and backward baseball cap were intended to convey geekiness.

Sam endured dinner smiling through somewhat clenched teeth, and every time Marty looked at him she had to laugh. Poor Sam. While this was okay, and especially fun when their table won the grand prize, scavenging for the costume pieces had been a blast. Sam had missed all that. Even the crew had joined the fun, some going to extremes, as when their waiter Vincent stole the executive chef's hat for Marty.

It was hard to believe this was only their fifth night onboard, and Marty said so to Christine and Sam as they

111

wandered among the photographs displayed in the Promenade Deck lobby after dinner. The ship's photographers shot passengers as if they were rare leopards spotted on safari, at every activity, every meal, every port disembarkation. If you wanted to purchase the prints, you had to find them in this display. Ten dollars each, three for $25.

"Well, I can believe we've only been here five days," Christine said. "I've eaten enough food for two weeks."

Sam patted her red-vinyl bottom and whispered to her.

Marty pretended not to notice.

"I know. I keep trying to walk it off. You two need to make sure you get all the pictures you want before you leave at Eleuthera."

A film drop box reminded Marty that she hadn't had any of her own pictures developed yet, and she suggested a return to their rooms to change and to get her film. Christine was enjoying the attention her costume was generating, but Sam and Marty weren't, and majority ruled.

"Besides," Marty said, "I have a meeting with the chef at ten-thirty to review your wedding dinner plan, and I can't very well show up in his hat."

Christine went with her mother to Marty's stateroom on Caribe Deck, while Sam went to their mini-suite on Baja. Christine had moved some things into her mother's room for the night, including the wedding gown that precluded closing Marty's closet door. Marty, in her Women Fly shirt, had rushed back from her Orient Beach adventure via the Philipsburg bus just in time to dress up as a champagne bottle for dinner, and had found her cabin in this tornado whipped state.

They changed into slacks and pastel cotton sweaters. Under her mother's direction, Christine scrubbed off "at least the top six layers" of makeup. Marty glanced at the closet safe as she burrowed under Christine's gown to hang her bottle dress and thought of the necklace she'd tossed in just before dinner.

Since Christine had decided to sleep in Marty's cabin on this night before her wedding, Marty planned to present her gift just before they went to bed. She could barely wait! The necklace was so precisely Christine. Marty's throat caught as she imagined how different life would be without her. How different life would be from here on out, period. Well, all too overwhelming to consider right now. She gathered exposed film from her camera case, and, arm around her daughter, headed back down the two flights to Promenade's gallery.

Sam caught up with them on the stairs. They dropped off Marty's film and started searching photo boards in earnest. Marty scanned a wall of pictures from their first formal night. Just as she found one of herself and Christine, she came across another familiar face two rows below. Garrett Maxin, glasses off and eyes sparkling, stood alone by a carved-ice unicorn at what looked like a midnight buffet. He wore a tuxedo, and the picture might have been taken just after their gold star meeting on Lido Deck. They were all arranged according to event, and in her own picture, she wore the gold gown she had worn that night. He looked happy. She plucked the photo from the rack for a closer look, and felt her face flush when a voice came from behind her.

"What a handsome devil *that* is! Almost worthy of a drink with the Goddess Korbella. Maybe even a dance."

Marty took a second to gather her composure—why did he always seem to pop up behind her?—and replaced the photo before she turned to greet Garrett.

"How did you know?" she asked. "I didn't see you at dinner. And what do you do, anyhow, lurk in the shadows?"

"Zee doctah, he know all," Garrett intoned, still, she noticed, sparkle-eyed. Then he came clean. "Stopped by your table before dinner, but you were late. Long day at the beach?"

It dawned on her that he had probably heard Donna's "topless" report, but before she had to answer, Christine and Sam joined them. Christine held a sheaf of photographs. After a quick re-introduction to Sam, Garrett congratulated him, and then congratulated them all, saying he had seen the costume parade and heard the announcement of winners. Because they were blocking traffic, they moved to sofas in a nearby lounge area and spread their photo choices on the coffee table for review.

A waiter came by, and Garrett expressed mock horror that the Goddess Korbella would choose diet cola over champagne. Marty explained that she had wedding business to attend to in half an hour.

"I guess the chef can only sleep while we're in port, so we get to have these late night business meetings."

"It's a busy galley," Garrett said. "While we're eating dinner, they're cooking the midnight buffet."

Marty thought of her old kitchen, remembered how she'd loved to start baking just after doing breakfast dishes.

"You know, I really wish I had thought of baking wedding cookies and bringing them on this cruise."

"That's logical, Mom. I can see it now. Especially getting sixteen boxes of cookies from the airport to the ship."

They both laughed at this vision. Garrett and Sam looked confused.

"You had to be there," Marty said.

Marty and Christine had flagged down separate porters simultaneously at the Ft. Lauderdale airport, and before they knew it, each half of their luggage was headed in a different direction. Marty's porter didn't speak English, and she'd ended up running between them, trying to pantomime instructions.

"You can't even imagine," Christine was telling Sam, "how important homemade wedding cookies are in Pittsburgh. Fire hall or Sunbeam Heights Country Club— doesn't matter—you always have a dozen female friends or relatives showing up with plates of their cookies."

Marty nodded. Discomfited silence descended for a few seconds, then Christine and Sam drifted back to sorting photographs, with Christine relating more details of the trip before his arrival. The waiter returned and put a tray of tiny pastries on the table. There was one mini cream puff, Christine's favorite. Marty ate it. Garrett gazed at his knees. Suddenly he excused himself, asking them to wait for his return. Twenty minutes later he did come back, with the air of a bad poker player holding four aces.

Christine was trying to lower Sam's eyebrows with an explanation of just exactly how she happened to be photographed sitting between two men in a hot tub.

"It was my bachelorette party," she said righteously.

"Well maybe I need a bachelor party then," Sam countered.

Garrett immediately offered to host one, and Sam thanked him and accepted. Christine warned Sam that there "had better not be any strippers jumping out of cakes," and Marty remarked coyly that she thought Garrett had other plans for the evening.

"Didn't I hear something about a drink—and maybe a dance with the Goddess Korbella?" she teased.

"Certainly did. I'm hoping for a raincheck though, since *you* have other plans."

"I do? Besides the wedding menu? What are they?"

"A surprise," he answered. "But first let me take you to the galley. You said you had wedding business with Enrico at ten-thirty?"

"Enrico?"

"Chef Enrico. Hatless guy in the galley?"

In response to Marty's surprised look, he added, "Small ship." Then, "So, how was your afternoon over Orient Beach?" Marty ignored the remark. As much as she wanted to brag about parasailing, she preferred to avoid the details.

Christine said she'd review the wedding menu with her mother and the chef, "since the bachelor man will be partying."

Garrett was obviously simmering some surprise, so all four entered the galley together.

116

A young woman in chef's garb stood at a vast counter with a large knife. One by one, she stabbed five live lobsters, helpless with their claws banded, in the back of what Marty presumed to be their necks. At least forty of the creatures did a futile rapid rock on the stainless steel, awaiting the same fate.

Marty had to look away. She heard a man screaming before she saw him.

"Idiot! Idiot! We need shells! You have hour only to prepare bisque!"

She looked up, shocked to suddenly realize that this—the chef they'd met at the captain's dinner—was also the naked fat man from the beach who met Nan at Chez Mare. Christine did not appear to recognize him from Orient Beach, and Garrett was laughing.

"Out of his way. Enrico is on a mission," Garrett said. "We're used to his temper. Don't worry, he values his blade edges too much to use his knives on people."

The group watched as Enrico scooped lobsters into a five-gallon pail, then dumped them into the nearby vat of boiling water. Marty winced as they struggled before succumbing to the boil.

"I just thought it more humane," the young sous chef muttered, even as she got herself another pail to join him.

"Humane? Humane is a thousand starving people waiting for their bisque? You want to tell them is nicer to kill lobsters one by one than all at once boiling? Ten minute only."

117

"Ho!" he called to another young woman. "You help. Get three more helpers to shell. Now!"

Marty realized why Enrico had looked familiar when he joined the congressman's wife at Chez Mare. She pictured him at the captain's dinner, waiting impatiently for Truce to finish her shopping story.

The other sous chef hustled around the kitchen to draft more help with the lobster bisque preparation for the midnight buffet, and Enrico wiped his hands on a towel hanging from his apron. He turned to Garrett.

"So, this beautiful bride and beautiful mother," Enrico said, a different person entirely now, his voice exuding gentle wonder.

Almost before they knew it, the wedding picnic menu was finalized and, aproned and hairnetted, Marty and Christine were enjoying Garrett's surprise. They stood before their assigned counter, a mass of cookie dough, a stack of gleaming trays, cookie presses, icing bags and containers of fruits, nuts, jams, sugars, and icings at their fingertips. They had bid farewell to the bachelor party after reviewing the menu in Enrico's office, and been directed to follow yet another sous chef whom, Enrico promised, "give what you need."

This young man left them alone to prepare their cookies, and advised them not to touch the oven; that he would return for the baking.

"Be careful what you wish for," Marty told her daughter, and reached for a rolling pin. Christine responded with a mock glare. She started kneading nut chips into a fist-sized portion of the dough.

An hour later, when the sous chef returned, the women directed him proudly to six dough-dotted trays. He nodded approval at the silver sprinkled bell shapes, then frowned at the dozen little pockets of apricot, their fillings leaking a bit. Wetting his fingers, he re-sealed them deftly without a word. Marty winked at Christine, who had made that batch.

The sous chef busied himself with cleanup, and refused their help, so the women stood by the oven as their cookies baked.

"You didn't recognize Enrico, did you?" Marty said.

Christine was obviously puzzled, and her mother explained.

"Boy, this gets weirder all the time. So Enrico the chef is friends with or lovers with or the naked father of Olivia's stepdad."

"I think we can forget the gay lover possibility. Joseph is married."

The sous chef turned then, and Marty realized they had been discussing his boss. "Don't be so sure," he said. And that was all he said, removing trays from the oven and providing platters.

Marty lowered her voice. "Okay, so Enrico and Joseph are either friends or father and son."

"Probably friends," Christine said. "If Enrico was at Chez Mare, and is Joseph's father, I think Joseph would have introduced us to him."

"Yeah, but Enrico was in a tête-à-tête with Nan, who seems to be honeymooning without her congressman-husband," Marty said. "Also, remember, Joseph said he worked somewhere as a chef's assistant?"

Christine nodded.

"So maybe that chef was Enrico."

"The world can't be that small."

"Sure it can. It is, Marty said. "Think about Enrico being there with Nan, whose honeymooning congressman-husband is honeymooning with Joseph's wife."

"Boy, this whole thing is a convolution. Sam better honeymoon with just me. He's not leaving my sight on Eleuthera."

Marty and Christine were exhausted by the time they finished arranging, and icing, two dozen of their baked wedding cookies. They stored the filled platters in a pantry as instructed, then wound their way through the galley to exit. It was past midnight, and the only remaining clatter of activity came from the dishwashing room. Both women prepared for bed when they reached Marty's cabin.

Christine sat against pillows, sheet pulled to the waist of her pajama shorts. "I wonder if the bachelor party's over yet?"

"You have other things to think about tonight, dear," Marty said, diving under the wedding gown into the closet. She reached for the safe knob, forgetting to punch in her code, and was surprised when the tiny door opened easily.

"Well that's great! I put it in the safe, then don't even bother to lock it."

"What's 'it'?" Christine called.

Marty wasn't all that surprised by her forgetfulness these days, but was relieved to see the tiny white box in its place. She removed it tenderly.

"I have a little present for you," she told Christine, "but first, I want to give you a poem my Grandma Mary gave me when I was about your age.

"I was four when you were my age."

"That's right. I must have been younger. When I saved this, I planned to give it to you when you went off to college. That wasn't a good time. Not a time for letting go any more than we had to."

"Letting go?" Christine sounded worried.

"Well, actually, it's a nice letting go. Kind of an offer to stand by. I guess it's about family, or friends. Being there, but not controlling."

"Oh yeah, Mom. Like our family's famous for *not* controlling."

"Okay. But maybe it's time we should try."

She handed Christine a much-refolded, yellowed paper, and Christine opened it gingerly and read aloud.

My Promise
If darkness should fall
while you're walking alone,
you have only to reach out your hand,
and I'll take it and lead you
the best that I can,

But first, I'll ask where you were going.

If you're laden with burdens
and see me downtown
and ask me to tote one or two,
I'll take those and no more
for as long as you need
And return them when your need is through.

If you stumble and fall,
I'll hoist and dust off
and wait till you're well on the road.
You will look back to see me
smiling with pride
glad you can walk on your own.

These things are good things
when I know where to stop...
Please remember I'm up to the task.
I've been there, I'll be there,
I'm able to see there,
and I know that someday I will ask...

And you'll tell me...

If darkness should fall
while you're walking alone
you have only to reach out your hand
and I'll take it and lead you
the best that I can
But first, I'll ask where you were going.

"Oh Mom."

Christine looked up from the page with tears on her cheeks, and Marty squeezed in beside her on the bed for a hug.

"That's exactly right," Christine said. "Thank you so much."

Marty wiped her own tears on Christine's sheet, then smiled and handed her daughter the white box.

"This," she said, snuggling Christine to her side, "has pearls for your purity, diamonds to symbolize your strength, and," she patted one finger on her daughter's collarbone, "a heart of gold to match the one right here."

Christine removed the lid and looked inside. Marty watched her eyes shift to an odd expression as she reached into the box.

Disappointment?

Christine looked up.

"What's the gun for?"

———

He'd decided to risk one at the Wheelhouse Bar, had just ordered it, in fact, when he spotted the bone. He considered staying to eavesdrop. There was enough plant crap in this place to hide himself. Nah, not worth it. If the bone did catch him, the plan would be harder to implement, and so far it was going off without a hitch. Better just slip out the side.

———

10

Morning Six, St. Croix

Marty woke remembering her decision to forget. Her horror, and Christine's bewilderment over the silver gun charm clipped to the fine chain of her necklace, had been temporarily resolved by what she described to her daughter as an "executive decision." Marty had demanded the issue be tabled by an act of will because there was no time to deal with it on Christine's wedding day. She had been astounded when this fiat, this ultimate "because I said so," satisfied Christine, but after crooning her favorite lullaby "... sleep my child, and peace attend thee...," and watching it do the magic of twenty years ago, she had realized that she was, indeed, still the mother here.

Amazing. Her daughter was snoring like an adenoidal angel when Marty herself got up at seven. She sat cross-legged in the twin bed closest to the balcony and rubbed her forehead. The tiny bit of silver, not an inch high, was unmistakably a pistol. Someone had clipped it onto the chain beside the symbolic gem Marty had chosen especially for Christine. Olivia, the girl who had confided in Christine about her boyfriend putting a gun charm on her necklace, had to be involved with this, but how?

She rang Paras and requested coffee in a whisper. Christine's necklace was on the nightstand. Marty removed the gun charm and put it into the safe. She jerked the combination dial.

She eased her vanity chair out and sat to gaze into the arched mirror. Older eyes than yesterday's stared back. She glanced toward her still sleeping daughter, then picked up her brush and decided to do everything in her power to prevent this day of beginnings from being spoiled. Just as she became aware of the pain she was inflicting on her scalp, there was a soft knock, and she put the brush down to get her coffee from the steward. His gentle smile was reassuring.

On tiptoe, she crossed the stateroom again, slid the door gingerly, and started out to the balcony. But she was not quiet enough; Christine stirred. Somehow, for Christine's sake, she had to put this gun charm out of her own mind. With a deep breath, she turned and smiled brightly, a major feat before coffee on even a normal day.

"Good morning bride!"

Christine groaned. "Cookies. You had to bake a million cookies in the middle of the night."

Could she have forgotten?

Christine looked toward the necklace on the nightstand, and emotion flickered across her face.

No, she hadn't forgotten.

Halfway out the door, Marty brought her cup to her lips and watched her daughter decide to pretend that the gun charm hadn't happened.

"Well, I am going to have my shower first. It's a good thing we woke up; my hair appointment is for eight," Christine prattled. "I'll have to eat when I'm done. Don't forget, you promised to have breakfast with Sam."

Marty took a plastic chair, shifting it to avoid the sun's glare, and talked to Christine through the screen.

"I took a few liberties," she smiled. You'll be in the salon till lunchtime, so you might want to have your breakfast served there."

"What liberties?"

"Don't worry, there's no facial. Sometimes they make your face break out on the first day."

Christine didn't answer.

"And there's no worse zit than a zit on a bride."

Marty peered through the screen at her daughter's face, hoping she hadn't said the wrong thing. But Christine's face looked fine and clear today.

"Well, what then?"

"Oh, let's see. Marty sipped her coffee twice, pretending to struggle to remember. "There's a pedicure... and a manicure..."

"Mom, that's great! I never had a pedicure."

"Well, I haven't either, but I just might start. After you're gone and life as we know it is over."

She smiled brightly again, to show that she was only fake whining about her impending empty nest.

"And, hmm, let's see, a massage and a special deal called aromatherapy."

"What? No mud bath?"

Christine came onto the balcony to kiss her mom. Both were startled by a loud flap of wings and a "ha, ha, ha."

"Ohmygod! It must be a laughing gull! I read all about them," Christine exclaimed, obviously pleased with her research about St. Croix.

The island seemed to loom above the balcony as the ship drew closer. Humped green hills threatened to avalanche the harbor town of Frederiksted. Arched Spanish style buildings of cream and yellow came into view. Red roofs peeked out from green palms and mahogany trees like Christmas ornaments.

"I think I smell mangoes." Christine inhaled.

"You smell bacon," Marty laughed, indicating the balcony next door where they could hear breakfast being served.

"Can I really have breakfast while I'm getting a pedicure?"

"You can't have anything unless you get a move on."

Christine hustled back inside and Marty tried to relax. This is going to be a perfect day, she told herself. No matter what.

Marty escorted her daughter to the spa on Riviera Deck by way of three stair flights to work off the anticipated breakfast—Christine was now deciding between eggs Benedict with sausage and pecan waffles with bacon—and to avoid any chance of running into the groom before the wedding. Then she took the elevator all the way down to Emerald Deck, where she found her son-in-law-to-be at a window table in the Regency dining room.

Sam jumped to his feet with a grin, and Marty sat to face him with her back to a room divider. The sun in her eyes made looking out at St. Croix difficult, but when Sam offered to exchange seats, she refused.

"You Arkus women are stubborn. And traditional. Two of Christine's best qualities, to my mind. Irritating sometimes, but on the whole..."

When Marty merely smiled nervously, he continued. "So where is my bride-to-be? And how many cookies did you two bake?"

Marty looked into Sam's green eyes, at his open, Irish smile, and felt reassured. Christine would be happy with this honest, intelligent young man.

"Christine's having beauty treatments this morning," she responded. Then cautioned, "you are not to go *anywhere* near Riviera Deck."

Marty looked around her. The table for four next to them was empty. "And we baked more cookies than we would have needed if we'd had this wedding at home. We didn't finish until after midnight. How was the bachelor party?"

Sam grinned again. "Different."

"How different?" Marty suspected this would be interesting.

"Well, think about it. You usually have bachelor parties with your best friends, guys you've known all your life, or at least more than five minutes. So it wasn't really a bachelor party. It started as a good time though. Garrett is a nice guy. It was nice of him to do it.

"Where did you go?"

"The Wheelhouse Bar. Not quite as swingin' a place as Christine's hot tub.

Marty cringed a bit for her daughter, but Sam laughed and continued.

"Enrico showed up later. We split a pitcher and talked about marriage. Garrett tried to be positive, but I think his divorce experience was tough. He *could* still be in love with his ex."

This was probably intended to be a tactful warning for Marty. She felt a little stab. Sam was a protective sort, which was fine, in Marty's opinion, for a man marrying her daughter, who had little enough protection in her life. But she sure didn't need it herself. She shifted to dodge the sun's dazzle and tried to divert Sam from the subject of Garrett.

"At least you didn't drink too much. One pitcher of beer for three guys isn't bad."

"Oh. Well. I should say Garrett and I split a pitcher. Still not too bad. We were there about two hours. Enrico, your hat owner and cookie fairy—no pun intended, you're gonna love this—polished off half a bottle of tequila. He did not talk about marriage. At least not how you'd expect."

"What did he talk about?"

Marty wanted desperately to focus on anything other than the gun charm, Olivia, and Garrett's still being in love with his ex-wife.

"Well, first off, he's gay. Said maybe I might want a fling on my last night single. Said that with a man, it wouldn't be cheating on my fiancée. This was early on, and he was joking. Not about being gay, but about the pass."

"You're kidding."

"No, not kidding. Okay, so that's fine. Real funny, ha, ha. But then, he starts getting really drunk, and Garrett's trying to get him to leave. He's not going anywhere, and Garrett doesn't want him to embarrass the line and himself in front of passengers—it's already too late about me—so he's stuck."

Sam threw up his hands.

"And I'm stuck because Garrett's bought me beer and I don't want to leave him alone with this on his hands."

Marty really was distracted now.

"Okay, so he finally agrees to go back to his cabin, but now Garrett has to go to the bathroom. He tells Enrico to wait, so he can walk with him, and it's obvious he wants me to stay and watch him. So here I am babysitting this guy you hoped was Joseph's father. And he's wasted."

"Hope he kept his clothes on." Marty recalled the vision from Orient Beach.

"Oh, he did. But he sure wore his heart on his sleeve. First, he starts worrying that I took his pass seriously. Then, to prove he was only joking, he starts telling me about his one true love, a guy he used to work with in a restaurant on St. Martin. Next thing you know, he's crying."

Sam looked genuinely anguished and Marty could imagine how uncomfortable he had been, but her mind was wandering back to the gun charm and Olivia.

"Seems this guy—this love of his life—is married. The guy's best friend was a pregnant woman with no husband. So, he married her. Now he loves Enrico, but he's stuck with a wife. According to Enrico. Don't ask me."

Marty hadn't planned to ask. Who knew how people figured these things out?

"Maybe it was a cover? I mean the married guy. Gay people in the closet marry sometimes, to look like they aren't gay."

"Probably. It apparently happened a long time ago, the marriage. Fifteen years, he said. More gays did keep it quiet then. And, supposedly, the guy's wife knows. Anyway, the guy—Enrico's lover—won't leave his wife now because she needs him, her daughter needs him, and so forth. Also, she has money, at least more money than Enrico."

"Wonder why the wife needs him?" Marty thought about being needed—and not being needed. This could be her last day of the former.

They had finished a pot of coffee between them and the waiter seemed impatient for their orders. He brought a white orchid in a blue vase. As Sam discussed the merits of cane syrup, Marty excused herself, saying that she wanted to check on Christine.

"Afraid she's making a run for it?"

"Run? Oh. No. I just want to see how she's doing."

"Whoa. What's up? Is something wrong?"

Marty, now getting very anxious, admitted that there was. Against her better judgment, she agreed to tell Sam about it when she got back.

"Just order me a grapefruit."

True to her plan, Christine was tipped back in a pedicure chair with bright blue sponges between her toes while she munched pecan waffles beside a windowed vista of St. Croix. This kid never fails to grab the gusto, Marty thought, smiling. Relieved, she didn't disturb her daughter, and she hurried to her stateroom. Breathing heavily by the

132

time she got to the door, she couldn't bring herself to open it until she spotted a maid bustling down the hallway. The safe was still locked and she carefully spun the dial and removed the charm. She couldn't wait to get out of the room, but first she glanced into the bathroom and then assured herself that the balcony door was locked, wished there were track bars, thought of her broomstick in the condo back home. Finally she checked the safe lock again, then headed briskly back to the dining room.

Sam was plowing into a Paul Bunyan-sized stack of hotcakes smothered in syrup so thick it almost gave off sugar fumes.

Marty's grapefruit, cheerfully topped with a trio of plump raspberries, presented itself in a blue ceramic bowl. She flanked the bowl with clenched hands on the white linen cloth. Then she opened her right fist to reveal the silver gun charm.

Sam glanced at it and smiled curiously at Marty.

"What's wrong? And what's that?"

His pink face darkened as Marty told him.

"Well," he said when she finished. "What do you make of it? What does Christine make of it? Is she okay?"

"Christine's fine." Sorry to have upset him, Marty added, "And her toes are a beautiful shade of peach."

Sam looked even worse.

"Peach for the beach, she'll probably tell you."

Sam ignored her attempts to be light.

"So someone was in your room. In your safe. And they had to know about the necklace. Was there any kind of note or anything?"

Marty shook her head. She stared at Sam's yellow golf shirt to shade her eyes, sorry she'd told him any of it.

"Who would do this? Why?"

"The only thing that seems certain is that there is some connection to Christine's new friend Olivia. She must be mentally disturbed. But I can't imagine how she could get on the ship. She's not a passenger. She's staying with her mother and Joseph on St. Martin. The French side, she said."

"Did you call the police?"

"What police? And when? Do you realize Christine's getting married today?"

Marty's last question was almost serious.

"Well, maybe the captain?"

"No. I decided last night, and I told Christine, that we just aren't going to think about it. We aren't going to deal with it. At least not today. This is a once in a lifetime day."

"Every day is," Sam said.

Marty ignored the comment. "Sam, I've only told you this because there won't be time later and I felt I had to. Just in case. Christine is ignoring it, I'm trying to, and the best thing you can do for Christine is forget it for this week. She won't have to be in my cabin alone. I won't have to be there after tonight. You'll both be off the ship tomorrow. I'll do something after that."

Sam reached out and took the charm. He fingered it thoughtfully, then handed it back to Marty. "You're right. We can only do what we can do. Let's not ruin the day."

The waiter came to take their unfinished breakfasts, and Sam said he needed some exercise. As he left his seat to head for Promenade, Marty moved her coffee to his place and switched her chair to try to contemplate the view without the sun in her eyes. She settled into Sam's chair, and looked over the room divider, straight into the eyes of Congressman Richard Brasheer.

Why had Olivia lied about knowing a congressman, Marty wondered, sure he had heard her conversation with Sam, and immediately turning her gaze to the island. She could feel a slight jarring beneath her as the ship was moored.

Suddenly, Commodore Mascellino's voice boomed the port announcement over the loud speaker. His clipped tone indicated that he was reading from a text:

"St. Croix is the largest of the U.S. Virgin Islands. As you stroll the Romanesque piazzas and visit the churches, be sure to notice the mahogany, bread-fruit, mango, tamarind, and palm trees. Enjoy the beautiful hibiscus and orchids everywhere. We have toucans and parrots, and laughing gulls. You are in the tropics. Notice the arched buildings. People speak English and are American citizens here, but they can't vote for a United States president."

Then, more natural sounding:

"The other end of this island is actually the easternmost point of the United States. But we're in the western part, the most beautiful part of the island. A few miles north of here you'll find the rainforest. Christiansted is

135

seventeen miles from here and the tour is preparing to leave now. There's a harbor in Christiansted, but it's not large enough for Mare Majestic. Closer by, you might enjoy the St. George Village Botanical Garden of St. Croix, where the ruins of a nineteenth-century sugarcane workers' village are being restored, and where you'll see an Eden of tropical flowers."

Marty half expected the announcement to mention that Christine's wedding would take place at St. George Village Botanical Garden, but of course, it didn't. As the captain continued about possible port excursions and shopping expeditions, she lifted the delicate orchid in its vase and brought it close to her nose, then turned to look over the room divider again. The congressman was gone, but there had been no mistaking his focus. He had heard the part about Olivia. Maybe he even knew the story about Olivia's boyfriend. Maybe that *was* just a story.

———

"I'm sorry, Sir. We don't actually rent them here. They come from Black Tie Options in Ft. Lauderdale. When you booked your cruise, you should have had an opportunity to order a tuxedo. Black Tie delivers to the ship, and just as a courtesy, we deliver to staterooms.

"Your daughter's wedding? What a shame! Here. Put down your sizes—jacket, trousers, and shoe—and we'll see what we can do. I'll check with entertainment's wardrobe department. If we have no luck there, possibly we can help you on St. Croix."

———

11

Afternoon Six, Wedding at St. Croix

Expectant strains of "Trumpet Voluntary" caressed the small group in St. George Village's sultry breeze. Marty realized there could be no more idyllic set for a wedding than this enchantingly tropical botanical garden. The people from their regular table had come, as well as the group from the captain's dinner, except for Nan. Only the male half of the honeymooners attended this time. Apparently, they were taking the art of separate vacations to a new level. Richard Brasheer stood with Garrett, looking as though nothing out of the ordinary had happened, and acting as if he were a long time friend of the family. Even Commodore Anthony Mascellino had come.

Christine is perfect, Marty thought, determined to think of nothing else. This is a perfect day.

The bride seemed to float in a diaphanous puff of white. She took her mother's arm to glide through the lush grass with the band's not-quite-recognizable version of "Pachabel's Cannon." Sam and the minister waited just past a bower of tropical flowers. The band, more accustomed to zook reggae than classical music, didn't matter. Everything was perfect.

Like brightly garbed players from opposing football teams, two great birds—one royal blue with a tangerine belly and a black bill; the other with a white bill, scarlet body, and tar black wings—swooped in to perch on the fragrant bower. Marty wondered if they were domesticated mates, part of the wedding package ambiance. She and Christine paused on cue.

The multi-talented minister, an island resident with a personality that had impressed Marty by phone when she talked with him from the States, stepped forward to sing "There is Love." His rich tenor, accented like that of a Brit who'd lived in Mississippi too long, wrung every ounce of poignancy from the lyrics.

"Oh, a man shall leave his mother and a woman leave her home..."

Marty's eyes filled, and she hugged Christine before stepping back to make room for Sam at her daughter's side. She felt an arm around her, and for a second, let her body rest against Garrett and her mind drift back to her own wedding day. The thought stiffened her spine, and she scanned the group behind her quickly, straightened, and stepped a bit to the side. Garrett looked at her, puzzled, and she smiled graciously and patted his arm.

They stood together, with Truce close at Marty's other side, while Christine and Sam spoke aloud what they had chosen to vow to one another. "Always" and "forever" were in it, Marty noticed, but also "support," "love," and "gentle." These, she knew, were qualities her daughter definitely had, and qualities they had every reason to believe Sam shared. It would make all the difference.

The band attempted "Ave Maria" then, and Christine picked an orchid from the arbor, took it to her mother—in lieu of the Blessed Mother statue that presided over the left alter of St. Sebastian's—and kissed her. Both women had tears on their cheeks. Christine returned to Sam.

The ceremony was drawing to a close. Truce stepped forward to bustle Christine's train, and Marty recalled doing the same thing just before they left the stateroom that afternoon. She had looked up to see her daughter's hands behind her neck, fastening the gift from Marty. When she reached up to help, Christine, in a soft and shaky voice, said: "It didn't change the necklace," and Marty hooked the clasp with a prayer of thanks.

"Mr. And Mrs. Samuel Joly" were introduced to the small congregation, and they walked together across the lawn as the band, a tad more in its element now, swung into "The Hawaiian Wedding Song." As planned, the guests threw birdseed, and the couple approached a cake- and cookie-laden table. All gathered round, glasses were filled, and the captain toasted the couple. Someone commented on the Dom Perignon champagne, and Marty was somewhat alarmed. Then Anthony explained that a case of the fine champagne had been a gift to Christine and Sam from Congressman and Mrs. Richard Brasheer, and that Christine had asked that it be served.

Glass in hand, Richard Brasheer was worked his way through the impromptu receiving line Truce had established, congratulating Sam, kissing Christine, thanking Marty quickly. She thanked him for the champagne.

"But it's far too much," she added quietly. I can imagine what it cost."

"Not *nearly* enough." John Brasheer smiled and patted her hand.

"Oow, he is good," Truce whispered. "Better than a vibrator that kills spiders and opens jars."

Marty frowned and nodded. She vaguely remembered Nan's enthusiastic acceptance of her invitation during the captain's dinner, and wondered why she had not come but her husband had. Maybe that's how politicians and their new wives are, she thought. Oh well, lots of things had no explanation, and for today, at least, it was probably just as well.

Guests were served an island picnic, then Christine and Sam cut their cake—a scrumptious looking concoction of white and apricot and flower petals by one of Enrico's pastry chefs—and fed it gently to one another. Marty-Mom nodded her approval, and at first, thought that was what sent the bride and groom into such gales of laughter. Then she saw. One of her daughter's newly installed nail tips had flipped off in the process, and Sam had just pulled it out of his mouth. Marty joined the laughter, and soon the three of them were holding each other and their sides as Christine told Sam about what had happened while she was dressing. Getting her pantyhose on had been impossible with her new long nails. Ruining the first pair, she had asked Marty to put the spare pair on for her, rather than risk another run. Two women and a dress comprising 30 yards of silk and lace, did not have much room to maneuver in a ship's stateroom. Pulling pantyhose on one's self was hard enough, but dressing another in them was a challenge beyond hope. Sam stopped laughing first, and Christine said you had to be there, and he admitted he was glad he wasn't. Charlie and Leon said they wished they had been, and the band started playing again.

A 16-foot square of hardwood was unfolded behind the dessert buffet, and the guests circled it while the bride and groom danced to an old Buddy Holly tune, "True Love Ways." Garrett was still at Marty's side when Sam invited his new mother-in-law to dance, so it seemed the most courteous and convenient thing in the world for Garrett to have this second dance with the bride.

————

His stomach churned bile at the thought of that interloper dancing with his daughter, taking the center stage position that was rightfully his. The bitch allowed it, caused it. She should have been dead before this. It would be so much better if she'd just do it herself. Maybe she had by now. And why wouldn't she? She had to know this was the end of the line.

————

The little group broke up to facilitate a garden tour before reboarding *Mare Majestic,* and Marty waved the bride and groom off while she gathered the small pile of presents into shopping bags. She tore another bag into pieces to wrap the Baccarat crystal champagne flutes from Truce and Donna. The box had apparently been disposed of, and there was no choice but to tuck them into the bag gently with a small, embroidered pillow and some bubble-boxed figurines. A ceramic sculpture of the Virgin and her infant barely slipped alongside. Garret offered to cart the remaining champagne, and Marty teased him.

"I think we better count those bottles first."

She watched, smiling, as Christine and Sam disappeared from sight, and Garrett followed with the case.

"You coming?" He turned back to Marty.

"I'll be along."

He nodded understanding, and went on without her.

————

It was good to have a few minutes alone in this beautiful place where a big part of life had ended and a new one had begun.

Her high heels were sinking into the damp turf so she strolled to the walkway, bag looping over her wrist.

I've been there, I'll be there, she thought, smiling.

There was a cracking sound from the brush along the walkway about twenty feet behind her, and she turned, still smiling at the beauty of it all, expecting more exotic birds to appear.

Floyd stepped from the hedge.

"May I have *this* dance?" He sneered.

Marty looked around quickly. There was no one else in sight. Floyd was wearing a tuxedo.

"How did you get here?"

His lips spread over clenched teeth in a hideous cackle. He reached into his chest pocket.

"Oh, God, no," she gasped. "Please!"

"Oh, there's plenty of time, Baby. Plenty of time."

She raised her hand to her face, shielding her chest with the shopping bag that hung from her wrist. She bit a sob into the back of her hand.

He took a flat, white, shiny object from his pocket and waved it abruptly in a horizontal arc, level with Marty's neck. She heard the words "bride mother bitch."

Was it a knife? A white knife? Flinging her arm out to the side, still dangling the bag, she started to run. Floyd spun in place, cackling again, as she ran wide around him and back toward the walkway, now clutching the shopping bag of presents to her chest. Her heel caught in the earth just before she reached the stone path, twisted her ankle. She overbalanced and pitched forward onto the bag, scraping her knuckles and cracking the sculpture beneath her chest.

On hands and knees, she crawled along the path, bag dragging from her wrist. She looked back. He hadn't moved.

"Don't beg for it, baby. I told you there's plenty of time." He threw back his head and laughed a hideous laugh.

Marty scrambled to her feet, but instead of running away, ran toward him. She grasped the loops of her sack with both hands and wound back, then smashed the bag of broken porcelain down on his head with a howl of fury. He laughed as a group of tourists followed their guide around the bend and approached.

Floyd stopped laughing and spoke loudly. "You really *are* a lunatic, you know. You should get some help." Then he whispered. "You perfidious bride mother bitch."

The tourists stopped and stared. At her.

Marty ran.

12

Day Seven, At Sea

In the dream, Marty wore rosary beads around her neck and around her waist and lugged a suitcase containing everything she owned.

She walked a precarious track that ovaled a cigarette-shaped building. There were doors with stained-glass portholes, and Marty was trying to gather the courage to open one and go in. She knew that, inside, there might be a place to sit. There might be a place to put her suitcase down. The track she walked wouldn't hold it. The suitcase had wheels, and the track, suspended by ropes, jounced and tilted high over water. If she put the suitcase down without a guardrail, it would skate itself over the verge.

Sidling closer to the building, she peered in through the clear edges of stained-glass portholes as she passed them. In the first one, she saw a long empty aisle strewn with white-stemmed, red-thorned white roses. At the next, she heard a woman singing "Killing me softly with his song," but when she looked through, Kris Kristofferson was strumming a guitar. He turned in her direction and Marty was terrified. She ran, thinking he would chase her, but when she rounded the building and came to his window again, he was sitting, strumming.

Kris looked out at her and smiled, then motioned her to come in. Exhausted and defeated, she shouldered the door open. The guitar player's smile widened as he watched her approach. When she got close enough to see his white teeth become a knife blade, she swung her suitcase back, gathered momentum, and heaved it forward, knocking him and his guitar backward with the chair.

She was immediately sorry, and didn't know what to say. She wondered if he'd believe it was an accident.

She woke. Kris Kristofferson? Alone in her cabin, Marty shivered. It had been years since she and Floyd had gone to hear the country singer. She stumbled to the bathroom over the presents that littered her cabin. Christine and Sam had received lovely gifts from their wedding guests; now Marty had to figure out how to get them to Raleigh.

The carefully wrapped crystal had somehow survived her encounter with Floyd, but the expensive figurines were completely destroyed. She poured the porcelain fragments into the waste basket. She didn't know what she'd tell Christine, just knew she wouldn't be telling her until after the honeymoon. During the night since Christine's wedding, *Mare Majestic* had put at least 500 welcome miles between Floyd and the rest of them, and she had no intention of telling Christine that her father had been there. She was entitled to this respite. Christine needed and deserved a new life, beginning with two nights in the suite on Baja Deck and then a honeymoon on Eluethera Island. Marty thought about Christine's comment that she'd be honeymooning with her mother, and decided not to leave her own stateroom today. There was much to be decided, much to be done.

How in hell had Floyd found them? Marty asked herself the question for the fiftieth time. And what, if anything, could she do about it?

She'd come straight to her cabin when she'd reached the ship after their post-wedding encounter on St. Croix, and telephoned Christine's steward. Assured that Sam and

146

Christine were in their suite, she'd called Paras and ordered a bowl of soup. He had asked about the wedding while he arranged her table, and she'd started to cry. Then he'd done something extraordinary. After opening the napkin and spreading it over her lap, he squatted beside her and tenderly lifted a spoonful of the soup to her lips. After one sip, she took the spoon from his hand and thanked him. He patted her shoulder before he left. "The sun will shine tomorrow," he said, closing the door quietly. "Light be coming through."

Marty had smiled at that. When *didn't* the sun shine in this part of the world? Feeling better for this gentle human kindness, she'd finished the soup then gone immediately to bed, and somehow, to sleep.

She stared at the few noodles stuck to the bottom of last night's soup bowl on her nightstand, thought of Paras's sweetness, then of Floyd and the post-wedding horror. So far, Christine had been spared little. Marty would spare her this. The gun charm was bad enough. And what could that possibly be about? Some connection with Floyd? Even after his appearance on St. Croix, Marty dismissed the thought. That was just too coincidental. It must have to do with Olivia and her psycho boyfriend gun charm. She couldn't imagine a connection between Olivia and Floyd. But why? And why Olivia? She wasn't even on the ship. She was staying on French St. Martin with her mother and Joseph.

Marty tried to remember. Olivia and her mother had been with the congressman on St. Thomas, apparently just for the day. Then they were meeting Joseph at Orient Beach on St. Martin, the place Christine had arranged to meet Sam. Just after Joseph was walking nude with Enrico the chef. And while Enrico met with the congressman's wife. There was something Joseph said to Sam, about a French restaurant where he used to work. Maybe Joseph was trying to get a job on the ship with Enrico?

Marty knew she was going to have to find a job. If there had been any doubt in her mind about starting a new life, it was gone now. If Floyd was determined enough to come this far... She shivered.

So what *had* Olivia and her mother been doing on St. Thomas? Why were they driving around in a Jeep with Congressman Richard Brasheer? Could Floyd have some connection to him? To any of this?

The four remaining bottles of Dom Perignon sat on her floor in their case. She put them into the small refrigerator, then took one out and popped it to toast her survival till morning. She drank straight from the bottle. Seemed more festive than from one of the water glasses. Quite a gift, she thought, realizing the case must have cost close to a thousand dollars. I wonder why? He doesn't even know us. Is this a bribe of some kind?

The congressman had certainly heard her conversation with Sam. He'd know about the gun charm, and that Marty thought Olivia was mentally disturbed. He has some kind of connection to Olivia himself, Marty thought, and, unlike Olivia, he *is* a passenger on the ship.

She chugged some more bubbly and opened her laptop on the vanity and plugged it in. There used to be a resume in her personal folder. Yes. She opened the document and read it over. The fairly recent college graduation date would make her seem younger than she was. The newspaper was good experience, but she really didn't want to be a reporter, and she wasn't qualified yet to be an editor or a columnist. Well, maybe for a smaller paper she would be. Small towns, small papers. But where? Somewhere near Raleigh? No, Christine would feel like she was being followed. And Floyd might think of that. This was a conundrum. Called for another gulp.

Katherine had advised her not to stay in any one place too long. But she'd have to work. Even the large sum from the divorce settlement wouldn't last more than a few years if she actually lived on it. How could she hold a job and move around at the same time? And what kind of a life would that be? No friends, no relationships, no future. Relationships, hah. She'd been living like a cloistered nun for three years. But at least there had been her job and Christine to provide purpose. And she'd pretty much been numb most of that time, getting over the shock of her decision to finally leave Floyd. Now that she'd met Garrett, Marty felt the awkward but unmistakable stirrings of her own sexuality again, almost like those she'd experienced in adolescence. But now she was a mature woman. Maybe not too far past her prime. At least the French boatmen hadn't seemed to think so.

There was a knock on the door. For a few seconds, she froze, staring at the computer screen. She tried to speak, stopped to clear her throat, finally got out, "Yes? Who is it?"

The doorknob moved and the door opened as far as the chain allowed, revealing Paras in the hallway. She moved to let him in to clean the cabin, and stepped onto the balcony with her half-full bottle of Dom to be out of his way. She drank and watched as he made up her bed, noticed his dark, muscular arms in practiced motion. He couldn't be more than 25. Very polite. Brilliant, sincere smile. Extremely nice and extremely nice looking.

Marty decided to seduce the cabin steward. For practice.

But how? She'd never actually seduced anybody in her life. Still, she had read a few issues of Cosmopolitan Magazine. Music and candlelight wouldn't be factors here. Direct was best. Men are visual. Marty was still wearing her sleepshirt. Paras usually folded her nightwear Origami-style into birds and animals that greeted her from the center of her bed each evening when she returned to the cabin. She stood on the balcony now, watching as Paras entered the bathroom to clean up there. She felt an again-familiar aching. She wouldn't give herself time to think about it. One more long sip of champagne, and she stepped out of her panties and placed them on the balcony chair, then stepped into the room and pulled the nightie over her head.

If Paras was surprised when he emerged from the bathroom with dirty towels, he didn't show it. He smiled as if she were handing him another towel, and took the sleepshirt from her hand. Marty resisted the urge to cover herself now that her hands were free, and clasped them behind her back instead. She smiled nervously, tried to look lustful. Paras scanned her naked body with obvious appreciation, put down the towels, continued smiling, and *folded her sleepshirt into a swan.* He made no move to touch her, but placed the cotton swan on the bed and continued his work. Marty stood frozen in rejected humiliation for nearly a minute, then moved past him to the bathroom.

"Is there anything else, Miz Arkus?' He came up behind her at the mirror, looking over her shoulder and into her reflected, tearing eyes.

"No, Paras. Thank you."

150

He moved closer, and she could feel his breath on the back of her neck. "You are welcome," he said. "If I may say, you are a lovely woman."

She tried to meet his eyes in the wall of mirror, but he was looking down at the reflection of her breasts, and she joined him, watching them change. Seeing herself blush, she looked down. There were a few drops of water on the vanity between her hands, and she tried to focus on them. Her eyes had closed and she was close to crying when she felt him turn and lift her. With one arm under her shoulders and the other under her knees, he carried her out to the bed. "I'm not allowed," he whispered.

"It's okay," she told him.

She was dizzy and felt the breeze come from the balcony, then felt the pillow behind her. As long as she kept her eyes shut, she was exactly where she was supposed to be. He was a stranger, close against her. He held her, he was broad-shouldered Garrett. He moved on top of her, slow, then powerful, urgent, and he was the Floyd that existed when she was seventeen.

And when he tucked the cool sheet under her chin and kissed her forehead, he thanked her. And she thanked him back and slept some more after he let himself out.

When Marty woke again, she had a pounding headache and was hungry. She took two aspirin. She didn't want to leave her cabin, but it would be too awkward to call Paras for room service. She couldn't imagine what he must be thinking about her behavior, then decided that the more important issue was what she thought about it herself. She should probably be ashamed, but she wasn't really. More like astounded. How was it possible that the second lover of her entire life was someone whose last name she didn't know? Someone a thousand years younger, with whom she'd never had a date or even a real conversation. A stranger, albeit a kind one, when you really thought about it. Someone who could well have AIDS. Yes, she should definitely feel ashamed. Or at least regret. But she didn't. She'd had enough guilt.

So much of her response to Floyd's harassment had been crippled by morality, Marty thought. Was justified anger really so abhorrent? Was that immoral? Was she really so perfectly moral? Obviously not. It was something else entirely, she recognized now: fear of the guilt that would smother her if she were to retaliate at full strength.

She'd done that before and had paid the price. Likely in a fit of three-year-old rage, she had pushed her baby brother over a stair rail. Unforgivable. She'd known it even then, and she'd lived with it ever since.

Little Marty had been praised extravagantly for fetching diapers and washcloths to "help with Baby." Before he'd come, Marty would wake her mommy—hers alone, then—each day by scuttling down the hall and climbing up onto her parents' big bed. The second morning after her new brother was home from the hospital, she'd thought to include him in the ritual. She'd pushed the nursery rocking-chair's wide, wheeled ottoman to the crib. Climbing up, she'd wrapped her arms around and under the tightly-swaddled seven-pounder, then dragged him carefully over the low cribside and onto the ottoman beside her. It was much harder than Marty had expected, and by the time the proud big sister staggered into the hall, her brother had become too heavy to hold.

That was the part she remembered most. The weight. Leaning the weight against the railing that overlooked the foyer, shoving it higher to balance. The tipping, the release, and yes, the relief. It was relief *from the weight*, she suddenly realized.

That memory of that feeling had always haunted her. She'd assumed it was relief at getting rid of the intruder. *It was probably just the weight!* But even if there had been more, if the little girl had been angry with her new brother for usurping her parents, it would have been a justified anger. Hardly "justified," punishing an infant, at least to a reasoning mind. But at three, Marty hadn't reached the age of reason, of responsibility. But her parents certainly had. *And they should have taken steps to protect me from the guilt.*

The doctor had called it a "lucky freak" that Teddy wasn't killed. When he hit the carpet ten feet below, he'd rolled several yards down the hallway in the tight swaddling. The baby's right side was severely bruised, but he'd suffered only a slight concussion. Teddy's subsequent "slowness" and his dyslexia were never absolutely attributed to his fall. But Marty's parents had seemed to feel it necessary to believe the accident responsible.

It was nearly 2 p.m. She could wait to eat until dinner time. Another cabin steward was usually on duty from 4 until 8, presumably giving Paras time for his own dinner. She wondered what hours people normally worked on cruise ships. What skills were required. How well it paid.

She showered, dressed, and remade the bed, then returned to her computer and stared at the resume again. "1998-Present: Cruise slut," she typed. Then she laughed and deleted it. She was beginning to feel ashamed, but drew herself up, determined not to dwell on it.

What kinds of work would she qualify for onboard a ship? Well, somebody must write the daily "Majestic Muse" distributed to passengers. That was probably done at corporate headquarters in Ft. Lauderdale. The ship had a library, but it seemed to run on the honor system, there hadn't been a librarian in evidence. Cruise directors surely needed degrees in related fields, but what would those be? Gym? Hospitality management? Cheerleading? Psychology?

No. Basically, the only jobs she might do would be in housekeeping or food service, and those were parts of her life she was glad to leave behind. Oh, what did it matter? If she'd contracted AIDS or HIV, she might as well just go home.

At 4:15, she called to order a sandwich. It was a different steward, and by the time he arrived, Marty had worked into a tizzy worrying that Paras had told him. But this young man seemed perfectly normal and businesslike. While he set her meal up on the table, Marty glanced down at the wastepaper basket near the bed and saw Paras's discarded bright green condom. She was torn between mortification that the steward had noticed it too and relief that she most likely hadn't caught HIV.

Now that she was doomed to live, however, she had to get back to figuring out how and where. And it wouldn't be a bad idea to figure out how a gun charm ended up on her daughter's necklace.

13

Day Eight, Eleuthera Island,

Bahamas

Marty tried to absorb the peace-soaked beach atmosphere without the intrusion of fear. The menace might lurk near this sea, but after two nights and a day, she was surely over 1,000 miles beyond it. She *hoped* Floyd was still on St. Croix. It wouldn't be hard for him to learn *Mare Majestic*'s next port, but this section of Eleuthera Island was actually owned by the cruise line. It would be difficult to reach by air and ground transport, even if you knew where to find it. Marty had decided to accompany the other passengers ashore on that theory, but also to avoid running into Paras or losing her mind in isolation. Christine and Sam would disembark here. She'd like to catch a glimpse and say goodbye. Who knew how long it might be before she would see Christine again?

The beautiful cay (pronounced "key," she'd learned when Truce corrected Charlie) was a just a tiny section of this small Bahaman island. A number of cruise ship lines owned similar beaches to use for day stops such as this. The blue water shone clear as an airless cube of ice. No jellyfish or bottle caps marred the white sand. Rope hammocks swayed beneath towering palms. You could reach a wooden lookout deck by either the rope ladder or the convenient stairs behind it. A pig roasted alongside the picnic shelter while passengers scrambled to rent snorkels and kayaks. The whole effect was Disneyesque. Nature ruined, some might say, but to Marty's mind, it was nature enhanced. Clean. A postcard. Safe.

She opted for a beach chaise and tipped her blue straw hat low to discourage conversation. It mattered not a bit.

"Here y'all go! Tried to call you yesterday. Where were y'all?"

A frothy peach drink was thrust toward Marty. The phone in her stateroom had rung several times yesterday, but she hadn't answered. Truce prodded her midriff with the icy glass until she grasped it. Giving up, Marty tilted the hat back and watched her new friend settle into the chaise beside her.

"Thank you, Truce."

"No problem. You enjoy." Truce looked around, then bounced back up and distributed towels, beach bag, and purse over the four nearest chaises. "Have to get these quick."

Marty didn't see anything like a run on the chairs. Most of their fellow beachcombers were already in the water with various paraphernalia. A few waddled by in flippers, carrying masks. Resigned to conversation, Marty settled back with her drink and smiled at Truce.

"Thanks for coming to Christine's wedding," she said, "and for all your help. I wasn't sure what to do with all those people. I was kind of surprised they came."

Truce acknowledged the appreciation with a nod. "Being mother of the bride isn't easy. If Donna ever gets married, I'll hire a wedding consultant. After all, you raise the kid, you deserve time to party on the big send off day."

Marty nodded. "I'm just glad it's over."

"What? The raising or the wedding?"

Truce seemed genuine in wanting to know, and Marty answered her quickly. "Absolutely the wedding. I'll miss the raising." Even as she said it though, she felt a twinge of guilty relief.

"I'm not sure I did much raising. Donna always had a nanny."

Then, by way of explanation, Truce launched into her life's story. It was obviously her life's excuse as well, but you had to grant it.

It had happened on a Thanksgiving morning in Charleston, she explained. Her mother was carrying laundry in a pink basket from the kitchen, and Truce was dusting the living room in preparation for their holiday guests. Her brother and two of her sisters were coming home from college, and her other two sisters were coming with their husbands and one new baby apiece.

They'd had to work fast, Truce explained. Her mother had a closing the day before and another listing that night. She usually worked seven days and a few nights each week. Truce used to go to her grandmother's big house on Meeting Street when her mother and daddy were at work in the daytime. Grandmother used to walk up King Street to watch her when her parents went out or when they both worked late, but the year it happened, Truce was fourteen, and big enough to watch herself when it was light out. Grandmother came a lot of nights because Truce's daddy was at the bar whenever he wasn't sleeping or at work.

Marty thought she knew what was coming, though what it had to do with Donna's having a nanny, she couldn't guess.

They all missed her daddy a lot, Truce confided, herself especially. Her mother was usually angry, but "I could tell she loved him anyway."

He hadn't come home at all the night before, and Truce was afraid that if he missed Thanksgiving, her mother would never forgive him.

Truce said she remembered that her mother had shifted the laundry basket on her hip and smiled. Noticing that Truce was rubbing the leg of the old fancy carved table, she said "good job!" They heard a car door, then another. Someone opened the front gate without stopping to knock. Two sets of feet crossed the veranda that ran along the side of the house, and Truce's mother looked toward the door still smiling, "and kind of, you know, quizzical, it was so fast." Then her face had changed so that Truce "just knew there was a monster outside on the veranda ready to bust in."

Truce paused for effect. Marty said nothing.

"There were two monsters. Police. Come to say Daddy was dead."

"Oh. I'm sorry, Truce."

"Suicide. Gun."

"Oh, God no!"

"In one of those no-tell motels."

Her mother's face had changed again, Truce added, from frightened to angry, "and it stayed that way for the rest of her life." She never cried, so Truce did it for her.

Marty was ready to cry.

Four years later, Truce's mother remarried. By then, Truce, at 18, had a two-year old without a father, "some stupid kid in my history class." Her mother moved away with her new husband and gave Truce the Charleston singlehouse and enough money to live comfortably until Donna was old enough for school and she could go to work.

Truce banked the money, which by now was "sizable," she told Marty, and went to work as a waitress immediately, hiring "a mentally retarded—just mildly—girl to watch Donna for fifty cents an hour."

Although Marty didn't express disapproval, Truce started to sound defensive. She'd earned three times that much before taxes, she explained, and at least triple her hourly wage in tips. In only four years, she was day manager of the restaurant, then she quit a year later to sell real estate.

In her spare time, Truce beat breast cancer, but not before turning her home into a bed and breakfast in case she didn't, and Donna, at 15, would need an independent income. Men could be charming, and lots of fun, Truce said, but she didn't want her daughter "ever thinking that you have to, or can, rely on one."

Marty could see the danger there.

Now, Truce kept the B&B going, but had dropped the Southern breakfasts since Helen, Donna's old nanny who had always cooked them, took ill two years ago. Truce substituted make-your-own-Bloody-Marys and boxed donuts, lots of wine at teatime, and cordials before bed. Nobody seemed to mind.

"People who vacation in Charleston don't really like to get up for breakfast," she drawled with a wink.

Truce went on. She and Donna had cared for Helen, whom they had moved to one of the six "traditionally appointed guest rooms," until her death last month. Truce scheduled this cruise, their first vacation ever, a week after Helen's death. She hoped it would help Donna get over losing Helen, and it could double as a 40th birthday gift to herself.

An extraordinary hubbub exploded along the beach in front of Marty and Truce. A parade, if that's what you'd call it, came bounding by, its participants in all manner of fantastic costume and mask, shaking cowbells, beating goatskin drums, and blowing whistles.

"What the heck…" Marty watched in amazement as they passed on down the beach.

"Don't you watch your Majestic TV station?" Truce asked. "Those are the Junkanoo Dancers. It's a colorful ritual for our enjoyment," she added with a touch of sarcasm.

At this point, Truce flagged a beach waiter and ordered two more "peach watchamacallits." Marty started to protest, but, as her straw made a slurping noise, realized her glass was empty.

"What the heck," she said again, this time in mock resignation. "These are on me," she added, reaching into her bag for the cruise card. "And happy birthday."

Charlie and Leon strolled up then. "Whose birthday?" Leon asked.

"Nobody looks old enough to have a birthday," Charlie said, laughing at his joke.

Marty was taken aback when Truce claimed to be celebrating her 35th. Surely, Truce didn't look that young, and besides, Donna—now trudging toward them through the sand with a bag of chips—looked every year of 24, and they knew she was Truce's daughter. But she soon realized the men didn't believe Truce anyway, or couldn't add, or didn't care.

Almost before she knew it, Marty had relaxed enough to join the whole gang on a snorkeling expedition. The water sparkled so brilliantly she hardly needed her mask to be astounded by the world of life beneath. Christine and Sam turned up in the glassy space right next to her, and laughed at Marty's concern that she was somehow invading their privacy.

"You'll be back on that ship and out of here in a few hours," Sam joked, "We can probably stand you 'til then."

They all dived again, just through the surface, to marvel at the colorful scene. Marty was starting to think she had found a fascinating new hobby when she noticed the baby shark. Reasoning that, as with bears, a baby means a mother isn't far away, she panicked, motioning for Christine and the others to follow her to shore. Christine and Sam, and then Truce, started to smirk as they realized what was happening, and the more frantic Marty became in her efforts to get Christine out of the water to safety, the harder they laughed. Finally, Marty herself was laughing, and she and Christine sucked water into their masks and had to get out.

"Mom, come on. Wait up." Marty turned to see Christine remove her flippers to catch up. Marty stopped and flopped down in the sand to wait for her daughter. She was half angry and half frightened, but she couldn't catch her breath to explain. By then, the whole group was sitting on the sand with them, and Christine, Truce, and Donna were howling and holding their sides. The men didn't quite get it, and Truce explained it was a mother-daughter thing.

"I still say," Marty, having joined the laughter and now consumed by it, tried to gulp the words out. "Where there is a baby shark... and when she smells humans..."

Truce leaned against her, weak, still holding her sides. "Give it up."

"Well, this baby smells pork barbeque," Christine said, and, still chuckling, she and Sam headed off for the picnic shelter.

Leon, Charlie, and Donna followed them, gathering everyone's snorkel gear to return to the rental stand. Truce and Marty kept laughing until Marty started to cry. Truce put an arm around her and held Marty's head against her shoulder. "I know, honey. I know. It will be okay."

"It's funny," Marty said after awhile. "They like knowing you're protecting them, but they like to make fun of you for doing it."

"None of it makes sense," Truce agreed. "I know I've been a selfish person, a selfish mother, and I know Donna resents that. But my own mother was so damn selfless before Daddy died. She always seemed like such a martyr, and I resented that."

Truce pushed sand over her gold-painted toenails.

"It made me responsible for her life, and I always thought I should make it up to her somehow. It was a relief when she remarried."

"Tell me about it." Marty agreed. "They resent your self*less*ness. They resent your self*fish*ness. But I guess they love you just the same."

She looked down at her knuckles, still raw from her fall near the stone path on St. Croix. Truce followed her glance, and inquired.

Soon, Marty was telling her about Floyd, the stalking in Pennsylvania, his appearance on St. Croix after Christine's wedding, her fear that he really might kill her.

"What a manipulative bastard!" Truce muttered every few minutes. Then, "Why do you let him get away with it?"

Marty was dumbfounded.

"What can I do? He's always smart enough to avoid committing an actual crime. Or, at least, to avoid anything that's not just my word against his. Besides, sometimes I'm really afraid, and sometimes I think he's just trying to scare me. He's always kept me off balance."

Marty related one example. It was a mild one, considering some of Floyd's stunts—if that was all they were—but some of them were still too embarrassing to discuss.

"I think he cheated on me, but I was never sure. I know at least one time, he tried to make me think so—that he was cheating—and he wasn't. He surprised me with this spa day. Not a gift certificate, but an appointment all set up. It was a full-day treatment, massage, facial, hair, makeup, and for a day when he knew I had plans for Christine's swim meet."

"Considerate bastard."

"Yes. Well, when I wanted to change the day, he was furious. Said I hadn't cared about him or myself since the day she was born. I knew he'd start taking it out on her.

163

Also, I thought maybe he had a point. Anyway, a friend took Christine to her swim meet, and I went to the spa."

Marty rubbed the back of her neck and shook her head, remembering.

"When I got home, I knew right away there was something weird. I could actually smell some strange perfume as soon as I walked in the door. Really strong. Our bed was all rumpled. I'd made it before I left. Floyd was just out of the shower. When I re-made the bed, I found an earring—not mine—under the pillow. What would anybody think?"

Truce just stared.

"He acted like I was crazy. Accused me of not trusting him. Refused to explain the earring. I had a fit and he did too."

Truce shook her head.

"Afterward, later that evening, I was out on the porch trying to decide what to do. He came out with this gift box. All wrapped. It was the other earring. Then, he gave me the sales slip to prove he bought them that day. Said he must have dropped one on the bed while he was wrapping them to surprise me. Said it was too bad I wasn't the kind of woman who appreciated a surprise."

"That is one sick puppy."

"Well, honest to God, I thought he was right. I felt awful, like, here he was, finally doing something truly loving, and I'd messed up the whole thing. It didn't even occur to me—not until I found one of those little sample perfume vials in the trash a few days later, empty, in a bag from the department store where he bought the earrings—that the whole thing could have been a set up.

"He might be doing that now. Just trying to set me up to think I'm crazy. Or to make other people think I am. What can you *do* about something like that?"

"Kill the bastard! Have him killed. I don't know. But, you don't sound crazy to me, unless you take this sitting down. You can't let him suck your whole life away!"

Marty looked at her. "He's Christine's father."

"Yeah, well some pimple-faced sperm cell from Charleston is Donna's father, if that's all it takes. Think I'd roll over and play dead for that creep? Think Donna'd want me to? Think that would be a good example for her even if she did?"

"This is different. He's been a big part of her life. At least until college. Sometimes a good part. She loves him."

"Then why not in college?"

"I think it just got too hard. He bugged her all the time. Said awful things about me during the divorce."

"Sounds real loving. Maybe she just got smart. Isn't that what you sent her to college for?"

Marty reflected. "Anyway, I try not to talk about him to her. I hope they'll find their own peace someday. I don't want to hurt the chances of that."

"Oh, yeah. Help her find peace with the pig who's trying to kill her mother or scare her to death."

Marty looked down at the sand.

"Ah, motherhood. Let's go *eat* pig." Truce bounced up.

Marty slid her new cruise card into the lock of B310, and opened the door to Christine's old suite on Baja Deck. Everything was in order. Marty's luggage had been moved in. Sam's and Christine's things had been taken to their honeymoon "hale"—a thatched roof cottage that Christine had been proud to report, had "no phone, radio, or TV"— on Eleuthera Island. She and Sam would leave the island next week to start their new life together in Raleigh.

Marty dropped her beach bag in the tiny foyer, kicked off her sandals, and took a quick look in the mirror. Her long hair had dried, straw-like, in the sun without brushing. Wild island woman, she thought.

She sat on the flowered peach sofa and rested bare feet on the glass table in front of her. A bouquet of white gardenias brightened the matching side table next to the aqua club chair, their sweet scent overpowering her coconut sun oil and salt-watered hair. A note from her new Baja Deck steward was clipped to a receipt on the table. Great. The wedding presents had been packaged, and would be shipped directly to Raleigh. And if God was good, she wouldn't have to face Caribe Deck or Paras again.

Marty couldn't wait for Christine to get to her new home and find her bridal registry choices waiting there along with these gifts. Marty had purchased them all, to make up for Christine's missing out on a big wedding and the several bridal showers that would undoubtedly have preceded it. There would be a blue and yellow comforter with matching sheets and dust ruffle and a full set of china with the whimsical octagon shape on which Marty had failed to dissuade her daughter. They were very pretty, but Marty had worried that they wouldn't endure, and it was unlike Christine to make an impractical choice. After all though, it was her choice, and not her mother's. Besides, she thought now, fingering the receipt, who was she to say what would endure?

Christine's choice of stemware was a different thing entirely. Waterford's Colleen pattern was gracefully brilliant, and Marty herself would have selected it. The exquisite crystal would be a wonderful match for the china Christine would choose at some future date when she came to her senses, Marty thought. The same went for the simple traditional flatware pattern. Christine had followed her mother's advice there by choosing a pattern in which round, cream-soup spoons, and even iced-tea spoons, were available—stainless, not silver, "because you'll never keep it up. I wouldn't either." Blue and white towels, a stand mixer with every attachment—you never knew when you'd want to whip up some homemade sausage, they had joked at the Bridal Registry desk, a full set of premium cookware— "while you're still young and strong enough to lift it"—and a wide-slot toaster. Christine and Sam already had the basics, and Marty hoped they'd be thrilled with this big surprise. She should probably replace the broken Madonna and Child too, but that could wait.

You really didn't need that much to set up house, Marty thought now, looking around her. The suite's décor was much like that in her cabin on Caribe Deck, but it definitely had a more spacious, comfortable feeling. A curtain that matched the sofa could be drawn between the sleeping and sitting areas, and both sections had double sliding-glass doors to the balcony.

Marty walked out now and the difference in height was noticeable. Only one deck above Caribe, Baja Deck was four stories above the water, quite a bit too high for a comfortable lean over the rail, had the rail been low enough to lean over.

Marty tried to reenter through the bedroom doors, but found the slider locked. Good, she thought, then wondered immediately about the invader who had placed the gun charm on Christine's necklace. How had she—Marty realized she was convinced it had been Olivia—gotten into the cabin, even if the safe had not been properly locked? The stateroom doors all locked automatically, so it didn't matter if you forgot. You had to have your cruise card to unlock them.

Cruise card! Richard Brasheer had retrieved Marty's beach bag when it fell from the jitney wagon above Magens Bay on St. Thomas, and he had been in the Jeep with Olivia and her mother. The key had actually been in their possession, but for what, ten minutes? And it was hardly likely there was any way to duplicate the card on Magens Bay.

Marty chided herself. Ridiculous. Olivia was only 15 years old, too young to drive a car. She had no way of getting to the ship or on the ship. No way of locating Marty's cabin—or even knowing the necklace existed—and no way of getting in.

Calypso music undulated far above her, probably two stories up on Riviera Deck where the band usually played at the poolside bar. Just as they broke into "Anchors Aweigh," Marty felt the subtle lurch of the ship, taking her away from Christine. She wouldn't go up to wave from the deck. She had said anticlimactic good-byes to Christine and Sam after

168

the pig roast. The real goodbye had taken place when she kissed her daughter in front of the wedding arbor.

Sand was still sticking to Marty's feet, and she decided to clean up. She retrieved her bag from the suite's entranceway and took it to the bedroom. She surveyed the queen-sized bed and lighted vanity before opening the drapes to the balcony, and then the door, to let the warm sea breeze into the over-air-conditioned room. She took her damp bathing suit directly to the bathroom and draped it over the side of the whirlpool tub. As nice as a water massage would be, she had to wash and condition her hair, and the separate step-in shower was more practical. Hungry already, she made a quick call to have dinner delivered to the suite. She ordered just an entrée; too much of the delicious food on this cruise was going to make her regret it. The 8:30 seating was still two hours off, and she wasn't up to the chatter. She'd wrap up in the fluffy terrycloth robe, wind a towel around her head, and dine on the balcony in the company of sea and sky.

The water was wonderfully hot. She let it spray her stomach for a long time, while cream conditioner did its magic on her sun-brittled hair. What should she do about Floyd? She'd puzzled about it yesterday, in and out of sleep, but no reasonable action occurred to her. She'd considered making the standard call to her hometown police, her "for the log" call, but that seemed absurd. Also, there was the fact that he had not actually touched her. She'd hit *him* with the bag. And in front of witnesses. She could call the St. Croix police, she supposed, but if she were going to do that, she should have stayed on the island. Captain Mascellino? He probably couldn't have done anything, but he might have known what *to* do. Garrett? Well, that was silly. What could he do? Go beat Floyd up? Of course not, and he would most likely think she was a fruitcake.

Floyd couldn't possibly be connected to the gun charm appearing on Christine's necklace. Not that it wouldn't be right up his alley to do such a thing, but how in the world could he know about the story Olivia told them? Two gun charms, entirely separate, would be far, far beyond the realm of coincidence. It must have been Olivia. But how could Olivia have known about the necklace, gotten to and onto the ship, known what cabin to go to, gotten into the locked cabin, and opened the probably locked safe?

Marty rinsed conditioner from her hair. It would not be impossible for Olivia to have known about the necklace. So many people—Truce, the purser, Garrett, the jeweler, and anyone who happened to be in the jewelry store, around the purser's desk, in the beauty shop, or in La Patisserie would, or could have known, as well as anyone that any of those people might have discussed it with. So, it was definitely a stretch, but not impossible, that Olivia was aware of the necklace's existence.

Okay. Could she have gotten onto the ship? Well, maybe. She obviously knew the congressman, who was a passenger. Another explanation, possibly, but still a stretch, for Olivia's knowing which cabin they were staying in, especially since Christine had moved into her cabin.

But then, that's where the necklace would be, in Marty's cabin. If Olivia knew about the necklace, she would have known it was to be a gift, and that it would be in Marty's possession. So, okay, suppose somehow she knew about the necklace, knew it was in Marty's cabin, got onto the ship, and knew which of a thousand cabins was Marty's. And suppose she was mentally disturbed. Why would she want to frighten Christine who had been so kind to her? Jealousy? The fact that Christine was getting married, that her boyfriend *had* worked out? Or some connection to Floyd?

It really didn't make sense. But what else did? And if it had been Olivia, how did she unlock the cabin door? Just as she turned off the shower, Marty heard a click. Someone knocked on, then opened, the cabin door. Floyd? Marty sucked her lips between her teeth and folded her hands against her chest. Slowly, she made a sign of the cross.

"Miz Arkus?" It was the cabin steward, bringing the dinner Marty had forgotten she'd ordered.

Marty breathed.

"Yes," she called, stepping out of the enclosure. "Just leave it on the coffee table. Thank you."

When the door clicked shut, she leaned her head forward against the ceramic tile in relief. Her heart was pounding, and took a few minutes to settle down. She whispered a prayer of thanks, and soon was terry-wrapped as planned. She decided to watch a little television and eat on the sofa.

The Majestic TV station showed a taped broadcast of yesterday's line-dance lesson, and then, the midnight buffet. Marty remembered the food in front of her. The steward had spread the coffee table with plain peach linen, and the napkin matched. The setting included a flowered peach napkin snuggling three different types of tiny dinner rolls, three pats of butter molded into miniature horses—*Mare Majestic*s, she supposed, although "mare" was French for "sea"—a glass of ice, a pitcher of water, and a pot of coffee with a cup, and sugar and cream in china. She lifted the dome from her dish. Marty would not have thought a piece of flounder could be gorgeous, but here was one. A crushed pecan crust coated the fish, and it was topped by nickle-sized slices of tiny yellow and red tomatoes. Bright asparagus spears were accompanied by hollandaise sauce in a separate warming pot. Oh well, she thought. I tried to order light. She tucked the peach napkin into the front of her robe and dug in, resolving to skip all appetizers, soups, pasta courses, desserts, and even salads for the next week of the cruise. Obviously this was enough. More than she usually had for dinner at home.

Taking her coffee out to the balcony with a banana from the fruit bowl after dinner, she was relieved and satisfied. This was certainly a beautifully indulgent way to live. Maybe she'd try the cruisercise program this week, or the daily stroll-a-mile. Yes, this would be very nice indeed, and she intended to enjoy it. She'd forget Floyd, she'd forget the gun charm, she'd forget maybe-still-in-love-with-his-ex-wife-Garrett and her anomalous encounter with Paras, and she would bask in luxury. It was Saturday night. A week from tomorrow, the cruise would be over. Next Saturday she'd figure out what to do with her life.

Marty intended to stay in for the evening, so she dried her hair, moisturized her skin, and pulled on lounging shorts and her loose tee-shirt with lady angels that said "Women fly while men are sleeping." She wasn't sure what that meant, but she remembered suspecting as a child that her baby dolls came alive while the family slept, and she liked the idea.

As night moved in, the outside air cooled down quite a bit. She locked up and sat at the sitting room desk, which was well supplied with cruise ship stationery. Who would she write to? There was so much to write! So much beauty on these islands! Before she knew it, she had opened her laptop and her fingers were flying. Just as she ended her descriptive essay about beautiful Eleuthera Island and its birds and music and soft, soft sand, there was a knock at the door.

Her heart seemed to quiver. Then she recognized the chatter in the hall outside her door and checked the peephole. She unlocked and opened it.

Truce said they'd missed her at dinner, and so she had brought Leon and Charlie over to say goodbye. The guys would be disembarking early tomorrow with most of the other passengers when the Eastern Caribbean cruise week ended back in Ft. Lauderdale, but Truce and Donna, like Marty, were onboard for the full 15 days, which would include the Western Caribbean as well.

"Congressman Brasheer and his wife are staying on too," Truce now informed Marty, who was calling for party service—a room service delivery of cheese, nuts, coffee and liqueurs—and bringing a chair in from the balcony to provide enough seating for her unexpected guests. "I haven't seen his wife—that's Nan, right? —for days."

Marty nodded. "Neither have I. She didn't make it to Christine's wedding."

"Yeah, I know. Isn't that odd, him coming alone and bringing all that champagne? I just assumed he knew you and Christine somehow. I mean, how rich can you be, to throw money around like that?"

"That's all women care about," Leon grumbled. Charlie agreed. Neither Marty nor Truce cared enough to argue.

173

Donna was watching the television. "Hey, cool! They're showing the art auction. Look! There you are, Mom." They all looked, and, sure enough, there was Truce in the audience, waving her cruise card to bid.

Marty froze. A cruise card! That's what Floyd had brandished. She remembered the flat, shiny object in his hand. Not a white knife. A cruise card.

Floyd wasn't on St. Croix.

He was on this ship.

"Hope you got it," Charlie said.

"Actually, I didn't. People get nuts on a cruise ship. It was way overbid."

"What was it?" Charlie said he wished he had gone to the auction.

"This spectacular Emile Baer print. I would have sworn it was an original."

"How do you know it wasn't?" Leon asked.

"Well, for one thing, the auctioneer said so. For another, there's no way an original Baer would be auctioned on a cruise ship."

"It's naked women raping a horse," Donna said, rolling her eyes. This returned the attention of Charlie and Leon, who had drifted into a discussion of how good it would feel to be back behind the wheel after a week of not driving at all.

"Oh, it is not. They're just wrestling the horse in the water. It's just as well anyway. The thing was immense. You'd need a fourteen-foot wall to hang it.

174

"You know," Truce went on, fingering a tanzanite earring, "it's surprising that Nan wasn't there. I mean they are really into art. Are you going to see their collection tomorrow?"

Marty stared through her. Truce snapped her fingers. "Hey! Earth to Marty!"

Marty shook her head. Can't panic, she thought. Floyd is on the ship. I have to take action. I have to think. Now she responded to Truce. Yes, she remembered the invitation. At the captain's dinner, Nan had invited them to stop by for tea at the congressman's home in Ft. Lauderdale. It was a way to get off the ship, away from Floyd. "I suppose."

"Yeah, after all that champagne." This was from Charlie, who, it was just as well, did not know there were still three bottles in Marty's mini-fridge.

"The congressman stopped by our table at dinner," Truce fiddled with her earring some more. "He didn't mention the tea. I wonder if she mentioned it to him."

"Mother, he's probably busy," Donna said. "They let their wives handle social things."

"Well, I don't know. And I don't think Nan was at dinner. I watched Richard go back to their table and she wasn't there."

"He probably threw her overboard," Leon laughed, "because he found out she invited half the ship to his house when all he wanted to do was watch the ballgame."

Marty was hoping they might all leave so she could think, and praying they wouldn't, so she wouldn't be alone. Then the steward arrived with the goodies and she had to play hostess. "What did Richard talk about?" she asked Truce.

"Not much really. Something about making sure we had our valuables locked in our safes. Apparently there's been quite a bit of theft onboard this cruise."

Marty looked at her. "Really?"

Another knock brought Garrett to the party.

"Long time, sea," he greeted them. He munched some nuts but refused coffee and a cordial, opening Marty's refrigerator in search of a soft drink. He makes himself at home, Marty thought. Garrett closed the refrigerator quickly. Too late.

"Hey! I thought I drank all of that," Charlie said, spotting the three bottles of Dom Perignon.

"Sure did!" Garrett acted the host, and amicably poured him a small brandy. "Marty's holding these three bottles for Christine and Sam's first, second, and third anniversaries. Isn't that what you told me, Mar?"

She nodded, less put off by his assumption, grateful now for his presence.

As if on cue, Truce started to herd her group out. Charlie was passing out business cards—"in case you're ever in the neighborhood" —and, black book at the ready, asked Marty for her address. She mumbled awkwardly, about how it would be changing soon, and could tell he was a bit put off.

When they had gone, Garrett moved the porch chair back outside for Marty, then sat on the sofa beside her. "Don't worry about it. Everybody asks for addresses at the end of these cruises. Most you'd probably hear from him is a Christmas card."

"I wasn't worried. It's just that I don't have…I mean, I don't know…" She took a deep breath. "I have no idea where I'll be living when this cruise is over. None."

If he had asked a question then, she would have told him nothing. But he didn't. He just reached out and patted her hand, looking at her with such pure empathy and acceptance that she told him the whole story.

"I knew there was something. Something bad, but not this bad."

"How?"

"Don't know. You seemed afraid. And like someone who would want a big church wedding for her daughter. Someone with lots of friends and family. Like someone hiding. Doing it this way because you're hiding."

"Apparently not hiding very well. I can't believe he found us. Do you think the captain can do anything?"

"Not sure. If the police can't… He buys a ticket, gets a stateroom. You say he waved the cruise card. Do you think he's just trying to scare you?"

"I think he's trying to kill me. If making me think that is scaring me, then I guess he's succeeded."

"I'll stay here with you tonight."

"Oh, no. That's not necessary. It's not your problem. I just thought maybe you'd know if the captain…"

"We can talk to him. Let me sleep on your couch."

"Absolutely not. I'm not sure you understand. If you stayed here, and somehow, he knew…"

"But you can't be afraid to protect yourself."

The psychologist's words came back: "Why won't you protect your daughter?"

And the attorney's words, about the protection order: "I agree with you. This could set him off."

No, she had to do this herself. She had to trust her own judgment.

"What would help," she said, "is if you could check the passenger manifest and find out what stateroom he's in. I'd also like to know if he's been here all along, or if he replaced that seasick passenger."

"Done. And remember, this cruise ends tomorrow, so he's probably getting off. You won't have to worry after that. But for tonight, I still think…"

"I'm sorry," she cut him off, "to dump all this on you. I can handle it. I'm just so… so distressed right now. I was even before I realized he was onboard. That island was beautiful, and Christine wasn't here, and I wanted to write it all down, capture it somehow, but there's no one to write to, or for."

She gestured to the laptop that still had her words on its screen. Garrett walked over and leaned down to look. Then he pulled out the chair and sat to read. Finally, he turned to her.

"You're a writer," he said. "I know. I'm a reader. We can tell." He smiled. "You don't have to work for a newspaper. You could write a travel book. You can live anywhere. Anywhere."

———

Just before 2 a.m., he called the steward for extra luggage tags, claiming he'd accidentally thrown his away. After they'd been delivered, he leaned from his doorway, watching until the steward entered another room. Then, muttering about the waste of time, he slid the already labeled bag and briefcase into the hall and re-locked his door.

———

14

Day Nine, Ft. Lauderdale, Florida

Disembarking 2,000 passengers seemed a complicated process until Marty watched Majestic's coordinators move that many people and reconnect them with their belongings once they were off the ship. The night before, all departing passengers had been told to pack their bags and place them in the hallways outside their cabin doors. This required some fancy stepping by passengers who closed the disco down at 2 a.m. and resulted in fancy breakfast outfits on the few who'd failed to plan. Alan, the new steward who had packed Christine's wedding gifts, assured Marty they would go with baggage for shipping.

People everywhere seemed tired, sad, or impatient with the process of leaving the ship. More than one tearful goodbye occurred in Marty's presence. Just as Garrett had said, many new friends—and in at least one obvious case, new lovers with hands in each others' back jeans pockets—exchanged phone numbers and photographs as they milled around the purser's desk waiting for release.

All in all, the cruise line did a good job of organizing the mob. After a person finally walked down the gangway, he or she had simply to head for the proper alphabetized-by-last-name section of the baggage terminal.

Garret had called early to report that Floyd was registered to the stateroom vacated by the seasick passenger and would disembark today. He was not registered for the sold-out Western Caribbean cruise beginning this evening. She toyed with the idea of hiding onboard until then, when she could be sure, but a congressman's home—with Garrett,

Truce, and Commodore Mascellino—seemed safer than the nearly empty ship.

What did one wear to a congressman's tea? Nan said "casual," but this was a woman who wore a church dress to a bar on a nude beach. Marty considered her new wardrobe of cruisewear. Not shorts, certainly, but maybe the pantsuit? No, too hot already, she decided, watching from Promenade Deck as passengers streamed off the ship. Obviously the more formal outfits would be out of the question.

Maybe she could find a simple summer dress like the one Nan had worn on Orient Beach. East Las Olas had a wonderful, if expensive, shopping area. She remembered buying a backgammon set in a game shop there when she and Floyd spent a week away from winter in this section of Ft. Lauderdale years ago. The congressman's home was just off East Las Olas, Nan had told them, next door to the house where the movie "Where the Boys Are" had been filmed years before. Marty recalled driving by that particular house on a tour. It was definitely an older yacht neighborhood, with dock-dotted canals running behind the homes.

Marty stopped by the purser's office for cash and was introduced to Majichecks, which could be written up to the amount she had on deposit. She left the ship without bothering to change. She would wear whatever she bought, and the necessity of wearing something would force her to choose. Sure she could find Nan's house on foot from the shopping district, Marty took a cab there. A quick scan of the bustling block revealed only three men; none was Floyd.

She entered the first women's boutique she encountered and quickly found some things to try. The saleswoman introduced herself and said she was a personal

182

shopper. This was fine, and she was actually a big help, but her questions were a bit unnerving.

"I'm just here on vacation," Marty tried to explain.

"Of course. That's fine. We ship. I'll be getting a beautiful pearl bracelet in, Mikimoto, it will go with this perfectly," she put a sharp charcoal blouse with pearl buttons on the dressing room hook.

"No. Really. That's okay. I don't wear them."

But the woman had rushed back out to look for more.

"I'll be glad to call you when we get more of these." She thrust in a skirt that was not Marty's size. "Sometimes I can spot just the right thing."

On it went, the clerk eager to get Marty's name, address, and phone number; Marty dodging the reasons for not providing them.

When she finally escaped in her new garments, the street was, again, nearly empty. She was feeling rather frazzled, but looking, she had to admit, quite sophisticated. The cream linen suit was treated to resist wrinkling. It slid lightly over a cream lace-trimmed silk half slip and a periwinkle silk chemise. The scoop-necked chemise served beautifully as a blouse with the short-sleeved jacket. Sheer pantyhose set off her suntan, and rich cream leather shoes felt like walking on cool sponges. Her new handbag—more basket than purse—was a weave of muted linen shades with a periwinkle thread. The slacks and summer sweater she had worn in earlier were neatly boxed with her sandals and old purse and packed into a shopping bag by the clerk. She had to admit that she'd never felt quite so ready for tea.

Except for her hair. Notwithstanding last night's conditioning, it was so wild after a week in the sun and salt water, the best she could do was buy a hat. The whole effect was elegant, in a Florida way, but hat wearing always required a bit more panache than Marty had. Strolling down East Las Olas now, she kept hold of its brim with one hand, pretty much taking the edge off the elegance, she thought. And how was she ever going to kill three hours until teatime?

The answer appeared on the next corner. Not the coffee shop she hoped for, but a beauty salon. Praying they might take a walk-in, she entered.

"Certainly," they could help her, a soft voice said, and before she knew it, the new clothes had been hung in a closet and she was perched on an upholstered chair in a teal spa robe, reviewing a list of available services. Three hours… She had time for the whole routine. She sure didn't look like a victim anymore; maybe she could stop feeling like one too.

"Manicure, facial, eyebrow shaping, makeup application, haircut—just a trim—and style, oh, and a pedicure if I can be done by three."

"Are you sure just a trim?" One of the stylists lifted a few strands by Marty's temple. "It's pulling your face down."

"Uh… No. Thanks. Just a trim."

The man raised an eyebrow, implying that he'd have to consider whether Marty was worth wasting his time on.

Just then, Marty heard a familiar voice from one of the small treatment rooms. It was Truce, and from the conversation, she was arguing with the manicurist.

"No. I told you. I do not want my cuticles cut."

There was a murmur in response.

"That's where you're wrong. I *will* tell you how to do your job when I'm the one who's paying you to do it."

Apparently, Truce's cuticles would stay put.

Marty raised her own eyebrow and looked directly at the hairdresser.

"Just a trim," she smiled.

On her way to the facial room, Marty poked her head into Truce's manicure room. "Funny meeting you here."

"Funny indeed. Guess we're both getting gussied up for the congressman's tea. I tried to call so we could share a cab. Guess you'd already left."

"Well, we can walk over to the Brasheer's together from here. What time do you expect to be done?

They made their plans, then Marty described the suit she'd just bought, but the esthetician moved her along, and she was soon tilted back in what felt like a dentist's chair, hair swathed in more teal terrycloth. The esthetician worked cleansing cream into Marty's forehead with light circular motions of her fingertips.

"Do you know his wife?" The question had a conspiratorial tone.

"Whose wife?" Marty pretended not to know whom she meant.

"Brasheer's. The congressman's."

"Oh. We've met, but just once." Then, remembering the mortifying taxi ride, "I mean twice."

"That poor woman. I guess that's how they do things in Washington, but around here... well, it's a wonder he keeps getting reelected."

"Why?"

"Well, it's probably the longest running affair a married man's ever had. I really don't know how she holds her head up. Guess it's for those two boys. Lots of women do it. Stay with a cheater to raise the kids. I don't know how she has the nerve to come in here—I mean, she has to know, and she has to know everybody else knows. Course she hasn't been in for a real long time. Maybe that's why."

"When was she in last?" Marty was curious now. She hadn't seen Nan since the captain's dinner—no—she had seen her, she thought, at the costume ball. Maybe. If she was dressed like Jackie Kennedy.

"Oh, I'll bet it's been over a year."

Marty tried to raise her head.

"Well, I mean," the esthetician pushed down on Marty's cheek and defended her customer's loyalty, "sometimes she goes to Washington for months, so it's not that unusual."

"I was told they had only been married a short time. The wife I met was named Nan. Maybe you knew his first wife."

"Oh my God." She sponged a burning substance over Marty's cheeks now. "That must be what happened. He finally divorced her and married his cutie. You know, I heard he had a kid with her. A little girl. Must be a teenager by now. Man, what a long affair. But I guess it was true love, to turn out like this.

Cooling wet pads covered Marty's eyes now.

"I heard she was really beautiful. A super tall girl, with straight hair all the way down to here."

Whatever gesture the esthetician made with reference to the cutie's hair was lost on Marty, who was now being troweled with clay. But she knew Nan wasn't tall. And she hadn't heard anything about a daughter.

The manicurist, apparently finished with Truce and her cuticles, popped in to see when Marty would be ready for her.

The esthetician filled her in on the latest gossip.

"You're kidding!" the manicurist exclaimed. "She was gorgeous. I did her nails once, and Reggie was dying to get his hands on her hair. She looked like an Indian, but her hair wasn't black. It was an odd shade of dark brown with gold running all through it. We thought she was an island woman, but she lives in Virginia."

"Probably close to Washington," the esthetician said, satisfied. "That's what he spends our tax dollars on. Keeping a mistress."

"I doubt he had to keep her. I think she's a famous artist. Maybe in the Smithsonian. Wonder why she'd bother with a married man, even if he was a congressman."

"Yeah. Seems like she could have done better."

"Well, you know what they say. Women who go after married men don't really like them. They're usually just doing it to get back at their own mothers."

"You read too much of that self-help junk."

"Maybe you should try it."

Apparently these two women were used to exchanging verbal slaps, Marty thought, since neither seemed upset.

"Well, at least he's married her now."

Marty, completely forgotten now, was suddenly frozen under her mudpack. Olivia's mother! Joseph had said at Chez Mare that she'd come to collect him. He'd called her Bethany. Bethany was unusually tall. Bethany had teak-colored hair down to wherever. And Bethany had a daughter. And if Bethany was the affair, Olivia could be the lovechild.

She decided not to tell these women that Bethany was not the congressman's wife now, but was possibly still his mistress. That would only fuel their gossip. And the whole thing was so bizarre. So distressing.

Marty could well understand how the congressman's first wife had chosen to endure the humiliation of her husband's infidelity—she herself had endured much worse. Not that either of them should have—just how one could.

It had much more to do with ego and idiocy than with the traditionally assumed "sake of the children." Oh, women could convince themselves that was the case, but the real reason was usually belief that they had more power than they did, that they'd caused the husbands' horrible behavior and could stop it whenever they really put their mind to it. By losing that extra ten pounds they'd kept since the pregnancy, by becoming more interesting, more beautiful, or by simply doing what "he" told them to do. And their self-esteem was so quickly depleted once they decided to endure after the first blow, they started to believe they deserved it.

Marty was fitted with headphones during her manicure and pedicure, and this discouraged further conversation. She was soon shampooed, hot-conditioned, and transferred to Reggie for her trim. By then, she had thought of a million questions, but she doubted that these people would know anything about Olivia, and how crazy or dangerous she was or wasn't.

Olivia had not chosen to endure after the first blow. From what she'd told Christine, this 15-year-old had immediately recognized that her boyfriend was a troubled jerk. Yet... Marty remembered how shy she had been, how completely lacking in confidence. It made her recall how Floyd had beaten her for having her hair cut on Christine's first day of school. It symbolized independence for her and he knew it.

"I've changed my mind," she smiled at Reggie, who was just starting to snip. "I'd like a wedge cut. One layer on top, so it swings."

It did swing. After risking her cervical spine by practicing in the beauty shop mirror, Marty flipped on her new hat and left with Truce.

"Floyd was on the ship." Marty said it quietly, looking around as they started walking up the fashionable block toward the congressman's neighborhood. When Truce did not respond immediately, she thought her new friend might have forgotten their discussion on Majestic Cays. But Truce was apparently thinking. She put her hand firmly on Marty's arm, and leaned to face her as they walked.

"You can't keep fooling around with this guy."

"I'm not!" Marty was incredulous.

"You are. Here you are, getting your hair done, going to tea, for Christ sake..

"But he's gone now. Garrett said…"

"Garrett shmarrett! That's another thing. I see it. You're getting all caught up with doctor boy there, and your life is on the line. Ya'll need to concentrate."

"Look," Marty said defensively, "I didn't realize he was on the ship until I saw you wave that cruise card at the auction on TV last night. When I saw the card, I realized the thing Floyd flashed at me after the wedding was a cruise card. You all left. Garrett was there. I told him. He checked."

Truce sighed. "Oh well." now her tone was sarcastic. "Just so somebody checked."

Marty stopped and looked around again. "He checked to see if Floyd was registered. He was. He boarded at Sint Maarten. He must have followed Sam. There was an empty cabin because somebody went home sick. But he had to leave today. And there's no space on the cruise that starts tonight."

"According to Garrett."

"Well, yes."

"So, even assuming that's right, and okay, it probably is, we don't know somebody else won't get sick and leave."

"I've thought of that. But *he* won't know I'm staying on for this cruise."

"And we do know he's probably here in Ft. Lauderdale right now. And here you are, walking down the street in broad daylight."

"You don't understand," Marty said. "In Pittsburgh, it was like this. I mean, I had to live. I couldn't hide."

"No. You're wrong. I do understand. You've told me enough about this lunatic. He's sick and dangerous. You've been lucky so far, but you can't count on luck. You can't count on cops. And ya'll sure can't count on a ship's doctor to protect you."

"Then, who...?" Marty wondered if Truce was offering to protect her.

"Only yourself."

"Truce, I've been through all that. I can't control this. I can't control him. I know that now."

"Nobody said you could. You just have to stop him. You have to protect yourself."

"But how?"

"How should I know? Only you know."

"But I don't. You said kill him. Remember, on the beach? You said I should have him killed. Well, you didn't really mean that, and yet, short of that...."

"If that's what it takes. Better him than you."

They were a fashionable 15 minutes late for Nan's tea. Nan, however, was not there at all. A servant said the congressman was out back on the canal with earlier guests and his yacht, and invited them to wait in the foyer. The women waited on a French settee, talking in whispers as they gazed at the seven-foot grandfather clock in front of them.

"Why wouldn't she be here? Do you think she forgot?"

Marty had other ideas, but she hadn't relayed the gossip to Truce yet, and this was not the place to do it.

With Garrett and Commodore Mascellino trailing behind him, Richard Brasheer strode into the room and greeted them warmly. Unless Garrett and the captain—both in dress whites—as well as she and Truce—both in elegant linen—had misjudged the appropriate dress for this occasion, the congressman had not been expecting company, his demeanor not withstanding. He wore baggy khaki shorts and a somewhat dirty red polo shirt. It looked like he had more likely been working on his boat than planning to show it off to guests.

He apologized for Nan's absence, but offered no excuses. He complimented the ladies, inquired about Christine, Sam, and Truce's daughter, Donna, then ushered them graciously into the billiard room, explaining that they had been doing some work around the house and that he would leave them "for just a minute, to shower off all this dirt."

Garrett was obviously on the same page as Marty, and suggested they might return at a more convenient time.

"I hope you'll all return frequently," the charming politician laughed, "but I'm really looking forward to our time together today. We back-to-back-cruisers who live in one of the ports aren't lucky enough to avoid housekeeping at the mid-point."

Marty thought he looked nervous, but you sure couldn't tell it in his booming voice.

192

"Let me offer you a cocktail. Then, I promise, I'll be back in a minute."

The uniformed butler stepped behind the bar and poured wine for Marty, a cocktail called a "Miami Vice" for Truce, and beer for the two men.

Garrett raised his mug in a toast and winked at Marty: "Tea?"

"Tea," she responded, as the congressman departed.

"You okay?"

"Pretty much. Kind of nervous."

"I told you. Two new passengers boarded at Sint Maarten," Garret said quietly to Marty. "One was Sam, for Christine's suite on Baja, and the other was Floyd Arkus, for the vacated stateroom on Aloha Deck."

Marty looked down at her glass.

"And like I said, he's not on the new list. Good news is, we're sold out. He *had to* disembark this morning."

Marty looked over at Truce.

"Well, let's hope nobody else gets sick and leaves."

Garret nodded and raised his glass to her. "My business to see that they don't."

Sipping in silence, they all perused the room. The billiard table centered beneath a long brass chandelier suspended from the lofty carved-plaster ceiling. A gleaming hardwood floor reflected bits of light from the chandelier's twenty-plus candle-shaped bulbs. Dark paintings covered three of the papered walls, and good luck symbols were spread throughout the room. A three-dimensional amber glass and copper star, about seven inches in diameter, housed a tea light and hung from a spiraling copper stand. Truce explained that this was a Moravian star lantern. One wall was bare. Leaning against it on the floor was a large—at least six feet by seven—butcher-wrapped flat rectangle. Probably a new painting, Marty thought. Truce had wandered over to the package, which was torn open on the side facing the wall, and she tipped it back to peek.

Just then, Richard Brasheer—hair damp, and now in a sports coat—reentered the room. Grinning, he refilled beer mugs and poured one for himself.

"You got it?" This was Truce, directing herself to Richard as she pivoted the heavy package from the wall to reveal a monumental painting of a horse and three nudes who seemed, to Marty, to be frolicking at the edge of the sea. "You outbid me at the auction!" Her smile was one of admiration and her tone was you-sly-dog-you.

For a second, Richard appeared to be disturbed. It seemed to Marty that he was upset that they had seen the painting, though he may have been—justifiably, Marty thought—concerned that Truce might damage the artwork by tilting it back and forth like that. But he recovered immediately, and said tactfully, "On the ship? They must have auctioned a print."

"Do you mean to say that this is an original Emile Baer?" Truce seemed nothing short of flabbergasted.

When Richard nodded, she turned to Marty.

"I know a bit about art. I have about two-dozen very fine artists' prints, worth several thousand apiece. They're all appreciating, I hope, at this very moment. But an original Baer..." she proceeded to tear it's wrapping further.

By now, everyone had gathered too close to the painting to see it properly, and they stepped back for perspective as a group. Truce though, bent to peer closely at the bottom of the painting.

"It was painted in France in 1943," Richard said. Then, like a docent conducting a museum tour, he moved the group quickly to another painting, then through eight-foot pocket doors to more original art in the living room.

"Luncheon is served, sir." The butler had returned.

Richard queried Truce about her art collection, as, glasses refreshed, they were seated on a tiled veranda with a view of his yacht and the canal. Commodore Mascellino— "Please! Call me Anthony"—chimed in about his own. Plates arrived with filet mignon on crumpets topped with bean sprouts next to tarragon dressed salads. A boat of béarnaise sauce was passed, and, as Garrett handed it politely to Marty, he said, "Tea?"

The festive group rode with the congressman back to the ship. The butler donned a driving cap for the occasion. There had been no discussion about Nan, and somehow, it would have been awkward to bring it up. Only when they arrived at Port Everglades did Richard mention her name.

"I'm ready for a seagoing rest," he said. "I hope Nan has a log on the fire."

Within minutes, Marty and Truce were alone at the check-in. Garrett and the captain had rushed ahead— apparently already late for shiply duties—and the congressman had simply disappeared.

"Original my foot," Truce said.

Marty was surprised.

"It would've been crated. I've certainly never seen valuable original art delivered in butcher paper."

Marty did not point out that Truce had just told them she only owned prints, and, in any case, the cruise card lady was upon her. They prepared to separate then because Marty had a cash account and Truce needed to go through a different line for credit card holders, but they agreed to meet for dinner.

"Don't know if I'll be hungry after all that tea," Marty said.

Truce seemed confused.

"Hey Truce," Marty called, as the woman walked away.

Truce turned.

"Thanks."

"Thanks for what? Butting into your business."

"No. For not saying he's crazy and dangerous *if* what I told you is true."

Truce smiled and waved.

Marty headed straight for her suite. An envelope was taped to her door. She opened the note.

Should be finished in time for the midnight buffet. Hope to see you there. Forgot to mention—the haircut is tres chic!

Garrett

She refolded the note, absently stroked it against the silkiness of her new chemise. Having already sailed away,

Marty elected to skip the "Sail Away Party" and nap. But her mind kept reeling. This leg of the cruise would stop at Majestic Cays the first day, and she hoped to see Christine to discuss this new information about Olivia. She'd like to see Nan before then, and maybe get a better sense of things. She would bring up the anti-stalking legislation if she had to. Maybe she could find out if Nan was aware of Olivia at all, or if she herself had a daughter. No. Nan might have had teak-colored long hair at one time, though it didn't seem likely, but she was surely never "super tall."

Hank and Philip were the new Leon and Charlie at their table, and Truce seemed very taken with Philip. A woman named Pat was in Christine's old seat, and Donna's chair was empty. "Pouting" was Truce's explanation for her daughter's absence.

After eating very little, Marty excused herself to wander the ship until time for the first night's musical revue. She planned to attend before meeting Garrett at the midnight buffet. She scanned the dining room on the way out in a deliberate search for Nan. The chair beside the congressman sat empty. Either Nan had gone to powder her nose, or these people just didn't associate. Some honeymooners.

A bit early for the 10:00 show, Marty stopped by the photography display and asked if they still had photos from the previous week's cruise.

"Decided you wanted some after all? Well, you're in luck," the clerk said. These weren't shredded in time to recycle in Ft. Lauderdale."

Marty situated herself on one of the sofas near the bar and began searching through the large carton the clerk carried out from a back room. The photographs were sorted into folders. She found one in "late seating" that included herself and Garrett at the captain's table. Nan was there, and Truce, Leon, and the captain. She searched for shots of the congressman's table. The costume dinner was hopeless unless you knew which costumes you were looking for. Most passengers had donned their masks for that shot. Most of those without masks were heavily made up. No Jackie Kennedys. Finally, she found a photo from another night when Richard and Nan Brasheer were seated together. Imagine that, Marty thought. They do spend an occasional moment in the same room. The same folder also included a photo of Marty in her gold gown. It must have been taken on day three, a formal night after a full day at sea. That had been the night she met Garrett on deck, Marty figured, remembering his remark about "pure gold." But that was it. No more of Nan. Unless they were in the impossible-to-identify costume party photographs after their day—or at least Nan's day—on Orient Beach at St. Martin, Nan and her husband had not been photographed together since the first formal night. Richard showed up in a number of photos, which were taken daily all over the ship, but there were only these two photographs of Nan, alone *or* with her husband.

Much of the entertainment onboard was not especially entertaining, Marty thought, as she munched cheddar goldfish at a tiny table and watched groups of performers sing and dance. She left early, stopped by her suite to freshen up for the midnight buffet. Regretting the garlicky snacks, she brushed her teeth twice and re-applied lipstick. Then she decided to cleanse her face and re-do all of her makeup. The new haircut surprised and pleased her each time she looked into the mirror. I really do look good, she thought, maybe even a bit younger. Then, noticing the wrinkles in her new outfit, she selected a glittery peach top, brown linen slacks, and strappy brown sandals to change into. Satisfied with a final look, she spritzed cologne into the air and walked through it. The telephone rang just as she picked up her purse.

"Marty." It was Garrett. "Can you meet me in the Wheelhouse Bar, forward on Promenade? I want to talk with you, and it's quieter there than it will be at the buffet."

"Of course, but what's up?" She was concerned. Garrett usually didn't sound so serious.

"Rather tell you there. I'm heading over now."

"Okay. See you in a sec."

Garrett was waiting at the door. There was none of their usual banter as he led her across the dark English pub to a quiet table in the back. He left her for a minute while he went for the coffee they had both decided on. When he returned and sat on the edge of the club chair across from her, Marty could see that he was distressed. He leaned forward and jumped right into it.

"Nan Brasheer is missing."

"You mean she didn't get back on the ship?" Marty asked.

"I mean missing. Never got off today either."

"Well, I haven't seen her. I'm almost certain I haven't seen her since Sint Maarten," Marty said. "In fact, after she wasn't at her tea today, I started wondering. I checked the photographs after dinner and the last one of her was taken—or at least it's the last one I could find—at the captain's dinner the third night. We were approaching Sint Maarten," she added.

Marty picked up her spoon and stirred the coffee in front of her, even though she'd added neither sugar nor cream.

"And I've only seen her onboard once after that myself. At the costume party, just before dinner."

"That's what they're checking now—all of the photographs taken aboard this and last week's cruise. We already know she did reboard at Sint Maarten. Night of the costume party."

"Some people object to being photographed." Marty was thinking aloud. "Maybe she's like that. And besides, how do you know she didn't just stay on the ship today?"

Even as she asked, she didn't think it likely. But so much about Nan and Richard's relationship was very strange for honeymooners. For any vacationing married couple, really. And after all she'd heard today...

"No way. Every passenger is checked in and out at every port. Disembarkation procedure at home port, even for people like you who are doing back-to-backs. In our case, that's Ft. Lauderdale. Nan wasn't processed through disembarkation there. And she didn't check on or off at Majestic Cays. We record tickets for the tenders there."

Marty recalled that *Mare Majestic* had docked about a mile offshore for the little island visit. She had thought she might be in the same tender with Christine and Sam, but tickets were issued by deck.

"I checked with Richard after dinner this evening. He admitted he hadn't seen her since the costume party. We were at sea then."

Garrett was grim, and it took a few seconds for Marty to comprehend his implication.

"So she might have fallen overboard? And he didn't report it to anyone? And acted like that today?"

Marty was incredulous.

———

He read her letter once more. He'd found it on the kitchen counter after work the day she took off and cleaned him out.

Floyd,

Please don't try to contact me. Mike is my lawyer and has filed for divorce on my behalf. Call him with any questions about that. I have taken only enough furniture to get by, and the court will divide the rest.

I'm sorry I had to leave this way, but you have made me afraid to do otherwise. I will tell Christine tonight, but she has surely seen it coming. So have you. You left me no other choice. I still can't believe your cruelty, especially to Christine. I hope that somewhere, deep down, you love your daughter enough to handle this properly. If you do, she will forgive you in the end. You are her dad and she loves you, but she knows better than to believe the lies you've told.

Marty

———

201

Then he reread his masterpiece, painstakingly photo-shopped from the original. It was a process he liked to call decoupaging. Selecting just the right handwritten words, copying each carefully from the scan of the original letter, then placing them perfectly into a new computer document. Smudge a few tears on the finished product, fold and refold. Elegant.

Christine, I'm sorry to end this way, but deep down I have no hope left. I told lies about your dad. Please forgive me.

———

15

Day Ten, Eleuthera Island, Bahamas

Unable to sleep by 2 a.m., Marty stepped from her bedroom to her balcony and into a fluttery night breeze. *Mare Majestic* churned through the dark Atlantic wilderness. Marty shivered, thought of Nan, the obvious, the impossibly horrific, and the connections. If Olivia was the congressman's daughter with Bethany, she could well have motive to harm Nan.

Olivia is on this ship. Somehow, she's on the ship. Somehow, she pushed Nan into the Caribbean Sea between St. Martin and St. Croix. And, somehow she got into our cabin and attached that charm to Christine's necklace.

Absurd, but what else could explain it all? But why would Olivia see Christine as an enemy? And, she wondered, why me?

The only enemy Marty had ever had, as far as she knew, was Floyd. Floyd boarded the ship the day she gave Christine the necklace. But he only wanted to hurt her, not Christine. He would have even less chance to get into the cabin than Olivia. Unless... Marty couldn't bear the speculation. She'd started to consider the possibility that Floyd had Christine's cooperation. She crawled back into bed and dipped in and out of sleep until dawn, unable to let herself think the unthinkable.

At six, she dressed in shorts and T-shirt and made her way to the Horizon Court on Lido where coffee was set out. She watched land emerge from the mist as crew members set up a breakfast buffet, and she read the daily "Majestic Muse" to force her mind elsewhere.

Mare Majestic had traveled 284 nautical miles southeast from Ft. Lauderdale during the night. Reading that a nautical mile was 15 percent longer than a statute mile, Marty tried doing the math in her head but decided it was too early to think. She'd take the newsletter's word that the trip took 14 hours at speeds just under 20 knots.

After today's stop back at Eleuthera's Majestic Cays, they would pass through the Bahamas and, essentially, circle Cuba. They would navigate the Windward Passage between Haiti and Cuba on the Caribbean Sea, then the Gulf of Mexico would carry them back to the Atlantic. Ports on this cruise would include Jamaica, Grand Cayman, and Cozumel Island, Mexico.

Marty could see land in the distance. She had to figure this out, face whatever it took. There was still the difficulty of Olivia getting onto the ship in the first place. Floyd had been on the ship. Christine would never betray her. The more Marty considered that, the more she was certain. But what if he'd tricked her? They might have talked by phone. Floyd could have—would have, Marty was sure—told his daughter that he loved her and desperately wanted to attend her wedding. He might have said that her mother would never have to know, that he'd watch from the sidelines and stay out of sight.

Already anxious to forgive her daughter, Marty reminded herself that Christine had no idea how very serious her fear of Floyd had become. It *was* possible.

Wait. Christine's cooperation could explain Floyd's showing up on St. Croix, maybe even joining the cruise at

Sint Maarten, but it did not explain the coincidence of the gun charm. Of course, Christine could have told him about Olivia, but Christine didn't know about the existence of the necklace in Marty's safe. Or did she? Marty thought about the bridal gown in her closet. The possibly-unlocked safe in the closet. Christine might have peeked at her present. No. She wouldn't have realized it was for her. Wait. Floyd wouldn't either. He would have assumed the necklace belonged to Marty. If he somehow got Christine to let him into the cabin, then, say, Christine had to go to the bathroom, Floyd could have looked into Marty's safe.

No! Christine would never let Floyd into Marty's cabin. That *would* be a betrayal, and Christine would see it as such. Besides, Marty remembered with great relief, Christine's cruisecard was for the suite. It wouldn't open Marty's door. It really must have been Olivia. Crazy people didn't need reasons. Olivia had decided to hurt or frighten her stepmother and Christine.

Marty finished her third cup of coffee and was first in line for the tender when *Mare Majestic* set anchor a half-mile off the southern tip of Eleuthera. She leaned forward at the rail as though that would hurry the little boat across the water to Christine. Hard to believe it was only two days since she'd been here.

She looked straight down into the blue water. Nan overboard? Marty closed her eyes and saw the beaded jacket, the silver earrings, the bracelet. The vision sent a quiver across her shoulders. An accident? Suicide? She doubted it. Her conclusion about Olivia made more sense, and that sick girl might not be finished yet. The danger to Christine seemed horribly real.

From the tender, Marty could see the rainbow of water toys lined up in wait on the beach, as well as the picnic shelter and lookout perch. Olivia was crazy. Dangerously crazy. If she had managed to get herself onto the ship, she could get herself off. She could be, this minute, on one of the tenders behind Marty's headed for Majestic Cays and for Christine. Marty had managed to gain passage on the first tender out—reserved for passengers with cabins on Riviera and Aloha decks—by claiming that she was ill and needed to get on land quickly. Even then, she was only allowed onboard because there was extra space. Apparently some of the upper deck passengers had continued their sail-away party into the night and were sleeping late this morning. After the initial transport, tenders would commute continuously between the ship and the island.

Marty was the first one off at the dock, and she ran to the picnic shelter, where she stopped to catch her breath and empty sand from her tennis shoes while she looked behind the shelter for the path. The aroma of roasting pork turned her stomach.

Sam had told her on Saturday that the honeymoon hale was about a half-mile from Majestic Cays near Bannerman Town, and that the path leading between them was nature's equivalent of a well-planned tropical garden. He and Christine had been taken by rickshaw with their luggage to the hale, but had walked back to join the pig roast and Marty's snorkeling hysteria.

Christine and Sam would go north by horseback to Davis Harbor on Tuesday and then a taxi would pick them up Wednesday for the longer ride to Northern Eleuthera's Gregory Town. There, in a more populated area, they would spend the last few days of their honeymoon as tourists, then fly to Ft. Lauderdale and on home. No one else knew their plans, Sam had said, but they wanted Marty to know they wouldn't be out of reach in case she needed them. Marty had chuckled at that, but felt better having the itinerary Sam handed her.

Surely, she thought now, she would recognize a thatched hut when she came upon it. Finding the path might be more difficult.

She needn't have worried. A parade of bicycle driven rickshaws and electric golf carts emerged from an opening in the lush tropical foliage behind the shelter. People were streaming in to help cater the picnic. Probably they lived in Bannerman Town. Marty waited for a break in the parade, which turned out to be the end of it, and hurried up the pathway. Her brief run through the sand had winded her, but she managed a brisk walk. Within five minutes, the only sounds she heard were unfamiliar. She hoped they were tropical birds, but a peculiar screeching made her uneasy. A monkey, perhaps? She scanned the pineapple trees overhead. Did monkeys bite? That led her to thoughts of snakes, and, head down, she broke into a run.

Clop, clop, clop. "Mom!" It was Christine. Christine and Sam, on the backs of two small black horses, were riding directly toward her. She stopped. When they drew abreast, she grabbed Christine's leg and leaned against her horse, gasping.

"What are you doing?"

"We were coming to…"

Sam and Christine interrupted each other.

Marty drew a deep breath. "You can't stay here tonight."

207

"What?" Sam sounded more irritated than curious.

Christine started laughing. "Mom! Talk about having trouble cutting the apron strings."

"No, I'm serious." Marty was settling down. "I think Olivia killed Nan. I think you're in danger. Can we go back to your cottage or somewhere to talk?"

"Oh my God. Nan Brasheer? Nan's been killed?" Christine turned to Sam. "She's the woman who was sitting with Chef Enrico when we met you at that bar on Orient Beach."

"That's right," Marty said, adding "She's the congressman's wife."

Christine relinquished the stirrups and helped Marty onto the saddle behind her. Marty hadn't been on a horse for years, but the process was smooth and automatic.

"How was she killed? I can't believe Olivia would kill anyone. There's some mistake."

"I don't know for sure that she was killed," Marty admitted. "But she has been missing since St. Martin—since the costume party—and she never got off the ship."

"How do we know she's not still on the ship?" Sam asked reasonably.

"We know," Marty responded. "Garrett says they check everything at Ft. Lauderdale. Otherwise, I guess they'd have stowaways all the time."

This brought her back to Olivia. "I'm not sure how Olivia got onboard."

They came into Bannerman Town, one narrow street with a few white stucco dwellings and shops. Sam's horse led the way, and Christine talked over her shoulder to her mother.

"You think Olivia got on the ship somehow? And that she's coming here tonight?"

"Yes."

They had arrived at a small stable, where Sam turned in the rented horses. From there, they walked to a drugstore that was also part grocery, part diner, and part bar, and sat in one of the two booths. They ordered pineapple juice and buttered toast, and Marty tried to explain.

She told them about the beauty shop gossip and that it seemed likely that Richard Brasheer was Olivia's real father.

"She already told you Joseph wasn't."

She told them about Richard Brasheer's odd behavior at the tea and the outrageous fact that he hadn't reported his wife missing.

"I think Olivia put that gun charm on your necklace," Marty said definitely. "I can't really explain how she did it, but I think I know why. She has been through some crazy times. Either with her mother's having an affair for all these years, and having to hide her father's identity, or with a nutso boyfriend." Marty sipped her juice. "Maybe both."

When neither Christine nor Sam responded, she continued.

"If she was crazy to start with, then with her father marrying Nan... well, the boyfriend might even be innocent. Olivia might have planted that charm in her own locker."

"Listen to you! How can you, of all people, blame Olivia?" Christine was angry.

Marty stared at her daughter. "How could you, of all people, let Daddy into my stateroom?"

"What?" Christine's incredulous expression told Marty beyond doubt that her daughter had nothing to do with this.

"What did you say?" Christine asked again, as though she couldn't believe her own ears.

Marty shook her head slowly. "I...nothing. I don't know why I said that. Forgive me. I think maybe it's the pressure."

"What pressure?"

"The pressure of Olivia having done this to you, of her having killed Nan, of you being in danger now..." Marty trailed off.

"Well, again, I don't know how you of all people can assume that about a girl who's been through what Olivia has."

Marty knew her daughter was right. She was the last person who should jump to a conclusion like this.

"Well, okay. If the boyfriend really did give her the gun charm, then that's maybe what made her crazy. Either way, I think she is mentally disturbed. She talked to you. She knew you were getting married. She could have heard about my planning to give you the necklace. Who else would have put that gun charm on your necklace? I mean, who would ever think it would have any significance?"

"I don't know, Mom." Christine sounded ready to cry. "I just know Olivia wouldn't do that." The boyfriend wasn't innocent. Remember, he tried to hit her with a car!" Now a little sob escaped her. "I even thought of Daddy."

Sam put his arm around Christine. Marty reached out to pat her hand.

"That doesn't make sense either, honey. Your dad and Olivia—both with a gun charm—no. And you don't really know Olivia at all. You just don't want to be wrong in your judgment. My only doubt has to do with how she could get onboard."

Floyd, of course, had been onboard. No! She wouldn't think it again. Marty considered telling Christine that her father had joined the cruise at Sint Maarten. That he'd been thirty yards away during the wedding. But she didn't. It made no sense unless Christine was involved, and she wasn't. Floyd could have had no knowledge of the gun charm. To protect her daughter, all she had to do was put her on alert. It wouldn't matter if Christine could just get away from Majestic Cays and Eleuthera Island.

"If Garrett's right, and he ought to be," Sam said, "she couldn't possibly still be onboard *Mare Majestic* and ready to get off here. She would have been caught at Ft. Lauderdale. I mean, if she could do that, Nan could do that—right?"

Christine was drying her tears on Sam's hankie. Marty leaned back on the torn red plastic seat.

"That is right." She considered further. "So, it's most likely then that Olivia got on and off the ship at Sint Maarten."

"Yeah, right, "Christine said. "This little girl, who's scared of her own shadow, sneaked onboard, right past the customs people and crew members who check you in."

Christine sat up straight, pulling away from her husband's protective arm. Her sarcasm thickened.

"She went directly to your cabin." Christine's finger traced a path on the table. "Unlocked the door with the key she just happened to have. Then she just happened to know the combination to your safe. She also just happened to know about the necklace, and where it was, of course. She put the gun charm on the necklace just to spook me because she had so much reason to hate me. Then she slammed the safe shut, ran out of the cabin, ran to Nan's cabin—she knew where that was too—punched Nan and knocked her out, then carried her out to the balcony—assuming they have a balcony—and threw her into the drink. Then she sneaked off the ship, past the guards again, and ran into the island night. Is that how it happened, Mom?"

"Now, you look here..." Marty stopped. By now, they were all confused, and she realized that it sounded ridiculous. She pinched her mouth with her hand. Maybe she *should* doubt her own sanity.

"But Nan *is* missing," she said, feeling tears starting to well in her own eyes, "and the gun charm was on the necklace. And we know there is a connection. There *has* to be. That's not ridiculous."

Even as she said it though, she was thinking: It could have been Floyd. If he followed Sam to the ship, to Chez Mare on Orient Beach. If, somehow, he overheard them telling Sam about Olivia and the gun charm... It really could have been Floyd.

Now they were strolling through the little town toward the hale. Christine wanted to show Marty around before she left.

"We don't know there is a connection," Sam said.

Marty bristled. "We know there is a connection between gun charms and Olivia, and appearances of tiny silver guns on fine jewelry are not common occurrences. And we know Olivia and Nan are both connected to the congressman."

They were silent for a minute, walking. It occurred to Marty that Sam might think she had lost her mind and put the gun charm on Christine's necklace herself. Could he really think such a thing? Would Christine?

But Christine spoke. "Mom's right, but I just can't see Olivia doing that, let alone being able to."

They arrived at the hale and did a cursory tour. It was, indeed, a thatched hut, with a well-dressed queen sized bed inside. There was a chest of drawers on the opposite wall, and two candle-topped nightstands flanked the bed.

"The kitchen." Christine gestured toward a stone barbeque pit in the yard as they left and turned back toward the path to the beach. "It's charming and quaint, but I guess I'm addicted to electricity."

"Okay," Sam said, walking again with his head down. "I guess we do know, or at least we think, there is a connection between Olivia and Nan."

"We do know there's a connection between them. Nan is married to Richard Brasheer. Or was. Olivia was with Richard Brasheer in the Jeep at Magens Bay, when they returned our bag. Remember," Christine added, "she said she didn't know a congressman. That, I did think she was lying about. But not the rest."

"And we think," Marty said, "that there is a deeper connection. We think that Richard is Olivia's father."

"But we don't know that for sure. And even if it's true, we have no idea of whether Nan or Olivia would know that," Christine added.

"I'm just afraid," Marty said. "I'm so worried about you."

"Wait. I have an idea!" Christine opened her tiny purse and removed a folded piece of notepaper. I have Olivia's address and phone number on St. Martin. Let's call." She led them back to the drugstore-diner-grocery-bar. There was a phone on the wall behind the counter, and Marty paid the proprietor in advance.

Christine tried to dial long distance, but was told she had to use the operator. She waited. "If she's there, at least you'll know that she's not onboard *Mare Majestic* or lurking in the oleander behind our hale."

They all waited.

"It's ringing… Hello, is Olivia there?… Uh, Christine. Christine Arkus. I mean Joly. We met at Magens Bay. She gave me the number. I asked for it."

Christine shrugged her shoulders and looked helplessly at Sam and Marty.

"Okay. No. That's okay. Just tell her I called. That the wedding was beautiful. She wanted to know. Thanks."

Christine hung up the receiver.

"I didn't know what to say. It was a woman. I think her mother. Wanted to know who I was and how I got the number."

"She wasn't there?" Marty touched her daughter's arm.

"No, she was. But in the shower. The woman offered to let me hold or have her call me back. So I'm sure she really was there."

If only, Marty thought, we could call to check on Floyd now. No, she told herself, it would be okay. He had to disembark at Ft. Lauderdale. He can't be here. He's not after Christine. If this wasn't Olivia, then Christine is safe.

When they got to the beach, the scene was much like it had been Saturday afternoon. Children ran through the pink and white sand, young adults punched volleyballs, and every beach chair and hammock held a body. Snorkels bobbed on the blue water and flippers occasionally splashed up a few feet behind them.

Marty invited Sam and Christine to join her for the picnic lunch, but they declined.

"It's really just for the cruise people, Mom," Christine said, "and we should be getting back."

"When you reboard," Sam added, "I think you should see the captain. Just tell him everything we know and let the authorities take it from there."

Marty just stared at him.

"We can wait with you," he offered weakly.

Marty felt awful. This was Christine's honeymoon, and here she was. She faced her daughter.

"No, I'll tell you what. I am going to have a nice big lunch, and then I'll steal one of those hammocks as soon as someone else gets up to eat, and I'll have a nap in the island breeze."

More seriously, she turned to Sam. "I'll tell the captain after we weigh anchor tonight."

Christine and Sam were obviously relieved, and Marty wished them a wonderful week, kissed and waved them goodbye, and proceeded to do exactly what she had said she would.

The ship's foghorn woke her just in time to hear the announcement that the last tender would leave in 15 minutes.

The laptop computer was still running when she reached her suite, and Marty's first thought was that she'd been wasting the battery for two days. Remembering that laptop batteries lasted only about four hours, she checked anyway to convince herself it was plugged in. Before he'd left her cabin Saturday night, Garrett had asked if he could e-mail a copy of her essay on the island to himself. She had agreed, knowing that he was only trying to make her feel better, but appreciating his interest all the same. Apparently he had signed off, but had not closed the file, and she had not looked at the computer since.

Marty sat. Somehow, she had to take this matter in hand. She keyed in the words "What we know now." When her list was complete, she telephoned the captain's office and arranged an appointment for 6 p.m. "to provide some information about the woman who is missing." She had no trouble making that arrangement. Then, since she had no printer, Marty asked the man for the captain's e-mail address and got it. She transmitted her list, and within seconds, felt *Mare Majestic* weigh anchor. She considered calling Garrett to ask him to join her in meeting with the captain, but decided against it. First, she barely had time to shower and make herself presentable. And, second, she needed to do this on her own.

———

He folded and refolded the finished letter. Then he opened it once more to read. So sad, so hopeless. Anyone who read it would see how she just couldn't go on. Christine would see. His daughter was intelligent like him. She would comprehend his truth.

———

16

Day Eleven, At Sea

After talking with the captain, Marty had her best night's sleep since discovering the gun charm. Now she woke feeling almost luxurious as *Mare Majestic* continued its way south. The telephone's ring startled her back to the worried present. It was Garrett.

"I was on duty all night with no calls, so I was able to sleep. I have a whole wonderful day to do your bidding. Thought we'd start with a Castro watch."

"A what watch?"

"Castro. We'll be passing by Cuba soon, and you never know when there might be a sighting."

"Oh." Marty smiled. She had been thinking Timex and Rolex. "Any word on Nan?"

"Unfortunately not. Join me for breakfast?"

Marty smiled again.

"Of course. I have to shower first though. I just woke up."

"Fine. How about I pick you up in half an hour."

"I'll be ready."

"Marty… I talked to Anthony last night."

"Um." She didn't know what to say to this.

"We'll talk at breakfast."

"Okay." She looked at her watch on the nightstand. "I'll see you at nine."

Garrett arrived as promised and, over poached eggs and smoked salmon in the dining room, related his conversation with the captain.

"Anthony likes you. I think he wants to hire you."

Marty laughed at this, embarrassed. When she e-mailed the captain, she had accidentally attached her island description first, and had to resend her "what we know" list. The captain must have read the first attachment thoroughly, looking for clues about the missing woman, and probably, she thought, deciding that Marty was some kind of flake.

Before she arrived though, Anthony had obviously read the second e-mail, and taken it very seriously. He had opened their conversation with a compliment about her descriptive writing, and the need for someone with this ability on the ship. Marty herself had the impression that he might want to hire her—and couldn't figure out why a cruise line would need a writer. But then he had gone directly to the list, and he seemed to share her concern.

"He agrees there's some kind of connection," Garrett said. "He's known Richard Brasheer quite a few years, but only casually. Bethany Pumphrey was onboard with Brasheer for his cruise last year. Remember, I told you there was a different woman I assumed he had married—and I was surprised to meet Nan?"

Marty did remember.

"Well, there was another woman Anthony met on that cruise who knew Bethany. A woman who worked with her at the National Gallery of Art in Washington, D.C. She told Anthony that Bethany is a brilliant art conservator. She repairs paintings and can reproduce them. Anthony said he never forgot that because it made him wonder how anybody could know if they were really buying original art."

Marty had wondered the same thing when Truce commented on the horse picture at the congressman's house, and said so now.

"I mean, most people who buy original art are investors, aren't they? Sure, they enjoy it, but how could an untrained person really know?"

Garrett wouldn't be sidetracked.

"Anyway, this woman said it was an accepted fact in Washington that Richard and Bethany were lovers. Had been for years. There were rumors about them having a child together, but the woman didn't know for sure if Bethany's daughter was Richard's. Said his former wife was probably always aware of the affair and cut her deal to stay married to a congressman."

"Well," Marty was thoughtful, "she also had a family to think about."

"Richard had two sons. Supposedly a devoted father."

"Doesn't sound very devoted."

"Remember though, he was politically ambitious. In his world it was acceptable to have a mistress but not to divorce your wife and break up a family with children."

Garrett scooped egg yolk with a toast triangle.

"He didn't divorce his wife until his second son graduated. After the divorce, Richard spent more time than ever, the woman said, and more openly, with Bethany."

"But Bethany was also married."

"That's right. Supposedly, Joseph Pumphrey was a joke in their circles. A convenience. Kind of a place-holder for Richard until his kids were grown and he could be free. Or until he peaked in his career."

"Did—does—Joseph know about the affair?"

"Supposedly. The woman said it was a marriage of convenience for him too."

"How convenient could that be?"

"Who knows? Bethany made money. A good bit, from what that woman said. He may not even have a job. The point is, or, at least her point was, everybody expected Richard to marry Bethany after his divorce. People thought that was why he got the divorce. Bethany's being married to Joseph was pretty much considered immaterial."

"Maybe he loves her."

"That's what everybody thought."

"Not Richard, Joseph."

"Nobody seemed to have that impression."

Marty thought about Olivia. She had told Christine that Joseph was "like a father, but not really." She had also said she didn't know a congressman.

"Wow. What a mess."

Marty shook her head and missed the caressing swish of hair along her neck.

"You'd think so."

"Does anyone know how Richard met Nan?"

"According to Anthony, Richard had known her for a long time. Nan was the daughter of a senator who died years ago. Popular Washington hostess."

"You'd think she would have known about Richard's affair with Bethany," Marty said. "I mean, if it were such an open secret. I wonder why she'd ever marry him."

"Like I said," Garrett explained, "Washington hostess. Maybe more concerned with the guest list that comes with a political husband than if the guy has someone on the side?"

Vincent had begun to hover, and Marty realized he had been kind to serve their breakfast half an hour after the regular seating. The other waiters had already set their tables for lunch and taken a break. Apologizing, she and Garrett left the table.

"Speaking of art," Garrett said, leading her by the elbow past a roped off area toward the far dining room wall, "what do you think of our Botticelli?"

"Really?" Marty gazed at the beautiful Roman painting and wondered if, indeed, a cruise ship would have a 15th-century masterpiece displayed above its champagne fountain.

"Course not. But some very well known artists have been commissioned to produce these in his style. We do have museum-class stuff here. Worth over two million."

Just then, Enrico came rushing by. Having passed them, he stopped abruptly and turned. "Galley

---

223

demonstration on Lido," he announced, turning again and chugging away, chef's hat bobbing.

"I think my good man Enrico is a bit uncomfortable," Garrett said.

"Well, he ought to be. Sam told me about the bachelor party."

Garrett looked directly into her eyes. "Probably not a person over twenty-five working on this ship who doesn't have demons to escape. Not a bad life. But it's usually not first choice. So, we're pretty forgiving."

He held Marty's eyes until she looked away.

They decided to watch the culinary demonstration in Horizon Court. This was the buffet style restaurant on Lido Deck that they should have chosen when they arrived so late for breakfast. The glass elevator took them up two levels, only as far as Dolphin Deck. There they transferred near the casino to another lift, running into Truce and Philip, who looked somewhat the worse for wear. Marty invited them to the demonstration, but Truce declined.

"We heard about Nan Brasheer," she said. "Have they found the body?"

Truce's question jarred Marty, who was so caught up in speculation about Nan's marriage, she had almost forgotten that Nan was missing.

"Is it true that the congressman is still on the ship?" Truce demanded.

Garrett responded. "Yes, Richard Brasheer is onboard. I think he's trying to help with the investigation."

"I'd think he'd be a suspect," Truce said flatly. "I mean, isn't it usually the husband?"

"No evidence of foul play, and no, Mrs. Brasheer has not been found yet," Garrett answered carefully. "The captain is in charge of the investigation because she was last seen here on the ship. Congressman Brasheer is certainly distraught, but he can be more useful here, with the captain, than back in Ft. Lauderdale."

Garrett didn't mention an opinion he had voiced to Marty earlier—that Richard was probably avoiding a media nightmare.

"I think we set a record for breaking even," Truce said, dropping the subject and tossing her head in the general direction of the casino, which, at ten in the morning appeared to be as lively as Marty would have expected it to be at midnight.

Truce and Philip had been gambling since just after the midnight buffet, they said. Truce had been lucky early on, then, started losing. Philip reported that they had taken a break in his cabin at that point.

"We decided to pursue more exciting activities before they forced us to wash our own champagne glasses," he said, with a comic-book leer.

Truce reddened, obviously distressed by Philip's crassness. Marty felt sorry for her, but since she could well imagine Truce making the comment herself, was a little surprised. What Marty had come to like most about Truce was her the-hell-with-what-anybody-thinks personality. Was it only a posture? Did Truce, too, want people to think well of her? And why shouldn't they? Truce had pulled a life together for herself and her daughter, and worked darn hard to do it. She was on vacation. If she wanted to have a little fling on a cruise, why shouldn't she? Marty tried not to wonder how Donna would feel. She put her hand on Truce's arm and said, sincerely, "I'm glad you had a good time."

Truce got the message and patted Marty's hand gratefully. Then she bubbled back into her subject. "By three a.m., I was back on top." She winked at the double-entendre. "But the last dog died a few minutes ago. I still have my three thousand dollars, but the one extra quarter I could have walked away with for a whole night's work just went into a slot machine."

Marty was impressed. "You won three thousand?"

"No. I gambled three thousand. I won another eighteen hundred. I lost eighteen hundred. I won six hundred. I lost six hundred. I still have three thousand."

"Oh."

"But think of all the free champagne they passed out at the tables," Philip chimed in, jovial; too stupid to know he was probably already history.

"Whatever lifts your skirt." Truce directed herself only to Marty. "I am tired. This getting nowhere is very hard work. See you tonight."

With that, she got onto an elevator that was about to close and left Marty and Garrett with her new friend Philip.

"That's one wild woman," Philip said. Neither Marty nor Garrett responded.

Marty expected radish roses, but was pleasantly surprised. Her favorite part of the demonstration was the pastry preparation. An almond paste called marzipan was carefully tinted, then kneaded and shaped into tiny peaches, strawberries, and pears. More food coloring was painted on for detail.

"These folks are actually artists," she said.

Garrett looked proud.

The show ended with a galley trivia quiz: "How much pasta is made daily on the ship? Four hundred twenty pounds."

Later, Garrett took Marty to Promenade, where they relaxed in deck chairs, watched themselves glide past Cuba, and didn't talk about Nan Brasheer at all, except to speculate about whether they should be offering comfort, condolences, reassurance to Richard Brasheer.

"It's really not appropriate at this point, we have no idea what's really happened," Marty said. "And his not reporting her missing does look bad for him."

"You're right. And there is nothing we can do at this point."

Garrett took a "Majestic Muse" from the counter and handed it to Marty. "Tell you what. Let's see how many "Day at Sea Activities" we can accomplish."

True to his word, Garrett was at Marty's disposal through the range of shipboard activities, most of which he said he had never tried before, "at least, not since I can remember." Marty took this to mean not since the woman he was "in like with."

They drove golf balls into a net in the sea from Riviera Deck, then mingled only with each other at the "Singles Mingles" in the Rendez-Vous Lounge where they shared the cocktail of the day—Chocolate Banana. Anyone who wanted this surprisingly good concoction was required to *sing* to the bartender, "Hey, Mister Hershey-man, blend me that banana," which Marty did with aplomb. After this, they decided to skip lunch and Garrett suggested a swim.

Great, Marty thought, facing the full-length mirror in her bathroom after pulling on her suit. The bulges at the tops of her thighs were no larger than they'd been when she was twenty, but they jiggled more. Well, at least her legs were tanned.

They met poolside after changing. Garrett seemed more appreciative than horrified by his first view of her in a swimsuit. He didn't say anything, just smiled and sparkled. They dived in together, competing with strokes Marty remembered from Christine's swim team days, until "Flip, Flop and Fly" started. They watched most of that spectacle, a diving competition with a number of Chocolate Banana-inspired competitors, then joined in the greased watermelon fight—a sort of football game that pitted men against women. The object was for one team to carry the slippery melon across the pool and out of the water on their goal side. The men won, but not by much, and Garrett made the touchdown.

"Probably shouldn't have," he told Marty, as they climbed out of the pool. "Forgot I'm not a passenger."

"Since when does being an official crewmember confer a watermelon-athletic edge?" she teased.

Then they took a free snorkeling lesson in the pool.

With just an hour to prepare for afternoon tea and the evening, Marty took the occasion to make a quick, zillion-dollar-a-minute, call to Christine and Sam. She didn't reach them, but was reassured by a desk clerk's saying they had checked into their Gregory Town hotel, but had "just walked out." She did not leave a message.

The *Majestic Muse* indicated it was to be a "casual" night. With no lunch and all that water sport, Marty and Garrett were both famished when they met again, and they ate so many of the tiny quarter-sandwiches and canapés the white gloved waiter brought around at tea that he finally put an entire plateful down on their table.

"You're pretty quiet this afternoon." She was asking a question. "Tired?"

"Just relaxed. Best day I've had in years."

"Well, sure. You got the watermelon touchdown."

He smiled. "You're a pretty comfortable lady to be with."

Marty felt herself blush.

"Didn't anybody ever tell you that?"

"No." She sipped her tea. "I don't think anyone ever did."

They each bought a Love Boat Lotto ticket and headed for Horizon Court to "Learn to Rumba with Randy." Truce wasn't around, but Philip was taking the lesson with a flashy twenty-something woman they had seen at "Singles Mingles." Marty glared at him as they dipped past.

They listened to classical guitar in the Wheelhouse Lounge, then moved to the Marquis Dining Room for a wine lecture and tasting. After learning that a quarter cup of ruby port, poured into a cantaloupe half and left to chill for thirty minutes, could be a tasty dessert, they moved on to a different kind of lecture.

"Either this, Dicey Horseracing, Water Volleyball, Pictionary, or an informative talk on Lladro porcelain," Garrett explained, leading her into a conference room.

"I love the lectures."

The talk was about Jamaica, where they would dock at Ocho Rios tomorrow. Marty and Garrett and the other passengers in attendance learned about Annie Palmer, the "white witch" who killed three husbands and a lover and was now said to haunt Rose Hill, a mansion open to tourists. They learned some history of reggae music, that "Mo Bay" was the Jamaican nickname for Montego Bay, and that jerk pork, a local specialty, was made with a paste of hot peppers, berries, and herbs. Another local specialty—rice and peas— was called the "Jamaican Coat of Arms."

The legend of an Arawak Indian girl named Martha Brae was recounted. People believed that she had changed the course of a river and killed herself and her captors to protect the location of a gold mine. The speaker ended by urging the audience to "walk good," an expression he said meant "Have a good day" in Jamaica.

By the time they left for dinner, Marty was excited about the impending visit to the island. The day had been wonderful, considering the circumstances. She felt so easy in Garrett's company now. Just as she was about to ask him to join her on one of the island excursions though, he mentioned that he would be on duty the following day.

"Wish I were on vacation too," he said, smiling. I'd like to climb Dunns River Falls with you tomorrow."

"Well, maybe Truce…"

"Probably Truce would like a visit to Annie Palmer's," Garrett said. "Good news is that I'm off all night tonight." He looked directly at her. There was a question in his eyes, and Marty's easy feeling washed away. The ladies room was just outside the dining room entrance, and Marty excused herself, urging Garrett to go ahead to her table.

The vanity area was crowded with last minute lipstickers, but once Marty was safely inside a stall, she covered her face with her hands and tried to think. Where was this going? Would Garrett expect to spend the night together? Well, so what?

She blushed, remembering the morning with Paras. But that was practice or drunkenness or craziness she wasn't going to waste years of analysis on. This was much different. Maybe it was what she'd been practicing for. Wasn't that what people did these days? Wasn't that what a date had become? Truce had obviously just done it, and with somebody she'd known a much shorter time than Marty had known Garrett. And Marty had felt okay about Truce, even defensive. But herself? How could she? It had been so long since she'd felt this way... maybe she had never felt this way.

Well, silly, she told herself. You've never spent a whole day with a charming man who was nice to you, and maybe it's time you did. She looked down at her white cotton hipster panties, almost bikinis, but not quite, though they did have lace around the top, and smiled. Truce probably wore a red satin thong just to do her laundry. Well, she thought, you just don't have the proper underwear. You are not prepared. Case closed.

She left the powder room in a more confident mood, fairly sailing up to the table. Truce had managed to make it down for dinner, but Philip was not in evidence. Hank and Pat were deep in conversation about the menu choices, including a crab imperial that Marty and Garrett both selected immediately, Marty pushing aside the memory of calories consumed at tea. She swore she would jog around Promenade twenty times after every meal, "starting tomorrow."

Truce was still tired and a bit depressed, so Garrett and Marty told her and Donna about the Jamaica lecture and the tours available. When Truce didn't bite on the Annie Palmer white witch tour, Marty winked at Garrett. Hank and Pat joined the conversation and decided to try Annie Palmer. When Donna tried to talk her mother into doing the same, Garrett winked at Marty, but Truce declined. Hank invited Donna to join them. Despite a sidelong glance from Pat, that Marty thought she couldn't possibly have missed, Donna accepted eagerly.

"None of us will be able to do any of these tours," Truce said suddenly. "The tour office is closed, and they're probably all full."

Marty looked at Garrett.

"No," he laughed. "I have no pull with the tour office."

"Maybe you could over-medicate a few people, so they'd sleep in," Donna joked.

"I'll sure try," he kidded back. "But don't worry, the witch tour isn't far, and the tour itself isn't limited. Only the bus. If it's full tomorrow morning, you can just share a cab. It might even be cheaper."

"Isn't that dangerous?" Pat asked.

"All travel is dangerous," Truce chimed in, mocking a bit. "Have you ever been to New York City?"

"Girls, girls…," Hank smiled. Pat smiled back. Truce looked at Marty and rolled her eyes.

Marty asked what Truce was planning to do in Jamaica, and when she had nothing specific, Marty proposed a Real Visit to the country.

"Something independent. Just catch a cab and head for the hills. See what we see."

"You're on," Truce said.

Now Garrett acted worried. "You know, it is a little more complicated than New York. You don't want to get too far from the port."

Marty and Truce laughed.

"Absolutely," Truce, his fellow Charleston native, said. "We don't want to stray from a nice port city. We all know the waterfront is the safest part of town."

"Touché," Garrett said. "Seriously, don't try going up in the mountains. It's a different world. You might not be welcome."

"Or they might be all too welcome," Hank added.

"Nine o'clock at the purser's desk?" Marty asked Truce.

"You're covered."

"Right now," Marty said to Garrett, "you are welcome to stay for dessert, but I'm going to escape temptation. It has been a wonderful day." She rose to leave.

Garrett pushed his chair back and prepared to follow her.

"Can't end a day at sea without a dance under the stars."

"The lady said she wanted to escape temptation," Truce said, accenting "escape."

Waving, Marty and Garrett walked off together. He repeated the invitation to have at least one dance on Lido where a band was playing now, but Marty thanked him anyway. She was really worn out from the day, and said so. He admitted that he was kind of tired himself and walked her to her door. As they said goodnight, he smiled and looked into her eyes. His expression was friendly and appealing. Marty was sure he would kiss her. She considered kissing him. But he took her hand and raised it to his lips.

"I am very flattered," he said, "that anyone would think I might be a source of temptation to you."

She waved him down the hall from her doorway and couldn't remember ever having felt such a delicious expectation.

"Bride bitch."

Marty spun left toward the menacing outburst and saw nobody, but she heard a door slam. She closed her own door quickly and twisted the bolt. Not Floyd's voice, exactly, and she might have imagined the actual words, just that vicious, guttural tone. But it was impossible. He left at Ft. Lauderdale. He wasn't on the list.

She tried to shake off the idea. There were plenty of brides, plenty of bitches, for that matter, and no doubt, plenty of nasty men. Still, that tone.

———

Two doors down in a stateroom just across the corridor, the man who slammed the door threw himself onto his cot and sobbed. "Bride bitch," he whimpered. Then, getting to his knees and wringing his pillow, he spat murderously: "Filthy bitch bride mother bride bitch. You will die. You will die."

———

17

Day Twelve, Ocho Rios, Jamaica

Like the adventurers they wanted to be, Marty and Truce hailed a cab at the port of Ocho Rios and directed the driver to the Blue Mountains.

The young Jamaican driver turned fully around in his seat and smiled curiously.

"Whe yuh waan go?"

"The Blue Mountains," Truce repeated, nudging Marty, "and step on it!"

The driver shrugged his shoulders and headed away from the terminal. He made a left on Main Street. Marty murmured to Truce about first asking the fare as they had been instructed. The driver kept going. Then, abruptly, he pulled over beside a market, shut off the ignition, and turned to face them again.

"Ladies shop?" he asked.

"Only for Blue Mountain coffee," Marty answered. How much will the fare to the Blue Mountains be?"

"Fifty American dollahs, maybe. Depend where in de mountains. Each." He pointed to the market. "Coffee right 'ere. Sixteen dollah ah pound."

"No," Truce said. "We want to see the mountains. We want to buy it there."

"Mountains," he said, gesturing toward their distant right. "Coffee," he added, "at market."

In Jamaican patois that they could understand only with the greatest concentration, the driver explained that he could not take them to the mountains because they could be hurt there. Only young men would he take, no "mammas."

Gathering the gist of his remarks, Truce took umbrage and insisted. Marty was getting nervous. She felt behind her for a non-existent seatbelt. The driver was telling them that going into the mountains was dangerous for women—and even for men who weren't young. Marty believed him, but she did share a bit of Truce's resentment. Finally, after he tried further to scare them off with the fact that "fifty American dollahs" was only the one-way fare, Truce left it up to Marty.

Where it came from, she couldn't tell, but suddenly, Marty was gripped by a real need to see this thing through. She wanted to avoid the tours that fellow passengers would be on. She did not want to return to the ship. She leaned forward and patted the driver's hand, which rested on his seat back.

"Thank you so much for your concern," she said, "but we want to go into the mountains. Can you suggest a good spot for lunch?"

Truce looked stunned and a little concerned herself. Marty noted this with some satisfaction.

"There's only the Lodge," the driver said, "and dem rob people up dere."

"The Lodge will be fine."

He tried once more. "Dirty. It dirty up dere."

Marty hesitated. Relative to what, she wondered, carefully keeping her hands from touching the sticky vinyl seat.

"The Lodge it is," Truce said.

The driver, not more than a boy really, shrugged again and dropped his old Chevy into gear.

"Ah, will you wait for us there? We could buy you lunch?"

Truce sounded nervous as the taxi began climbing a skinny path into the hills.

"Nah mon. Me wasn do to me bizness. I'll cum back in two hours."

The women settled back, or tried to. The scenery was breathtaking, but their nearness to the edge of the crumbling road was frightening and getting more so as they ascended into the mountains.

"What sort of business?" Marty was really curious.

The driver either didn't hear or chose not to answer.

"This reminds me of a dream I had last night," Truce said, and went on to relate it.

In the dream, Truce told Marty, she was flying on a seat of some sort. She could control her direction by moving a stick to her right side, like a gearshift. In the dream, she was not afraid to fly, and was having a wonderful time.

"Sounds like parasailing," Marty nodded. "I tried that at St. Martin, when Christine and I went to meet Sam on Orient Beach."

Truce grinned and Marty knew why.

"Well, I wanted to give them some time alone, so I stayed—"

Truce laughed. "Oh, we heard. Donna was out there. God knows what she was doing. But she told everybody at the table. The costume party, I think. Your doctor boy stopped over. Thought he'd die. He was probably kicking himself from here to East Buttbrain for missing it."

Marty grimaced and tilted her head twice in the driver's direction. Truce laughed again.

"He's no more my doctor boy than anybody else's."

"Yeah, right."

"No, I'm serious. Garrett's probably some kind of cruise ship playboy. I mean, how cliché can you get?"

"I don't think he is." Truce was not laughing now. "I think he's really interested. Remember, he's from Charleston, and I know Charleston boys."

"That's right! Did you know him? He grew up there."

"I knew his daddy's name, but we used another doctor. I didn't know Garrett before this cruise." She paused. "Maybe a few of his friends. So anyway, tell me about parasailing. This dream was as close as I'll probably ever get."

"It was really pretty great. Such a feeling. Until I got high—"

Now, Truce giggled and, imitating Marty's grimace, indicated the driver herself. "So, you were saying, you *got high*..."

"Look!"

240

Marty nearly startled the driver off the road in her attempt to subvert more of Truce's silliness. No matter how tempting it might be, she would never tell Truce about Paras. She'd never hear the end of it. They were still winding, still climbing. She pointed out the harbor below.

"Now, about your dream. You weren't scared at all?"

"No." Truce quit teasing. "The stick was connected to a man at control central, and he knew that when I moved it forward, for instance, I wanted to go lower, and he would make that happen."

"Obviously, only a dream, with a man at the controls." Now Marty was teasing.

Truce laughed at herself. "I pulled the stick all the way back and shot straight up. I did scare myself a bit there, but I adjusted. I practiced weaving back and forth, you know, like on a driver's test course around those orange cones. It was pretty real. I could see treetops and building tops and tiny cars on the road. Then, I flew out over the water and practiced going higher and lower some more."

"I vote for lower."

"In the dream," Truce continued, "I was deciding to buy this wonderful machine, and I was planning to try to make a deal. They wanted me to sign a contract for the *connection*, for the service of the man who made my directions *become* directions."

"Mmmm. Would that be something like a wedding license?" Marty asked, all innocence.

Truce glared at her. "They wanted me to sign a one-year contract, but I wanted to negotiate for a ten-year contract at a sixth of the price per year. After all, who knows what better technology might come along, and if I made a long commitment, I wanted a really good price. Otherwise, I might go for three months at a quarter of the one-year rate, I thought."

"This is great. You need to run to the nearest psychoanalyst," Marty said. "You might even be a case study candidate."

"Wait till I finish." Truce was chuckling. "I tried to radio my proposal through the stick, but nobody answered. I moved the stick left, but kept flying straight ahead. I tried right—no response. I screamed into the damn stick—no answer. Then I started to panic. I was disconnected from the guide man and flying straight out over the ocean with no way to change course or land." Truce sounded serious now, and Marty realized the dream had shaken her.

"I think," Marty said, "it sounds like repercussion from your lovely evening with the dear departed Philip."

Truce looked startled, and Marty thought she had gone too far, but then Truce laughed. Soon, she was telling stories about other men and Marty was almost wishing she could trust her with Paras. Before they knew it, they had reached their destination near, if not on, the top of Blue Mountain.

The Lodge was worse than what Marty had envisioned, even for "dirty" and "dangerous," but she had no intention of backing off at this point. The ramshackle structure was weathered gray. Faded blue paint spelled out the words "Blue Mountain Lodge" above a door that was propped open on a slant to reveal nothing but darkness inside. A middle-aged Jamaican man in dreadlocks stood talking to a young white man with shoulder-length dirty blonde hair who leaned against the façade of splinters.

Marty looked at Truce. Truce looked at Marty.

"Two-'undred dollahs," the driver said.

"What?" Both women exclaimed at once.

"Roun' trip. Fifty one way. Each lady."

"Here is a hundred," Truce said, handing him a crisp bill. "The other hundred when you take us back to Ocho Rios."

"And another twenty for your trouble," Marty said, scrambling in her purse and handing him another bill. She looked at Truce sheepishly. "A tip," she whispered.

"A bribe," Truce whispered back. "Good thinking." She checked the emerald-studded watch on her wrist. "See you back here at, what?" She looked at Marty.

"Two o'clock should give us plenty of time for lunch.

"Uh," she turned to the driver, "they do serve lunch here, don't they?"

"Best on de mountain." The driver smiled.

They got out of the cab. "It's the *only* restaurant on the mountain," Truce reminded Marty.

Their driver smiled again as he waved goodbye.

"Lord-oh-lord-oh-lord," Marty murmured, as she led her intrepid partner past the two men and into the dark interior of the notorious Blue Mountain Lodge.

Just through the door, they rounded a corner into a large room with better, though still dim, lighting. A pair of

Jamaican men sat at each end of the bar to their left. Marty walked around a jukebox toward four empty tables to their right, and Truce chose one next to the lone tree-shaded window. Sitting, they realized they had a wonderful view under the branches all the way to the sea. Marty looked across an old porch with several chairless white plastic tables. "Would you prefer patio dining?" she asked Truce.

"Well, it is a beautiful day…" Truce paused. "But what do you sit on out there."

The innkeeper, already at their table with menus, overheard.

"We tek these chairs out fuh you," he said, smiling a wonderful, wide smile. "Han we lave two vacancy. You would like room and meal, or room, or meal, or see yuh later?"

The women were confused, but a glance at the menu, which doubled as a hotel brochure, made it clear. The Blue Mountain Lodge boasted two rooms for lodging. "One with ocean view. One with indoor bathroom."

"We'll see later," Truce said, to Marty's surprise. "But first we'd like to take a look at your accommodations."

"Of course. Ladies cum wid me." The innkeeper bowed, took the menus back, and gestured for them to follow him. Truce whispered back to Marty, "You said you wanted to see things."

The three walked behind the bar, through the kitchen, and up a rickety staircase that ended *in* a large pine-board room; the one with the indoor bath. There were three beds, two double and one single, covered with bright raspberry chenille, and a large dresser with a clouded mirror and a red-fringed lamp. Jungle-like foliage pressed every inch

244

of the single curtainless window and a snappy disinfectant or insecticide assaulted Marty's sinuses.

She wiped away tears and tried not to breathe deeply as the innkeeper proudly opened a door to the indoor bath. Here were a yellowed, but freshly scrubbed, chain-flush toilet and pedestal sink. A cake of Ivory soap rested in its wrapper on a pile of folded blue washcloths *in* the sink.

"Very nice," Truce said to the innkeeper. "Very nice indeed."

He grinned and led them through the room's other door to the room with an ocean view. This room was even larger, with a similar arrangement of furniture.

"No hallway?" Marty asked.

"Yeh, yeh!" the innkeeper said, gesturing through the room with indoor bath toward the stairs. Just then, one of the Jamaicans from the bar came up the steps and entered what was apparently the only bathroom in the building.

"Very nice," Marty said. "Yes, very nice. But we're on a…"

Truce interrupted her quickly. "We'll decide later. Thank you for showing us around."

"Great. We're all chaired up," Truce said, as they were led to the patio. She gazed imperiously at the menu.

"Hope you weren't expecting one of Enrico's en croute-something-or-others."

"No indeed," Marty said loftily. "This is very nice."

Over a flavorful meal of brown stew chicken, peas (that weren't really peas at all but some kind of beans in rice), and fried plantain served on what looked like banana leaves, they talked about their daughters and about relationships with men. Over fabulous Blue Mountain coffee, Marty told Truce about her grandmothers, Martha and Mary. Truce reminded her of Grandmother Mary, and she told her so— adding that she was starting to remind *herself* of Mary this week. Truce's life was a textbook case for self-sufficiency, Marty thought—the good, the bad, and the heartbreaking— and all together worth it. She wished she'd had Truce's courage during all those more Martha-like years. Child rearing was another thing entirely though, and Marty knew she would not wish Donna's childhood on Christine.

Thoughts of Donna turned to her current white witch tour with their new dining companions, and to speculation about what costumes those folks might choose for the next costume dinner.

"My favorite was the seven-foot-tall guy who came as a pirate last time," Truce said.

"Seven feet tall—really?" Marty thought of Joseph Pumphrey right away. He might not be seven foot, but he sure was the tallest person she had ever met.

"Really. Or close to it. In fact, I wondered if it was someone on stilts."

"What was that table theme?" Marty wondered.

"Never saw him at a table. He was by the door to the kitchen talking to Enrico."

"Really."

Marty started thinking. She almost said more, but was interrupted by two characters bearing gifts from the bar. Without asking, the mangy looking men who had been lounging out front stepped onto the porch with chairs and placed coconut rum drinks in front of her and Truce. Before either of the startled women could say a word, they situated their chairs and sat at the table.

The young blonde man greeted them after he made himself comfortable. He tilted his head and stared at Marty through squinted eyes. She thought he might be drunk.

"What brings you ladies to the mountain?"

When Marty didn't answer, he turned to Truce and fixed his gaze directly on her wristwatch. The Jamaican with the dreadlocks grinned and joined his friend's stare.

Truce instinctively looked at her recently-purchased Rolex then covered it with her hand.

"Oh, almost two o'clock. Our driver is due..."

She looked helplessly in Marty's direction. It was only 1:15.

"Joe nah cum back fe yuh," the Jamaican said quietly, and Marty started to feel the onset of real terror.

She picked up her fork and tightened her grip.

"Joe will come back for us. But you'll be riding down the mountain with the Ocho Rios police if you don't get the fuck out of here right now."

The Jamaican spread his hands on the table and slowly rose to his feet. Truce burst out in nervous laughter and he spun toward her. She stopped laughing. Marty jumped up, fork clutched.

A door slammed suddenly.

"Okay mon. That enough."

It was the innkeeper, and he was approaching their table quickly. "Ah tell you before," he said to the two men, "yuh bizness somewhere else. Not here."

To Marty's surprise, the tiny innkeeper started swatting the large men with a dishtowel he carried over his arm. Laughing, they bowed to Marty and Truce, and picked up their chairs. The blonde man reached for the drink he had placed in front of Marty, but the innkeeper swatted him again.

"You say drinks for ladies, I make drinks for ladies."

Still laughing, the men re-entered the Lodge with their chairs.

"Yuh ladies enjoy your drinks? You decide to stay?"

"Uh, no," Truce said.

"Actually," Marty started to add, then stopped. "Thank you. They were very frightening."

The innkeeper apologized for his rude customers and explained that they would not really hurt anybody, "not while me 'ere."

He urged the women to enjoy the drinks, insisting that he mixed the rum and crème de coconut himself just for them.

"It is specialty of me," he added, smiling graciously.

Marty then explained that their cab driver was expected to return, and told him what the man had said about his not coming back.

"'im joking!" the innkeeper said, as though it was just a silly game and he was surprised they had fallen for it. He apparently took no offense at the fact that they'd had him go to the trouble of showing them his rooms with no intention of staying. They accepted the drinks gratefully.

"I can't believe you," Truce chirped. You were really going after him with that fork."

Marty didn't respond, but felt a little proud.

"You were going after him! And your language!"

Marty sipped and stared at the steep green hillside beneath them.

"Floyd may still be on the ship," she said quietly.

Truce stared at her. "Jesus," she said, and Marty wasn't sure that her tone of disgust was directed only to the fact. She told Truce what she thought she'd heard last night.

"Bitch bride? And this is the guy you're so worried about maintaining Christine's respect for? A man who's calling her a bitch?"

"I know. But here's the thing. I'm not positive I didn't imagine it. And, actually, I know he can't be on the ship. There was no room."

"Jesus!" This time there was no doubting the source of Truce's exasperation.

"How is it that you can kick ass with those guys over a stupid wristwatch, then wimp out when your life is on the line? This creep will have your hair in his hand and a knife at your throat, the photographer will catch it on film, your blood will be all over your blouse, and you'll still wonder if you're *imagining* it!"

Truce ordered more coffee, and Marty decided to tell her why it was all so confusing.

"You're wrong. I really might be imagining that. But there are enough things that I'm sure I'm not imagining."

Truce listened.

"When we were on St. Thomas, the day of the donkey man, you know, the pictures?" Truce nodded. "Well, I dropped my beach bag when we got back on the jitney, and the congressman was right behind us and he picked it up. When he gave it to me, there were two people in the Jeep with him, a teenage girl and a woman with really long hair."

"Not Nan?"

"No."

Truce looked ready to jump to a conclusion, but Marty held up her hand.

"Later that day, Christine met a girl named Olivia. Olivia told her this story about having a crazy boyfriend who put a gun charm on her necklace. Olivia turned out to the girl in the Jeep."

"And you think she imagined the gun charm?" Truce didn't say it cruelly. She sounded sympathetic.

"No. Let me finish. The night before Christine's wedding, I gave her a necklace. Well, you remember, you were there when I bought it."

Truce nodded.

"When I took it out of my safe to give it to Christine, there was a gun charm on it."

"What?" Truce shook her head as if to clear it.

"You heard me. A gun charm, a little silver gun charm, had been added to Christine's necklace."

"While it was in the safe?"

"Yes. I might have forgotten to lock the safe, but the necklace was in there. I put it in just before the costume dinner."

"Where was it from the time you bought it 'til you put it in the safe?"

"In my beach bag. And my bag was with me. Let's see. I went to the beauty shop as soon as I got back onboard, then I went to my room. The only time I left it was on the beach while I was parasailing."

"Was this Olivia girl at the beach?" Truce asked.

"Actually, she was. But she left before Christine and Sam. I was pretty sure she did. She was there with her mother and stepfather; a very, *very* tall man."

Truce did not react, so Marty continued.

"Her mother turned out to be the woman from the congressman's Jeep. It wasn't until after they all left that I went parasailing."

"What did the congressman have to do with Olivia and her mother?"

"Good question." Marty started to relate the beauty shop gossip, but the innkeeper returned to announce that their cab was waiting. It was only 1:40, but they paid the check with a generous tip and hustled out to the taxi. The men were gone.

The driver seemed relieved, and a little surprised to see them, and pointed out interesting things about the Blue Mountain rain forest all the way back. He even stopped and waited outside a tourist shop in town, without one I-told-you-so, while Truce and Marty each purchased a pound of Jamaican Blue Mountain coffee.

After stopping in port for two more rum coconut drinks that weren't half as good as their first, Marty was finally able to finish her story. At this point though, Truce seemed pretty drunk. Her stated opinion was that Floyd and the congressman probably threw Nan overboard and would be gunning for Marty next.

Truce and Marty were the last to re-board *Mare Majestic* at Ocho Rios. Crewmembers checking ID at the dock joked about pulling up the gangplank behind them. The two women joined the fun by linking arms and kicking their right legs out and crossing them back to the left— "Weee'rrre OFF to see the wizard..." then Truce made up a second line—"But we'd rather BE the wizard...." They were laughing hysterically as they finally let go to form a single file and board the towering ship. Marty stopped her stride abruptly causing Truce to rear-end her. The collision knocked the bag of coffee out of Truce's hand, and both turned to watch it gather momentum as it rolled down the gangway.

"Shit," Truce said.

"Oh, Lord," Marty added, as they watched the little sack's progress.

When neither had moved after a few seconds, Truce said "The hell with it," and they both turned toward the floating city, still above them, and leaned backward to gaze up.

"Wonder how he got onboard," Marty said. "I mean Joseph."

Truce said she didn't know who she was talking about and didn't much care because she was now forced to head for "that miserable casino" to recoup the loss of her winnings. They crossed Plaza Deck to the elevator.

"You coming?" she asked.

"No. I think a nice cup of tea is more my cup of tea at this point."

Marty got off at Promenade as Truce continued elevating to the "Grand Casino" on Dolphin, the next deck up.

A bulging moon quivered as Marty strolled along Promenade. The quiet, despite the dozen or so people in sight, surprised and pleased her. These passengers had obviously chosen the peace of this spot over watching from Lido Deck as ship pulled away from port. A few couples were huddled against the rail, and when she felt the rumble of motor, Marty approached it too.

This was starting to make sense. She waved absently to everybody and nobody as the Blue Mountains of Jamaica began to back up. Why would Joseph be on the ship, unless it was to see Enrico? Surely he didn't come just to attend a costume party. Besides his brief acquaintance with Marty, Christine, and Sam, whom else did he know onboard?

It did make sense. Married or not, Joseph must be the gay lover Enrico cried about to Sam after the bachelor party.

But why would Joseph kill Nan? Granted, that would free Richard Brasheer to marry Bethany, which would, in turn, free Joseph to be with Enrico. But Joseph could leave Bethany at any time, couldn't he? If the woman from Washington, D.C., was right, if it was a marriage of

253

convenience, what was so convenient? If it was that Joseph was gay, and Bethany knew it, what would really hold him back? Did he still need to remain in the closet? In these times, that seemed unlikely.

Money, she thought. If Joseph simply left Bethany, there might be a money problem. But if he made it possible for her to marry Richard, and that induced her to leave *him*... No. Still didn't make sense. Richard was free after divorcing his first wife, and didn't marry Bethany then, so why would Joseph think he would marry her if Nan were out of the picture?

Marty's head was starting to throb, and she moved across the teak deck, out of the increasing breeze, and toward the nearest wooden deck chair. A festive light pried its way through the edge of the heavy draperies covering the glass door beside her.

"Two sixths of a mile."

Marty turned right. Was it Garrett, approaching from forward deck with a tray balanced at shoulder height on his fingertips?

It was.

"Since when did you join the waitstaff?" Marty asked him, rather wanly.

"Since I figured milady could be missing her little girl and starting to hanker after some of those delicious leftover wedding cookies."

He bowed to present the tray with a flourish.

"Not now, thanks."

When he noticed her bag of coffee on the table and tried to chat further, Marty cut him off. Her head was pounding now, and she was more abrupt than she intended.

"I was actually looking for some privacy and quiet out here."

Garrett put his tray on the table and looked at her. He seemed hurt.

"I didn't think it was a good idea for you to be alone."

"Look, I'm sorry. I'm used to having a lot of time to myself and there doesn't seem to be much of that around here."

Garrett was obviously offended, probably even angry, but he exaggerated to make a joke of it.

"Adieu, milady." Raising his tray and his nose, he continued aft.

Marty flopped into the chair. She realized that her feet were killing her and kicked off her shoes. Getting old, she thought, pulling a small plastic vial of Tylenol™ from her bag and swallowing two capsules without water.

She leaned back in the lounge chair and made a mental note to bring a book out here to read sometime. The slatted chair had looked uncomfortable, but it supported her back perfectly.

Jamaica was fast becoming tiny lights in the Caribbean distance aft, and a drift of clouds floated sadly across the huge moon. A young waiter took her order for tea, and Marty realized suddenly that the other passengers had moved from the area. There was no one left in sight. Why would Garrett think she shouldn't be here by herself?

She stood.

The sound that came from over her right shoulder was the door to the inside of Promenade Deck. Dread welled up. For a second, she couldn't turn to look.

"Okay, what's this I hear about you wanting to be alone?"

At the sound of Truce's voice, relief sank Marty back into her seat.

"Who do you think you are, Greta Garbo? And if anybody should avoid being alone right now," Truce looked around, "especially out here—it's extra creepy with that moon—it's you."

She scudded another deck chair up close to Marty.

The boy returned with Marty's tea and placed a steaming pot on the small table beside her. Her headache was starting to wane, and she was glad Truce had come. She selected an Earl Grey bag from the partitioned wooden box presented, and took a packet of real sugar instead of her usual Equal.

"Thought you were going to the casino?"

"I was, but I ran into Garrett on the way. Then he came to the casino to tell me you were up here by yourself. It didn't sound like a good idea."

She raised her arm and called to the departing waiter.

"I'll have a cup of that too."

When he didn't turn, she added, "please."

Then, as the boy disappeared, "Sir?"

"A comforting cup of tea," Marty said in her mother's words, watching the pot as it steeped.

By the time she lifted the delicate, flowered porcelain to her lips, she felt like a vice had been removed from her head.

"You need more than tea," Truce nagged her. "You need a bodyguard with a bazooka."

"I am a little bit nervous, but not about Floyd. Garrett checked. He's not on the ship. Even you said Garrett could be trusted."

"Fine. We trust Garrett. But there's already one woman missing from the ship."

"That's right. Now think about this. You said a tall man, really tall, was talking to Enrico the night of the costume party."

"Right. I think he was a Pirate. Maybe on stilts."

"Why would a Pirate be on stilts?"

Truce shrugged. "Well, you just don't see people that tall—"

"I think it was Joseph," Marty interrupted. "Olivia's stepfather. Remember, I told you he was tall. Seriously, he was close to seven feet."

"Well, maybe he's a passenger. A basketball-playing passenger."

"No, I think..." Here, Marty stopped. She didn't want to betray Sam's and Garrett's confidence about the bachelor party, about Enrico being gay.

"Joseph is not a passenger. And he is not—at least I don't think—a basketball player. He used to be a chef, or a chef's assistant. If he really was onboard at the costume ball, Enrico must have helped him. No one was likely to get past security to board this ship."

Truce squinted.

"Remember when we got back on tonight? The crewmembers obviously recognized us, but they still checked our IDs, even in all the rush."

"So?"

"Well, Enrico could have helped Joseph board. Crewmembers might not question the executive chef."

"Okay. But why would he want to. I mean, why would Joseph want to be here and why would Enrico help him?"

"Christine and I saw Joseph and Enrico walking together on Orient Beach. While we were waiting for Sam. Then we saw Nan, later, in a bar with Enrico."

"What? While her husband was off with Olivia's mother?"

"No. That was a different day."

The waiter had apparently heard Truce after all. He returned with tea and also set down a tray of tiny pastries. Truce thanked him profusely then waited until he was out of earshot.

"Okay. Assume Joseph was onboard that evening, the night someone tampered with Christine's necklace. That's what you're getting at. Maybe Olivia told Joseph about her conversation with Christine. Joseph would know the significance of the gun charm. But why would Joseph want to do that to Christine? And how could he know about Christine's necklace?"

"Who knew about Christine's necklace? Well, you were there when I bought it, the jewelry store man, the purser, the people in the beauty shop, Garrett..."

"Well, I sure didn't..." Truce bit into a cherry tart.

"Of course not. The point is, anyone could have heard about it and about my plans to give it to Christine before the wedding. But a ship's employee was more likely to gain access to my stateroom than Joseph, and the only ship's employee who seems to be connected to the Richard, Nan, Joseph, Bethany, and Olivia thing, is Enrico."

Truce dabbed her lips with a small peach napkin. "But why in the world Enrico? We have Nan overboard and Floyd, if he's not on the ship, he sure knows you are. Wouldn't it be more likely that Floyd..."

"Forget Floyd for a minute. He probably doesn't know I'm still here. At least, not if he's not here too. And he's not on the list. Let's figure out this necklace gun charm. Let's say that, for some reason, Enrico wanted Joseph to leave Bethany, Olivia's mother."

"Why would we say that?"

Marty held up both palms. "I'm sorry. I can't tell you. Just believe me that it's possible."

"Okay, but I think we're wasting time."

"Joseph might have convinced Enrico that he couldn't leave Bethany and Olivia because they needed him," Marty said. "And Enrico would not necessarily know that Nan had not been Richard's wife all along. He might well see

259

the elimination of Nan as the only possibility of Joseph leaving Bethany. He would expect Richard to want Bethany if Nan was out of the picture."

"My God, Marty said, "that is what happened. Enrico killed Nan. Probably poisoned her first, or threw her into his lobster pot, then tossed her overboard just before they got to Ft. Lauderdale. He was a nasty man. You should have seen him the night Christine and I made cookies when he wouldn't let the lobsters be killed humanely."

Truce was shaking her head as though her new friend had lost her mind. Marty felt a bit giddy now. Except for the lobster pot, the theory really could make sense. She poured herself another cup of tea and they sat quietly as an entwined couple walked by.

As soon as they passed, Truce spoke. "Okay, assuming that made any sense whatsoever, now what about the necklace? What would his motive be there?"

Marty leaned back against the wooden slats and covered her face with her hands while she tried to think. After many months of therapy and dozens of "but, why would he's?" she had come to believe that the most likely true motive for anything was the thing's result. She thought awhile. One result was hers and Christine's fear. But who, other than Floyd, would want to make either of them afraid?

Considering Floyd, she thought back to the "bride bitch" voice she'd heard—or thought she'd heard—last night. Again, she dismissed the thought.

Okay, fear. The gun charm had made them afraid. So, what was the result of their being afraid? The result of that had been that Marty suspected Olivia, did not try to help Olivia as Christine had asked but, instead, distanced herself and encouraged her daughter to do the same. Who might want that outcome?

She sat forward and looked at Truce.

"That charm really spooked us. It scared us half to death, and nearly ruined Christine's wedding day. It made us both afraid of Olivia. Enrico and Joseph," she added slowly, "would both have good reason to prevent Christine or me from being friendly with Olivia."

"And Floyd would have good reason to spoil Christine's wedding day," Truce trumped her, "and I don't see how any of it ties to Nan overboard."

"Look." Marty spoke as one already convinced of her argument. "Joseph has been married to Bethany for most of Olivia's life. Regardless of his arrangement with Bethany, and I can tell you that it sounds like a marriage of convenience, it stands to reason that he genuinely cares about a girl he helped raise."

Marty couldn't imagine raising any child and not loving that child more than life itself.

"Joseph wouldn't want to make Olivia appear to be mentally deranged. But Enrico the lobster scalder would have no such compunction."

"And," Truce said, if the rest of this weren't so entirely off base, he might also want to convince Joseph that Olivia was crazy."

Marty thought about it. If Bethany left Joseph to marry a newly free Richard, and the stepkid was a dangerous nut, Joseph would be even more inclined to break all ties.

"That's right. And don't forget, Enrico is the only one who could probably get access to my stateroom."

The thought wasn't comforting, and as she and Truce left the moon washed promenade, Marty was glad to be heading back to Christine's suite, rather than the stateroom that had been violated.

"You're going to have to discuss this with the captain," Truce said as they parted. "Promise me."

"I will."

While she was at it, she would double check what she already felt certain was true: that Floyd had left the ship at Ft. Lauderdale. She dipped her cruise card into the suite's door slot and was startled by the hard slam of a door just down the passageway. Inside, she hurried the deadbolt into position. She tried to practice steady breathing.

Before bathing to turn in, Marty left a message apologizing for her abruptness and asking Garrett to please arrange a meeting with himself and the captain in the morning. She didn't say why, and did not answer her telephone when it rang a bit later. She didn't want to explain it again. Not to anybody. Not at night.

———

He pressed his eye against the peephole for at least a minute, imagined her seeing it, recognizing its color, absorbing its intensity.

———

18

Morning Thirteen, Grand Cayman

Island

Marty was dressed and waiting when Garrett called to say he had scheduled the meeting for nine. She paced the balcony, watching turquoise water swirl below, until it was time to leave. What would she say about Floyd? Garrett had already checked. He was certain Floyd was not on the ship. She regretted her rudeness to Garrett last night and did not want to insult him further. Anyway, why would the captain care about her personal problems? No, she wouldn't focus on Floyd. She would simply explain the possible Enrico connection to Joseph, and let them take it from there.

But she was afraid. She had barely slept, imagining shouts, hearing "bitch bride" voices in her dreams, and she'd have to get some reassurance on this score. She wouldn't focus on it though. She'd discuss what would most likely interest them, the parts that wouldn't make her sound like such a flake.

Yet the first thing she said after the secretary escorted her into the office where the captain and Garrett were already seated, was: "You have to make sure my ex-husband is not on this ship."

Anthony stood behind his desk and reached across to shake her hand, but Marty noticed his quick look toward Garrett who stood by a wingback chair to her left.

"Have a seat, Marty. Can you tell us why you think he might be?"

Marty sat slowly in the chair next to Garrett, who also sat, then squeezed his thin lips together and nodded.

"You need to tell him."

"Well," she began, "okay. The night before last," she turned to Garrett, "just after you left…"

Garrett shifted his eyes toward the captain.

"…well, I mean, just as I was going into my suite, there was this voice. It said 'bride bitch,' and it sounded like my ex-husband. I mean, I'm not sure, and maybe I'm just nervous." She turned to face the captain.

"It's just that, well, he showed up on St. Croix at Christine's wedding, but he wasn't invited because there's been trouble."

"Anthony knows you were stalked," Garrett said. "I'm sorry. I had to tell him. We had to make sure Floyd didn't reboard at Ft. Lauderdale."

"I'm sorry, Marty." Anthony looked at her kindly. "It must be hellish."

She went into more detail about Floyd's showing up after Christine's wedding, and waving what she later realized was a cruise card.

"He was really crazy. Raging. He called me something like "bitch bride mother.""

Garrett was nodding. So was Anthony.

"And I did check," Garrett said. "He boarded at Sint Maarten. Took a late vacancy."

"My son-in-law joined us at St. Martin," Marty added. "He probably followed him."

The captain directed himself to Garrett. "And you checked this cruise?"

"Absolutely. Fully booked. No Floyd Arkus."

"I believe he's very dangerous," Marty said. "He threatened, the voice in my hallway last night, 'bitch bride,' I think, well, I'm really pretty sure, and I'm afraid the voice was Floyd's."

"But he is not on the ship?" Anthony directed himself to Garrett again. Receiving an affirmative nod, he turned back to Marty.

"It's not surprising you'd hear his voice, after what you endured on St. Croix. It was late. Possibly it was someone else who—"

"I did not imagine this."

Marty thought of the Blue Mountain men, wished she had a fork. She grasped the edge of his desk tightly with the fingers of both hands. Her nails scraped into the waxed mahogany. Her teeth were clenched.

Anthony said he would check the manifest again.

"I'll check it myself," he added, and Marty felt guilty that he inferred she didn't trust Garrett.

"Or, Garrett could…"

Garrett reached over to touch Marty's left hand.

"It's okay."

She let go of the desk edge and sat back. Okay. Well, what else could they do? Still, it didn't seem like enough. She nodded agreement though, and launched into the story she'd thought she'd come to tell, about Enrico and Joseph and possible motives for Nan's demise.

They didn't buy her Enrico theory, or at least they didn't seem to. And with the light of a new day, as she heard herself calling the chef who'd helped her make her daughter's wedding more traditional a murderer, she started doubting it herself.

Garrett and the captain were both defensive about Enrico. They seemed to think the idea that Joseph and Enrico were gay lovers was plausible. In fact, they knew it, Marty was sure. They agreed that Joseph was Bethany's husband, and that Bethany was the artist with whom Congressman Brasheer had been having an affair for all these years.

"You are probably right about Olivia," Garrett said. "She could well be the congressman's daughter. And that gun charm thing, she's probably involved with that."

"And that was the night of the costume party," the captain added, as though all bets were off during costume parties, and that explained everything.

Both men even agreed that Enrico could obtain access to Marty's stateroom if he really wanted to, and that such a thing would be nearly impossible for anyone other than a ship's employee. The captain insisted adamantly that Joseph could not have boarded the ship without the aid of a crewmember, and Garrett admitted that Enrico, under the circumstances, might assist Joseph.

Anthony would not entertain that possibility.

"Passenger safety, as you might imagine," he said to Marty, "is not only paramount, it is Majestic's financial bottom line. Harm to any passenger—theft, food poisoning, man overboard, a fire, even a broken ankle from a slip on a wet passageway—can result not only in a lawsuit, but in very effective negative publicity.

"People who don't understand this don't work for Majestic," he added, giving Marty the impression that his supposed desire to hire her had ended.

"They don't work here to begin with. And we have ongoing training. A crewmember who would help a person who does not belong on this ship to board is unthinkable."

The captain glanced in Garrett's direction, then continued.

"Almost as unthinkable as Enrico Francill breaking into your cabin or doing physical harm to another human being."

"Anthony," Garrett said, "I agree with you about Enrico, but a crew member's mistake *is* thinkable. I've known it to happen more than once. In fact..."

Anthony looked at his ship's medical director sharply, and Garrett stopped mid-sentence. Marty was certain that Garrett had been about to confess to this infraction himself, probably the "in-like" woman. How stupid to think of that now. She wished she could forget about that woman, that Garrett was as new to this dating thing as she was. Were they dating? Marty wasn't even sure of that. Christine's warnings about the handsome doctor's practiced bedside manner came back to her. Christine. The thought of her daughter was enough to get her back to the subject at hand.

"I know the rest of it doesn't concern me," Marty said. "It just seemed to fit together. What I want," she cleared her throat, "is an explanation of how that gun charm got onto Christine's necklace in my safe."

She looked steadily at the captain.

"It is your responsibility to find one."

"I agree," Anthony said quietly. "I wish you had reported it immediately, but that doesn't absolve us now. We will find an explanation if that's possible, and I apologize for what you have had to endure on my ship."

The formality of his tone was chilling, but he looked genuinely sorry.

"I also appreciate your efforts in trying to solve the mystery of Nan Brasheer's disappearance. We are still hoping, of course, that she will show up, and that there will be some explanation. But I admit, with every day, it seems more unlikely that she will."

Now Garrett cleared his throat. "Marty, I'm sorry—we're sorry—this has all happened. But I honestly don't believe Enrico could be involved. I've known him a long time. To tell you the truth, I don't consider him a friend. Don't like the man much, never have. But I know him, and I'm sure he wouldn't do what you've suggested."

Well, that told her. Rising to leave, she shook hands with the captain.

"Let me know what you discover about the gun charm, any update would be appreciated."

Marty stopped.

"And about Floyd..."

"Of course." Anthony nodded. "We do feel certain that there is no Floyd Arkus aboard the *Mare Majestic*, but of course, I will check again."

"Yeah, don't forget those track bars."

"What?"

"Nothing. You might check the staterooms near mine, I think the voice came from the left. That would be... I'm in cabin 302. He might be using another name."

Anthony nodded again, but Marty sensed that he was not taking her very seriously.

"I'd like a list of the passengers registered to staterooms in that section. At least a list of men traveling alone."

Anthony's entire beard shifted upward as he sucked his top lip between his teeth. He seemed ready to tell her no.

"I'm sorry if this is trouble for you, but I'm afraid I'll have to insist." Marty faced him directly. The hell with the job, she thought, and suddenly, thought of something else.

"And if you're not concerned about me, remember this: Nan Brasheer was also a bride."

Anthony's eyes flickered. Anger or new interest? She couldn't tell. He nodded, and continued nodding as he clasped one hand in the other and rubbed it.

Garrett walked her to the door of Anthony's office.

"I'd like to talk." His voice was low. "Can I call you in an hour?"

Marty felt an inexplicable sense of relief.

"I'll be on Promenade in a deck chair. I could use some tea."

"See you there in an hour then."

They had docked offshore Grand Cayman, the largest of the Cayman Islands, and Marty stood at the ship's rail on Promenade waiting for her tea. The island looked bright and clean, even from this half-mile vantage point. White buildings with ski-jump roofs and yellow trim twinkled a greeting in the late-morning sun. Tenders would ferry passengers to shore at George Town on the long thin island's west coast. Marty hadn't checked the "Majestic Muse" yet, but the stretch of white beach to the left of the town looked like a great idea for such a sunny day; a better plan than a passenger tour or staying aboard.

Maybe she shouldn't have told the captain and Garrett what she had figured out. They were so defensive about Enrico. But her theory did make sense, damn it, and she certainly had a right to expect an investigation of the gun charm incident, and Floyd. Poor Christine. To have gone through, essentially, the loss of her father, to have been so gracious about having her wedding so far from family and friends, and then to have such a horrific moment as finding that charm...

Marty was getting angry again now. But the captain was right when he said she should have reported the charm right away. Why hadn't she? The wedding, of course. There was no way to get through that day and start a full-scale investigation at the same time. It would have meant meetings with the captain, probably police dusting her safe for fingerprints, and who knew what else.

Now, it was too late for fingerprint checks. But if they had done it—Marty was feeling an old suspicion—they could have checked Olivia's prints, and Bethany's. What was she *doing*? Just because of Anthony's and Garrett's loyalty to Enrico, and the captain's selfish concern about bad publicity, she was starting to doubt her own judgment. But, what *did* she know about Enrico anyway?

The waiter brought her tea and she moved to one of the wooden chairs. She knew he screamed at his galley staff and killed lobsters inhumanely. She knew he was involved with a married man and got drunk at Sam's bachelor party and humiliated himself. She knew he would have the ability to help an outsider sneak onboard, and that it would have been possible for him to get into her stateroom and safe, where Christine's necklace had been. But, to be fair, she also knew that he had been willing to arrange things so that she could bake her own cookies for her daughter's wedding.

She supposed she understood Garrett's defense of the chef, a fellow crewmember after all. Hadn't he said something about their being like family or all having problems and being forgiving of one another? She started to think of Paras. She hadn't seen him again. A little part of her, she realized, had hoped he would try to find her. Silly. If you're going to *have* a one-night stand, she chided herself, you have to *be* somebody's one night stand. She shoved the thought away. There probably was an element of escape in every person's decision to work on a cruise ship. After all, you became essentially homeless if you made it a career.

"How about that blue water!" Garrett sat beside her, and she raised her teacup in acknowledgement.

"It's beautiful."

"I'd say you're lucky to be alive to see it."

Marty furrowed her brow.

"Well, if you think it's that bad…" She stopped herself from asking why he and the captain wouldn't take more action if they thought it was this serious.

"I talked to Truce. You girls, ah, you women, took a foolish chance going into those mountains."

Oh. She considered before answering.

"Probably no more stupid than trusting the security on a cruise ship."

She gave him a level look.

"Sorry. I'm just glad you're safe. We all are."

Maybe he *was* referring to more than the Blue Mountain excursion.

"Anthony was headed for the galley when I left. Don't think he won't check this out."

Marty couldn't imagine what he would "check."

"I'm glad to have a day off in this place." Garrett gestured toward Grand Cayman. One of the best diving spots in the world. I know you don't dive, but even snorkeling here will give you a look at some fantastic sights."

"I don't snorkel, either."

"Nothing to it. You stay on the surface of the water. Remember our lesson?"

She cut him off.

"That was in the pool. I tried it in the ocean. I'm afraid of fish."

"Afraid of...?"

"Fish."

"Oh."

He watched her nod; they both burst into laughter.

"You are an interesting lady. With a warm laugh."

Practiced bedside manner, Marty remembered, but she blushed at the compliment.

A small plane flew over them.

"Did Truce tell you about her dream?" Marty wanted to change the subject.

"No, but I had a corker myself last night. Been trying to analyze it."

"Tell me. I'm really good at that. I love dreams."

"I don't know. You'd think I'm pretty weird."

"I already know you're weird. Tell me."

"Well, I was back in Charleston and working in the office. Dad was off on a cruise around the world, and the family practice was mine until he returned."

"I can already see why you're trying to analyze this. Go on."

"Well, okay. But it's pretty stupid, the more I think about it."

"Go on. I'd like to know you better."

"Great. You'd like to know how stupid I am."

"Not stupid. Just weird. Please, go *on*."

273

"Okay. Here goes. This lady was waiting, but as I called other patients to the examining room from this list Dolores gave me, she came forward."

"Dolores?"

"No. Dolores has been my father's nurse and office manager since my mother died. The *lady* never came when I called the names."

"When did your mother die?"

"When I was seventeen."

"Oh, I'm so sorry. That's an awful time of life for such a tragedy."

"It was. Not sure I... Hey, you want to continue this dive into my subconscious or not?"

"Go."

"For each name I called—and there weren't that many people in the waiting room—there was always somebody else. Started skipping men's names, just because I knew this woman had been waiting longer than anyone else and I wanted to get to her name. Couldn't ask her who she was because my father would have known and I was supposed to know too.

"I called out 'M&Ms,' like it was a name instead of a candy, and a young woman stood up to follow me. I turned to the half-dozen people still waiting and said, 'Did everyone sign in with Dolores when they arrived?' Everybody nodded.

"M&Ms looked a bit like my ex-wife, Millie, but I couldn't tell exactly why, because her actual look was different. Millie was, is, Jewish, and she looks Jewish. Small, dark, you know. This woman was small-boned, and she had

274

long blonde hair, eyes kind of like yours, actually I think it was you."

Marty rubbed the back of her neck. Then she looked at her cup and poured more tea from the pot.

"But she was like my wife, ex-wife. Even in the dream, I couldn't figure out how I knew that. Finally, I decided it was the way she looked at me when I talked to her. Kind of a disbelieving look. To convince her to trust me, I decided to confide in her about the woman in the waiting room. As soon as she understood me, she got up and ran back out into the waiting room and told the woman.

"The woman looked stricken. She—it was like slow motion—gathered up her purse and walked out the door. She seemed sad. I had to find a way to make her come back. I ran back to the examining room for an instrument that would do the trick. I picked up the otoscope, knew that would work! I ran down the sidewalk, waving the otoscope. Finally, I saw her back and touched her shoulder. She turned, and it was my mother."

"Wow."

"Analyze away."

"I'll have to think about it. Wow. Must have been a shock."

"You got that right."

He picked up the hottle and shook it.

"All out. Tell you what, are you ready to see Grand Cayman?"

"Well, I was thinking of the beach. Not swimming, just relaxing and looking at the water."

She put her cup down on the small table beside her and stretched. "Beautiful, beautiful blue."

"You can see the top of the water every day from this tub. I have a better idea. A surprise. Join me?"

"I'd love to join you," she said, meaning it more than she wanted to. "But I really don't want any close personal encounters with fish, and I think I've had enough surprises this week to last a lifetime."

"This is a good surprise. You won't touch any fish. And safe. Unlike the one you had yesterday."

He sounded a bit I-told-you-so-ish, but then, he was right. She was actually more frightened now, remembering the incident at Blue Mountain Lodge and imagining the other-than-happy endings it could have had.

"You've made your point. But it *was* an adventure."

"Okay. Enough said. You know, the older I get, the more the meaning of the word 'adventure' changes.

"How so?"

"Well, twenty years ago, your close call yesterday would have been an adventure. Now it's... well, not good. Now, an adventure would be what we're about to do now."

Marty had the impression that he wasn't just referring to an excursion on Grand Cayman, but she knew it might be only her imagination.

"Let's go, Fraidy Fish."

"I'll never hear the end of this, will I?"

"No."

After a twenty-minute tender ride, they walked along the coast at George Town. This island had a newer look than the others, Marty thought, and said as much.

"It's easier to thrive with the Crown's backing," Garrett said. He explained that the Cayman Islands had been territories of Jamaica until 1962, when Jamaica gained its independence and the Caymanians chose to remain British subjects.

"Expensive to live here," he added, "but it's a duty-free port with no sales tax, so if you know what you're doing, it's a good place to shop."

"I hate shopping."

"She's a woman and she hates shopping. She takes a Caribbean cruise and she's afraid of fish. She thinks *I'm* weird?"

———

By 11 a.m., he thought it was safe to step outside and consider which deck would guarantee sufficient height. Lido would be best if it came to that, but if she'd beg enough, and make promises—she always did keep promises—it might not have to. Nah. He wouldn't give her that chance again. Finding a few moments alone with her here would be difficult, probably only possible for someone as resourceful as him. But it would be worth it, waiting long seconds for the tiny splash that would show Christine once and for all.

Her mother was always the crazy one.

———

19

Afternoon Thirteen, Grand Cayman

Marty stepped into Garrett's surprise, hesitating a few seconds before descending the narrow triangular stair while her eyes adjusted to the relief of dimness. Whatever else it might do, this semi-submarine that he called a 'glass-bottom boat' would provide a bit of welcome shelter from the fiery Cayman sun. People were situated below-deck in two benchrows, back-to-back like children playing musical chairs, while they peered through portholes into the gigantic aquarium that was the Caribbean Sea.

They couldn't find room for two on either of the benches and so squeezed into singles that put them back-to-back. A marine life identification chart hung beneath each porthole, and Marty immediately found the orange and green creature with a blue mouth that was nibbling just two feet from her face.

"Look!" she cried, leaning back and half turning to Garrett. "It's a parrotfish."

"Have an *Astrapogon stellatus* over here," he said, relaxing against her back.

"A what?" She turned, and he slipped an arm around her stomach as she craned toward his porthole. He pointed. "The red one."

"And you know it's called a…, an astrofish?"

Garrett indicated the chart in front of him. "*Astrapogon stellatus.*"

Both returned to their own views, but continued to lean back against each other companionably.

In a minute, Marty squirmed. "Ugh!"

A young woman in dive gear swam past the boat. She released chum from a canister and dozens of fish immediately swarmed over her body to get it.

"Attracting the fish to our portholes," Garrett explained.

"Well, I know that, but they aren't the pretty ones. I can't even imagine…"

Garrett was still chuckling over what he now referred to as Marty's "delicacy" about the fish as they walked back through town toward Seven Mile Beach.

"We could parasail there," he suggested. "I'd love to see you try that."

Marty sailed past his intimation.

"I would land in the water with the fish."

"Thought you liked swimming?"

"I do. And I like it in the ocean. And I know the fish are always there. I just don't want to see them when I'm there."

"You just saw them and liked it."

"I do like them. I love seeing them. I just don't want to see them in the water coming at me where they can touch me. The water is too clear here."

Garrett laughed. Said he'd never heard anybody complain that the Caribbean waters were too clear.

Marty wondered if the way she felt about Garrett wasn't a lot like the way she felt about fish, but, back buddies or not, she wasn't going to tell him that.

Over a spicy lunch of turtle soup and conch fritters, Garrett told Marty he felt hurt.

"I understand why you didn't want to deal with the gun charm that day. You were so involved in Christine's wedding"—he refilled her wine glass—"and I know how important it was."

"But you don't understand why I didn't come to you."

"You got that right. I thought we were becoming friends. I could have gone to the captain for you, or tried to find out what was going on."

"I know you would have, but you have to understand what a shock it was. I mean it just made no sense at all. It still doesn't make sense, unless–"

"Unless your theory's right."

"Yes."

"Too hard to imagine. When you've known someone as long as we've known Enrico–"

"I know," she said. And she did.

It was nearly 2:30, and Garrett tried to coax Marty into shopping. "Tonight's a formal night, you know. Not that I'll get to see you in your finery, since I'm on duty at seven."

"I did enough shopping while I was hiding, waiting for this cruise, to last for years."

"Hiding?"

She realized she didn't want to go into it again. "Well, waiting." She changed her mind. "Yes, I was hiding," she reminded him. "For three weeks. That's how bad it was. That's why..."

"Anthony *will* check. And I think he'll get the list of passengers near your room. He *does* want to help."

Clouds had moved in to soften the hammering sun's blow by late afternoon, allowing the relief of a balmy Caribbean breeze. Woozy from wine and weather, they strolled out to the beach and back toward *Mare Majestic*. Garrett draped his arm around Marty's shoulders as they continued down the beach. It felt natural to have him close.

He stopped abruptly.

"I have an idea. If Milady will be kind enough to wait right here for fifteen minutes, we can make this a day to remember."

"It already is."

He put his hands on her shoulders.

"I know. I want to commemorate it."

"Well, okay, but what?"

"Wait here," he said. "Get comfortable."

He took off toward the row of shops that paralleled the beach.

Marty watched him for a minute, then sat in the sand facing the sea. What was it that Garrett had said about Enrico and anybody over twenty-five who worked on the ship? She thought she remembered exactly. "There is probably not a person over twenty-five working on this ship who doesn't have problems to escape. We're pretty forgiving."

She certainly had problems to escape. Would that qualify her? Would she be happy, so far from Christine? But Christine had started her own adult life. No, it was best to back off where Christine was concerned, at least for a while. Make sure she and Sam had all the privacy and independence they needed. She burrowed her hands, palms up, into the sand at her sides and sifted mounds of the sparkly grains through her fingers.

"Not a bad life," Garrett had said about shipboard work. "But it's usually not first choice." Marty wasn't sure she had ever had her first choice about anything.

Now she saw him, hurrying up the beach, white bag bobbling from his hand. He sand-skidded to a stop beside her and presented the little sack.

"Sorry it's not wrapped."

"S'okay."

She reached up to accept the bag. Garrett curled down close beside her.

Digging in, she found two pink boxes. When she opened the first there was a white and yellow enamel pin in the shape of a flying fish.

"To help you conquer your fear," he said.

She smiled.

When she opened the second box though, its content was exactly the same, another fish pin. She thought they must have made a mistake at the shop, but Garrett said

283

no, one was to keep and one was to hide—like a treasure— "until someday."

They walked to the edge of the ocean, where Garrett took out a notepad and pen to mark the time and date. He pointed to the building directly in their sight line as they stood with their heels at the water's edge, and described their starting position. Then they counted steps as they walked toward a stand of palm trees. He climbed about ten feet up a tree split in two sections and wedged the second fish pin tightly into the split. Sliding, jumping, then falling, he settled back in the sand and finished his notes. Together they drew a treasure map.

After reboarding *Mare Majestic*, Garrett walked Marty to her suite. Again, he didn't quite kiss her, but the clasp of both his hands around one of hers felt like something more than if he had. She double-locked the door and went straight to her bedroom, putting the pin in its box on her nightstand. The treasure map to its mate was folded under the box's cotton lining. That's where it will stay, she thought, until someday.

A rustle near the door. Marty froze with her hand on the box. Nothing else. She peeked around the bedroom curtain and, with relief, noticed a piece of paper on the floor. Probably the "Majestic Muse." She picked it up to find, not the daily news, but a computer printout. Oh! The list of passengers in her section. So, Anthony had come through after all.

She scanned the list of a dozen staterooms, the only one inhabited by a single man was #307, registered to "Raymond Venge." Could Floyd be using another name?

She ran a shaking finger over the names and numbers and stopped again at 307. Venge? As in vengeance? He would pick something like that. No. He'd be more obvious. If he was trying to say "vengeance," he'd pick "Vengeance." And why "Raymond"? That wasn't even his middle name, which was Edward. Marty knew her ex. If he was registered on this ship under a fake name, it would be something pointed, meant to scare her, like Edward Vengence or Edward Bitchater. Poor Mr. Venge. He was about to have a strange woman at door #307, just so she could reassure herself. What would she say? Just act like she'd knocked on the wrong room? She ran through the list again, paper getting damp from her nervous hands. The next stateroom was registered to "Donald and Lindsey Finch." She grabbed her purse and started to unfasten the lock. She'd just say: "Is Lindsey here?" and then she'd apologize for getting the wrong room.

She stopped with her hand on the lock. But what if it was Floyd? Suddenly, she was sure it would be, and her heart started to pound.

The telephone rang, reliving her of the decision. Probably Garrett. She walked over to lift the receiver.

It wasn't Garrett at all, but Anthony's secretary. He said that Commodore Mascellino wanted to see her on an urgent matter as soon as possible. When she paused, he asked if "now" was convenient. Agreeing, she asked if the captain would be coming to her stateroom. The secretary seemed surprised, and said that of course the meeting would be in the captain's office.

Wiping her face, hands, and feet with a washcloth in lieu of a shower, Marty's mind cycled through terrible possibilities. Had Anthony determined that Floyd was on the ship? Was he Raymond Venge? Had something happened to Christine?

Apparently, they thought it was safe for her to walk out into her hallway alone, but Marty suddenly didn't. When she was ready to leave the suite, she looked around. In a rush, she grabbed a pen and gripped it like a weapon. She slammed the door behind her and hurried down the corridor to the elevator, but saw nobody.

Anthony rose from his desk and walked toward Marty when his secretary showed her into the office. He took her hand and ushered her to a sofa. He sat beside her.

"Sounds like you were right," he said immediately. "I'm sorry to have resisted your theory."

Marty sighed with relief. "Finally. Thank God."

She couldn't believe it was finally going to be okay. Finally, someone believed her. Finally, Floyd would be stopped.

"Can you arrest him? Can you get him off the ship?"

"He's in the brig now."

"And he can't get out? You won't let him out on the ship?"

"No. Don't worry about that. He knows he'll be there until we reach home port. He did seem bewildered though. I doubt he ever meant to have it go this far, and it's still hard for us to believe he'd hurt anyone."

Good Lord, Marty thought, was he even able to charm these people? "What? How would you know?"

"Well, I've know him for many years—"

286

"Floyd?"

"Floyd? Oh, you mean your ex-husband. That's what you thought. No, I meant Enrico."

"Wait," Marty spoke slowly, feeling underwater. "You mean Enrico is in the brig, not Floyd.

"Oh. Yes. I'm sorry. I thought that's what… Oh. We did check. I thought they delivered the list to you. Mr. Arkus is not onboard. The only single man in your section was Mr. Venge. We did check Mr. Venge's credentials. Mrs. Arkus, Marty, I'm sorry. Your confusion is perfectly understandable in these circumstances. Divorce is always traumatic. Add your only child getting married…" The captain chuckled and shook his head. "It really is understandable. And he probably sounds a lot like your husband, your ex-husband."

Marty had realized how perfect a shipboard job would be for her. She wanted it. She wanted it on *Mare Majestic*, needed more time to get to know Garrett. The captain held the key to her possible employment onboard, but his patronizing tone cleared her head like a whiff of ocean air. Marty stood.

"No, Anthony—Commodore Mascellino—he doesn't *sound* like my ex-husband. The more I think about it, the more I'm sure he *is* my ex-husband. And I am not traumatized by my divorce or by empty-nest syndrome. There may be a dangerous psychotic on your ship under the name of Raymond Venge. His real name is Floyd Arkus. He is my ex-husband. He is here to either harm me or to frighten me, and I expect you to do something about it."

The captain looked doubtful.

"Marty, I…"

"How, exactly, did you check Mr. Venge's credentials?" She was angry and sarcastic.

"He has a passport."

"And you looked at it?"

"Yes."

"And that's all?"

"Well..."

"Well, to board this ship, you need a passport or a birth certificate. Don't you think someone traveling under a false identity would make sure they had a fake passport?"

"That would be a serious crime."

"This *is* a serious crime!" She said the words quietly through clenched teeth, but it sounded like a scream inside her head. The hell with the job. She strode to the captain's desk and grabbed a Post-It from the pad. She leaned to write and then thrust the tiny sheet into the captain's hand.

"Call this number. This is the local police department in Crafton, near Pittsburgh, Pennsylvania. Ask them to fax you their log entries regarding Marty and Floyd Arkus. Then do whatever it is you do to actually *verify* a passport," she spit the words now, "or I will call every newspaper editor I know, and I know several."

Anthony took the paper and stared at it. He walked to the telephone and dialed. Marty listened as he identified himself and made the request that Crafton fax the log. He listened for several minutes. "Twenty-four hours? Why so–? Okay." He wrote a few notes, provided his fax number, got the name of his contact, and hung up.

"I'll fax them a written request. Their chief must approve the release. It shouldn't take more than twenty-four hours."

Marty shook her head sadly.

"I'll have security verify the passport. That may also take some time." He started moving papers around on his desk. "I am sorry. You understand that, even if the log indicates harassment, if there has been no conviction and you don't have a PFA order, we can only go by the passport. If that's verified—"

"It won't be."

"Okay, Marty. We will check it out. I'm sorry about this. Once this Enrico thing started, my mind was on that."

"What made you change your mind about Enrico?"

"Joseph Pumphrey. Enrico implied to Joseph that the congressman was free to marry Bethany, *before* Nan was reported missing. So," Anthony sounded sad, "even if he didn't do anything himself, he certainly has information about it."

"How do you know Enrico said anything to Joseph?"

"Joseph reported him to the Sint Maarten police when he heard through Bethany, who heard from Richard, that Nan was missing. He had been concerned about Enrico's implication—said it sounded sinister—but, when he heard she was actually missing..."

"The Sint Maarten police were coordinating with Ft. Lauderdale police, who have been working with us. Nan has been missing since Sint Maarten. She returned to the ship there, but she has not been seen since the costume dinner."

Marty told him about searching the photo gallery box without success for a picture of Nan that was taken at a later time.

"You are quite the detective. I have to give you credit."

"Well, I need to find out how this involves Christine. And maybe her father. And I don't understand why the congressman didn't report his wife missing any sooner than he did."

"Richard didn't sound the alarm at first because he thought Nan might have learned about his meeting Bethany on St. Thomas and moved to another cabin," the captain said. "That was his best hope. If the worst *had* happened, he was afraid his daughter, Olivia, could have been the culprit."

"So he admits Olivia is his daughter?"

"Yes. He says he thought she was emotionally ill, partly his own guilt. Apparently, he let Nan talk him out of believing Olivia's story about the boyfriend and the gun charm in the end. He had put his career on the line when Olivia convinced him she was being stalked."

"Oh." Marty thought a minute. "So that's why the anti-stalking bill. He was doing that because of Olivia."

"Right. Then he decided to back off the legislation. He met with Olivia and her mother at St. Thomas and told them.

Marty tapped her palm against the pen that was still gripped in her left hand. "But that really isn't enough to explain why Richard Brasheer didn't report—"

"Also, remember, the media didn't have this yet. At least they hadn't pounced. Richard wanted to wait until we

290

returned to Ft. Lauderdale. He probably wanted to see his sons before word of Nan's disappearance got out. It's too late for that now."

The thread of a logical connection nagged at Marty, but she lost it. "I wonder why he'd take such a risk, meeting Bethany and Olivia like that on his honeymoon? I mean, he could have telephoned."

The captain shrugged. "So, tell me," he asked, "did you enjoy Jamaica?"

Marty was surprised by the question. Obviously, Garrett must have mentioned her little adventure.

"Well, I don't know if enjoy is the right—"

"Garrett told me. Very dangerous. But also very interesting. I understand you had a tour of the mountain lodge. Would you be interested in writing a description for us?"

"For Majestic?"

"Yes. The line is trying to revamp the port excursions brochure. They are adding a section called "On Your Own." It's aimed at passengers who say they are bored with tourist traps. The Blue Mountain Lodge would be an interesting addition as well as a warning."

"I might." Marty could barely keep up with this jump from murder and stalking to travel writing. She was amazed the captain would still consider her. Still, she didn't know what she was going to do, where she would go, and a new job would be a start. She needed time to think.

"Let's see what you can do about Floyd first."

Anthony nodded. "We'll do everything possible."

"When would you need the piece?"

"Soon, but I'm sure they could wait a week or so. Do you go back to work as soon as you get home."

"Actually, I've left my job. This is no joke. I *am* being stalked."

"I'm starting to understand that better. I'm sorry. I hope we can help. You know, a life at sea isn't a bad life. I don't know how much you've talked with Garrett, but he can tell you. If you're looking to start fresh, you might consider taking on more work for us, the pay is excellent."

"Excellent?"

"About a hundred dollars for this assignment."

She was too sad to laugh in his face.

"That wasn't 'excellent' ten years ago."

"Maybe two hundred for this one. You did have to risk your life…" He trailed off with a weak smile.

Marty matched his smile, relaxed a bit. The Blue Mountain excursion was nothing compared to daily life in Pittsburgh.

"You know," she said, bringing them back to the real topic at hand, "I'm still not clear about the gun charm. Was I right? Did Enrico put it there?"

"He denies that. But then, he denies everything. The fact that he told Joseph Pumphrey—or at least implied to Joseph—-that something had happened to Nan *before* she was reported missing indicates only that he is involved. We don't know specifically what he's done. We don't know specifically what *has* been done. It's a good bet though, as you said, that there is some connection with that gun charm."

"There has to be."

"I agree. And we'll get to the bottom of it. We put into Ft. Lauderdale day after tomorrow. Since that's Nan's home, the local police will take it from there, unless the FBI insists otherwise. I'm sure they'll want to talk with you. And Marty, I am sorry this has happened. It's a bad time for all of us. But we won't let you down again."

"I hope not."

"Enjoy Cozumel tomorrow."

He walked her to the door.

"Have another adventure, but make it a safe one."

Any adventure will be safer than staying in my cabin, she thought, if Floyd is on the ship. But was he? She was disgusted with the way her mind seemed to loop on this. One minute she was certain he was near, and certain that her doubts were some kind of twisted victim-psychology; the next she thought exactly the opposite: that she'd become paranoid.

He draped his jacket over the chair back, arranging the shoulders just so, and laid the items he meant to carry in a straight row along the dressing table. Handkerchief, photo driver's license with handsomely decoupaged print, doctored passport, wallet, flashlight, razor knife, and the trimmed and folded note. He stood back to admire the arrangement. Opened the passport for one more peek. Beautiful. He brought the note to his lips, kissed it tenderly, and smiled. Then he placed each item in a pocket of the jacket and patted its shoulders.

———

20

Day Fourteen, Cozumel, Mexico

Another sun sprouted, another port reached. Marty sighed at the "Majestic Muse" on her lap and pushed bare feet against the balcony rail to tip back her chair. The last thing she cared about was a Cozumel adventure. But she was not about to stay on the ship until after "Mr. Venge" had been thoroughly checked out.

Neither would she be on an organized port excursion, where Floyd might expect to find her, though she would have enjoyed the Mayan ruins of Tulum on Mexico's mainland. The "Majestic Muse" article related Maya predictions that the current cycle of history would be destroyed by earthquake on Christmas Eve of 2012. The Mayans were no dummies. They had devised a calendar more accurate than the one in use today, and just might know what they were talking about. The year 2012 was only a dozen years away. She'd probably have grandchildren waiting for Santa by then. Would she still be around to watch them grow? Would she be here tomorrow?

She rang Garrett to see if he might join her on Cozumel.

"I was about to call you. You talked to the captain?"

They discussed Enrico's incarceration, and Marty wondered aloud where the brig was located on the ship.

"In the hold. Down here, right next to the medical suite."

"Have you talked with him?"

"No. Only security and the captain can go back there. So," he added, "don't get any ideas."

"I wouldn't want to look at the creep."

"That's the spirit. Meanwhile, do you realize how much Anthony wants you to write for him?"

"Well, he said the line–"

"Don't let him fool you. There's real competition among these captains. Anthony has no control in establishing our ports of call, but he'd love a reputation for having the best excursions."

"Sounds more like he wants a travel agent."

"Nah, just someone to get them excited. People on their first cruise are happy with just about anything, but experienced cruisers get pickier all the time. And we get more repeaters every year. They're always looking for whatever's new and different."

"That's why I'm really calling. You're in the office now. Does that mean you're on duty all day? I was hoping–"

"Unfortunately, it does. In fact Paul—he's the physician's assistant—is a little under the weather himself. I had to cover for him last night."

Garrett went on to question her, rather closely, she thought, about her evening and the new people she'd met on this leg of the cruise. Did this mean he was jealous? As soon as the thought occurred to her, Marty chided herself for thinking like a teenager, then forgave herself on grounds of inexperience. But the idea made her smile.

She admitted she'd stayed in her suite, and she updated him about Floyd.

"So by this evening, Enrico could have some company," she ended.

She was surprised when he didn't comment. She twisted the phone cord around her wrist. "I really do think it might have been him. I think he could be on the ship." She waited for a response.

"Now about today," his voice took an authoritarian tone as he bypassed the subject. "There's a great beach at Playa del Sol to the right of the pier, and Pancho's Backyard is the best place to eat. Try the plantain and walnut-stuffed Chile rellenos. That's to the left. Cabs are right out front. That's probably enough adventure for you today."

"Doesn't sound new and different for those returning passengers."

"Maybe not, but you have to crawl before you walk."

"You don't think I can take care of myself?"

"Of course I do. But I'd like to share your next *big* adventure."

She couldn't argue with that.

"And Marty?"

"Yes?"

"In case you get lost, the Spanish word for ship is *barco*."

"Really? I'll have to remember that. Now let's see—left to the restaurant, right to the beach, spin around three times and yell, '*Barco!*'"

"Okay. Point taken. Have fun."

"Gracias. Adios."

With no answer by phone, Marty went in search of Truce. No luck. Walking down a lonely passageway to Truce's cabin unnerved her. She checked the casino and a few other Truce-prone locations. Her legs felt rubbery until she reached the crowds on Plaza Deck. Every tour was well on its way. Maybe Truce and Donna had taken one. Marty had to get off the ship, but would have preferred company. She'd have to see the island on her own. That would be an adventure, she reminded herself, and it would get her away from groups where Floyd would be likely to look.

Signs in the harbor directed her to every form of rental transport imaginable. She walked a few blocks among crowds in the market area to a sign in English: "Starlight Rental: Cheap!"

After wistful consideration of a shiny red motor scooter, she accepted the fact that she'd never driven one and this might not be the best time to learn.

She settled on a LeBaron convertible whose scrapes of white, not to mention navy blue upholstery, proved its green-yellow finish a garish repaint. The key was in the ignition and she checked it out in the lot. Neither the wipers nor the headlights worked, and the top was stuck in the down position, if it was actually there at all. She got out and went into the rental office to tell the agent. He didn't seem to think it was a problem.

"No rain." He pointed to the bright sky above them. "No night."

Can't argue with that, she thought, signing the agreement and walking back to the car. Tentatively, she pressed the clutch and wiggled the shift forward to where memory told her first gear should be. Okay. Now she pressed the gas gently and raised her clutch foot. Too fast. Stalled. Try again. This time, more gas.

The chartreuse convertible peeled out, just missing a group of pedestrians and burning what little rubber was left on its tires. Marty hadn't driven a standard transmission in 20 years. It felt more like the car was driving *her* as she headed north on the island's main road. She understood this road to make a 45-mile loop around Cozumel. Trusting that she would end up back at her starting point in an hour or two, she gave herself to the sun, the road, and the spirit of adventure—not to mention escape—as she glanced in the rearview mirror.

———

The clerk at Starlight rental stood at the side window and watched the blonde speed away, then turned back to the counter as a man dressed too warmly for the day rushed in. Raymond Venge produced a Pennsylvania driver's license and a passport, and asked to rent a vehicle. Since he hadn't been specific, the clerk stuck him with the old black truck. The man stared down the road while the clerk loaded the truck bed with a few gallons of water "for the radiator, just in case," then pulled out without so much as a thank you or a goodbye and headed north along the coast.

———

What a beautiful day this is, Marty thought, checking the empty road behind her in the rearview mirror, what a beautiful world. She murmured a prayer of thanksgiving—hadn't done *that* in a while. Just north of town, where hotels dotted the coast side of the road and bars and dive shops filled the other, she passed an airport and a military base and started to relax. Everything was quiet. Cozumel was as lavished with sun as Grand Cayman, but the LeBaron's clip breeze-brushed her hair, and low jungle growth did not preclude a seaside view of refreshing turquoise. This was a great idea.

The road ended at a beach. What about the circle? Well, maybe this was to be her adventure. She sputtered to a stop, removed the ignition key, stepped out onto a sand-littered dirt road, and walked toward the water. Taking off her sandals, she found the white sand marvelously cool to her feet. Odd. The sun was directly overhead and the air temperature was probably in the 90s. The breeze was slight and the humidity thick. Yet, the sand was cool.

She could see tropical marine life from the turquoise water's edge. Why bother snorkeling? This was like sitting in her dentist's waiting room while angelfish darted through the magnifying tunnels that connected two large aquariums.

Marty dipped in a toe. Could she? She stepped in bravely with both feet. Soon she was strolling knee deep, watching various fish scoot away from her path. Every so often a colorful one zipped by. 'Fraidy Fish.' She remembered Garrett's teasing comment and thought again of the pin—the treasure.

Where in the world was this going, anyway? Where was *she* going? *Mare Majestic* would dock tomorrow and she would have to get off. Christine wouldn't be in Pennsylvania. She had no desire to live there without Christine nearby. At best, there was simply no point. At worst, if they still couldn't arrest Floyd and he tried to find her, he would probably start there. He obviously hadn't followed her expensive fake paper trail to London. She had nowhere to return to.

Even if Floyd were on the ship and they could arrest him, what would the charge be? Anthony had said that falsifying a passport was a serious crime. Surely, he'd be convicted of that. Would that mean years in jail, or months? Or a just a fine? And how mad would he be after that?

The threat had seemed less real during her first six days in this other world. Just before the wedding, she had been thinking it just might be possible to go home. Back to Pittsburgh, rent another apartment. Maybe even back to her job. But it hadn't even seemed appealing. And when she remembered the roses on her bed—the roses that proved he could always find a way to get in—she'd known it was out of the question, at least for a long time.

Where would she go? Ft. Lauderdale, maybe? Miami? Nothing appealed, she realized, as much as strolling along with her new fish friends, water splashing the bottom edges of her shorts, and feeling the sun beat the top of her head.

She stopped for a minute and faced the horizon. Puffs of white cloud stood against the blue sky like the sticky plastic cutouts in a child's Colorforms set, too perfect to be real. The vast expanse of blue met the liquid turquoise that surrounded her in a distant straight line that went as far as she could see and beyond. She raised her arms up slowly and dipped them back to her sides so that her fingers just broke the ocean surface. She gasped, humbled by the enormity of it all, and breathed her second prayer of the day. There was a plan in all of this. There had to be. She *could* take care of herself with this kind of help. Maybe she'd just let it be. Live in the present for one more afternoon. Coast.

———

He backed the truck between tall stalks of sisal near the ugly green convertible and took care to avoid thorns as he climbed down from the running board, stretched, and faced the sea. Look at that. Not a care in the world. She was walking in the water, trailing her fingertips along, making careless wakes at her sides. He flexed his hands in and out of fists, thumb-knuckling a ring on his left. Yes, it was time.

He was well onto the beach before he saw the creature. Quickly, he ducked back among the jagged stalks.

———

"Shuffle!"

The man called from the water's edge so suddenly that Marty almost lost her balance. She stared. He was tall and fat and tan; topped, bearded, and chested gray; with an iguana perched on his shoulder. Marty scanned the otherwise deserted beach and walked faster through the heavy water. When she realized he was walking parallel to her, she turned and headed back, now against the gentle current.

He turned as well, and she saw lips pooch out from his tangle of beard, "Shuffle!"

What was he doing? Did he mean harm? She walked faster.

Now he came into the water, clearly approaching her. She started to go deeper but drenched the hems of her shorts. She wondered if Iguanas could swim?

The man waved both arms.

"You want to watch for the stingray. Shuffle," he shouted, and he smiled.

Marty stopped as he came closer, then she walked toward shore to meet him.

"What?"

She'd heard, but didn't understand. She stopped a couple of yards short of the friendly looking fellow and his weird cargo.

"I saw you walking along out there and figured you didn't know. We have to do the stingray shuffle in this water."

She took a step closer.

"What?"

"The yellow stingray. They're too small to see, and they hide in the sand. If you shuffle and bump them, they move, but if you step on one, you'll know it."

"Oh! Thanks."

She shuffled toward the beach, now following him in a kind of country line dance. New fish friends indeed.

On shore, she stayed to chat a few minutes about appreciating the information. She wanted to compliment his pet, but couldn't, and so pretended not to notice the creature.

"This sand sure is cool for such a hot day," she said, trying to make conversation.

The man laughed. "It's not sand, it's parrotfish poop."

Marty lifted a wet, bare foot and backed away a step. The man kept laughing.

"The sand never gets hot here—we call it air conditioned sand. When parrotfish eat algae from the corals, they inject some of the hard coral itself. They grind that up and eject it as waste. The coral stays cool. So, what we're actually walking on here—is parrotfish poop. No polite way to say it."

Now Marty laughed, too. She waited until the noise of a truck out on the road faded, and asked about the route that was supposed to circle the island. The man directed her back to the airport for a turn she had missed.

Back in the car with dry sand-poop feet, she found Cross Island Road and headed for the east coast. She detoured along the way when signs directed her to the San Gervasio Ruins. It turned out to be a small Mayan archaeological site where she took a guided tour. There was much to hear, if not much to see, and Marty learned a great deal about the history of Cozemul and the flowering and decline of the fascinating Mayan civilization. Extraordinary. Maybe 2,000 years after the big quake, another civilization would be digging up ruins from turn-of-*this*-century Americans.

What would they find of hers, Marty wondered, back in the convertible and shifting like a pro as she buzzed west again along Cross Island Road. Probably her resin porch chair, now stored in a Pittsburgh "Hold It."

The western coast of Cozumel was peaceful. Greenery pressed in from her right and, across the sandy expanse, refreshing blue water lay to her left with the mainland of Mexico in the distance. A bit too peaceful, she thought, without a restaurant or bathroom in sight. Just as she was becoming uncomfortable, Marty spotted a little cantina. It was shady inside. Cool. A black-jeaned waitress looked up from wiping one of the six or seven tables.

"*Baño?*" She was directed to the restroom, then had a fresh fish sandwich and a cola and chatted with the woman who served her, trying to fit in every one of the fifteen or twenty Spanish words she knew. She even asked for more cola that she didn't especially want, just to hear herself say "*más*" for "more."

She could see herself working here. She'd have a little bungalow and walk on parrotfish poop every morning before work. Christine and Sam could come to visit, maybe twice a year. She'd need a pet for company, probably one of those hideous iguanas. It would want to sleep in her bed. She would let it.

Marty missed another turn—this circle road was not as easy as it sounded—and arrived at a gate and guardhouse. The Mexican guard came out and approached her car. Just as she started to worry that she was unintentionally trespassing, he smiled and handed her an English map to the Punta Celerain lighthouse. She took a leisurely, independent tour, reading posted highlights and wondering whether lighthouse-keeper might be the best job for her at this point.

21

Night Fourteen, At Sea

An art auction was just starting at La Patisserie when she returned to the ship, and Truce was there alone. Marty sipped a glass of the complimentary champagne with her new friend and watched breathlessly as Truce bid $1,350 on a Martiros. When another art lover took it for $1,500, Truce didn't blink.

"I like it," she said of the painting. "But I never buy unless it's really a bargain."

Marty wished she could be as certain about anything. Well, she was fairly certain about her writing ability. And she did have an assignment. She was also certain that wanted to get out of the ship's public areas. With a quick goodbye, she was off to her computer, realizing as she entered her suite that she hadn't even told Truce about the arrest of Enrico—and in fact—hadn't thought much more about it all day. The whole thing was superseded by Floyd's possible presence anyway, and if she could just keep pushing thoughts about *that* down for twenty-four more hours...

Bride bitch? As she'd told Anthony and Garrett, Nan was a bride, too. Could Floyd possibly have pushed Nan overboard?

She called Christine immediately, and left a message, but remained firm in her resolve to protect her daughter's honeymoon. She would not breath a word about Floyd until

Christine had settled into her new home. By then, God willing, it would be resolved somehow.

Marty was proud of her ability to compartmentalize the terror in her life. Over the years she had learned to tune it out. It was that or turn into a blithering blob of fear. She started writing.

It was nearly dinnertime when Christine called back, and Marty was satisfied with her rendition of the Blue Mountain Lodge experience. She read it to her daughter, who heartily approved.

"Mom, this is perfect. Maybe you could just keep taking cruises for a while. Write about all the ports, only sell the cruise company first rights, then put all your articles together in a book, and—"

"We'll see. I just might do that."

This kid would do fine, Marty thought. No matter what she had to face about her father.

Marty brought her daughter up to date on Enrico, and Christine was in complete agreement with the theory. She said she was still worried about Olivia though, and planned to call her from Raleigh.

"Wait until this is over," Marty cautioned. "We don't know exactly how involved Joseph is, but I'm sure he was on the ship the night of the costume party. Pirate indeed."

"That seems like all the more reason—"

"Please, Christine. I understand. I'm just asking you to wait a few days."

"Okay, if it makes you feel better. I've really been trying not to think about it. After all, you only get one honeymoon."

"Usually," her mother responded.

"What's up with your doctor buddy?"

"I've spent some time with him."

"Mom, I know you know what you're doing, but just, well, just be careful of your feelings."

"Okay, okay. Don't worry. Now, you're on flight 2635, right?"

"I guess so. Whatever Sam told you."

"Fine. I'll call you in a few days."

"But where are you going when the cruise ends tomorrow?"

Why was she asking? Marty felt a shiver at the unreasonable suspicion she couldn't seem to shake completely. And shame. Maybe she was paranoid. But even if Christine wouldn't deliberately betray her—and she wouldn't, surely she wouldn't—the less she knew, the less likely it would be that Floyd could trick her.

"I'll let you know where I was," she told her daughter, "as soon as I get back."

"Now I'm starting to understand how mothers feel."

This was silly. Once Christine knew that Floyd had stalked her mother on the cruise, she'd understand. She'd be more careful. Marty didn't have to explain that now.

———

"Maybe London. When I know, you'll know. Don't worry! It might be a great adventure. Relax, honey. I'll call you. I love you. Bye."

Christine hung up and Marty e-mailed her article to the captain with a few short, hope-this-is-what-you-were-looking-for sentences. She added a note reminding him that he should be hearing from Pittsburgh and she'd expect the information they had discussed.

Marty had planned to skip dinner. Her suite felt safer, even though the passage of time without incident made it more unlikely that Floyd could be on the ship. Finally, too nervous with inactivity, she decided to chance it.

In a burst of take-back-the-night confidence, she removed the chair she had wedged under the doorknob, unlocked the door, and peered into the corridor. A family was walking by and Marty quickly fell in behind them and followed them onto the elevator. As she headed for the buffet on Lido, she felt relatively safe in the chattering crowd.

After gobbling a grilled chicken sandwich at an open table next to the food line, Marty took the few steps around the corner from the buffet to the elevator alcove, and found herself alone.

She suddenly and definitely didn't like that. She did not want to be anywhere public on this ship alone, had thought that was impossible. It was. A group of five or six young people nearly knocked her over as she hastened around the corner back toward the buffet. She reversed again, behind them, hoping to join them at the elevator, but they continued past it.

She couldn't bring herself to stay alone in the forward alcove, and so followed, hoping they would board the lift at the other end. By the time it became apparent that they were headed up the aft stairway to the paddle tennis table on Sun Deck, there was no one behind her, only the empty stretch of Lido above both sides of the swimming pool. She knew the Ping-Pong area and the basketball court behind it were often empty. If she followed the group up the stairs they would surely think it strange. She raced down the steps instead.

The aft elevator waiting area on Riviera was also deserted. Her suite was only two decks down, but it was near the forward lift at the other end of the ship.

Breathe, she told herself as she pressed the button. The people were out of sight now, and she could see by the indicator that one lift was at Promenade, five decks below, and the other was apparently not working, stuck here on Riviera with the doors shut.

Someone was running down the stairs from Lido. Maybe a young man from the group she'd been following. Maybe he'd wait for the elevator. Maybe she should ask him to.

But it wasn't a young man, and she knew it almost before Floyd leapt from the stairway, twisted her arm up behind her back, spun her around, and wedged the crook of his elbow against her throat.

"I'm done playing," he hissed, mouth against her ear. "You made a fool of me for the last time."

Marty tried to pull his arm from her neck with her free hand but couldn't. To punish her for trying, he bit a tiny piece of skin between her shoulder and her neck—hard. He

311

cut off her small shriek of pain by jerking his arm against her throat. The elevator door opened, and Floyd released her just as it did. The lift was empty and she knew he'd follow her in, if he didn't push her in. She turned toward the pool then, preparing to scream and run—swim if she had to—and felt the gun against the small of her back.

"Oh, please...God..."

"I told you I quit playing, bitch. But you never listen, do you? You never hear."

Marty couldn't breathe. She closed her eyes, ready for the noise, the blast. It wouldn't hurt. She'd read that somewhere. A gunshot didn't hurt. For a split second, her sensation was akin to relief. It would finally be over.

He grabbed hair on the top of her head and lifted it up and forward, prodding the small of her back with the gun's hardness, driving her away from the pool, toward the ship's rail.

"Time to take a swim, you suicidal bitch."

He slammed his knee into the back of her thigh and brought his lips close to her ear.

"Don't worry. Your little baby bride will understand that you just couldn't go on without her."

She stumbled forward and caught her breath. Suddenly, the will to struggle surged. Even if she couldn't get away, someone would surely come along soon. He wouldn't shoot unless he had to. That wasn't what this was about. It wasn't having her dead, it was about making his lies true. He wanted her to look crazy. He wanted Christine to think he'd been right all along. He was going to push her over the rail like he must have pushed Nan, and make Christine think she'd jumped.

Well, her daughter wasn't going to live with that. Marty wasn't going over alive. He would have to shoot her first.

He continued pushing from behind, and as she struggled to break free, he tripped over the side of a chaise lounge. They both fell to the plastic-matted deck beside the chaise, but he was on his feet quickly in front of her pulling her by the hair across the mat on her knees. She could see his free hand now. It wasn't holding a gun, it was holding a mini flashlight! Marty screamed and rammed his crotch with her head. As the group from Sun Deck came running down two flights of stairs, Floyd released her hair and ran into the elevator.

When the young people arrived at her side, Marty was sitting on the deck with her head in the chaise.

"Are you okay?"

"Was that you screaming?"

"What's wrong?"

Marty looked up. There were three men and three women, all about Christine's age. "Would you call the captain? No. Wait. Will you walk me to my cabin? I'll call him myself."

"Sure, but what happened?" One of the young women was sitting on the chaise now, patting Marty's hair.

"I was attacked."

"Oh my God! By who?"

"A lunatic."

313

One of the young men put out a hand to help her to her feet, and Marty stood, shaking. "There's nobody around," he said, looking forward toward the buffet and back toward the elevators. "Should we call the police?"

"The captain *is* the police here."

The group followed Marty past the pool to the forward elevator, and got off with her on Baja Deck. There was no one in the corridor as they walked to her suite.

"What did he do to you?" one of the men asked.

"Well, he tried to make me jump off the ship."

She noticed a disbelieving glance pass between her questioner and another of the men.

"It was my ex-husband."

"Why would he do that? I mean, why would he want you to jump?"

Marty sighed. Her neck stung, and she was still wiping tears from her face.

"Because he's crazy. That's all. That's the only reason."

The group was silent. Marty asked, and learned that they'd heard nothing except her scream, and had seen nothing, only her.

One of the women offered to come in with her while she reported the attack. Marty thanked her, thanked them all, but said no. Her hand was shaking so badly that the girl had to help her slide the cruise card to unlock the suite. She locked the door and wedged the chair as soon as she got inside. Most of her lights were still on, and she turned on the rest. A quick check verified that both sets of sliding doors were locked.

Marty sat on her turned-down bed and fingered the chocolate treat on her pillow with shaking hands as she dialed the captain. She got his voicemail. There was a security number on her telephone, but she was not up to explaining this from scratch. She really couldn't think right now. She rang Garrett.

In less than five minutes, she saw him through her door's security peephole, and three seconds later, was sobbing in his arms.

"I'm so sorry, so sorry."

Garrett tried to sooth her, but she couldn't stop. She pulled away, suddenly angry.

"I told you."

"I know. I'm sorry."

She sat on the loveseat, face in her hands. He stood in front of her, patting her head, her shoulder, then knelt and pulled her hands from her face. There was a knock at the door.

"Security. I called them."

Garrett let the man and woman from ship security into the suite and Marty detailed the attack. Garrett, still standing, followed with an explanation of what she'd told him and the captain, and where the captain was with her local P.D.

"You need to find him. Start with this Venge character in 307."

The woman nodded, but the man looked doubtful.

315

"I'll wake Anthony if I have to," Garrett told him. "This can't wait. If Venge is in his stateroom, bring him past this door and Marty can ID."

"Hey, if he has a passport..." the man started.

"I don't care what he has. If Marty says he's Floyd, he's Floyd."

Garrett reached for the telephone.

"No. That's okay. We'll bring him out."

Garrett stood just outside the suite, ready to tap a signal for Marty as they brought Floyd by. Marty would not have to enter the hallway. The security officers were knocking on 307. Marty watched the back of Garrett's head, which seemed yards, rather than inches, away from the glass tunnel against her eye. She heard some conversation, then Garrett tapped. She could see only him. Then, one of the officers came into view, and Garrett motioned with his hand for Marty to open the door.

"He's not there. No one answered 307, so they checked inside. Nothing. He's already packed."

The officers were just down the hall, reading tags on the bags outside of 307.

"This one's for pickup at the terminal," the woman called, lifting a briefcase, and it's his."

Marty had noticed suitcases along the corridor, reminding her that cruise would end tomorrow and passengers were supposed to pack and put their bags outside their staterooms by 3 a.m. with airline tags attached. She walked with Garrett to the officer, and looked at the tag.

"Look at the fake name," she said. "R. E. Venge."

"This is one sick puppy," the male officer said.

"Open it," Garrett directed.

"Sorry Dr. Maxin. That I won't do without an order from the captain."

"Wait here."

Garrett took Marty's arm and they returned to her suite. He deadbolted the door and went directly to the phone. Marty listened as he talked with Anthony, who apparently agreed to come. He returned to the door, spoke briefly with the officers, then sat beside Marty on the loveseat.

"Jamie will wait for Anthony and they'll get Floyd. Suzanne's going down to my office for some medicine for you. Nothing you need to do now. Get some sleep."

The next half-hour was a whirl of activity as Anthony arrived and Garrett went into the hall to talk with him. When he came back into the suite, he brought Marty a glass of water and a tiny yellow pill. She held them.

"Did they open the briefcase?"

"Yes. Some underwear and Floyd's real identification. We got him."

"You got him?" Marty took the pill. "Where?"

"No, we don't have *him* yet. Just what we need to put him in the brig."

Marty wished she hadn't taken the pill.

"Don't worry. You aren't alone. Now, try and get some sleep."

He walked her into the bedroom and pulled back the covers.

"I'll be right here. I won't leave the suite."

Marty nodded. Garrett closed the curtain to the sitting room, checked the sliding door lock again, and pulled the verticals shut. Marty went into the bathroom and changed into a loose tee-shirt and lounging shorts, then slid into bed. Garrett kissed her forehead and walked out through the curtain.

She lay down and rested her head against the cool pillowcase, wondering if she'd moved the chocolate. She was too exhausted to check. She should pack and put her bags in the hallway. What would the tags say? Could this really be happening? What would happen to Floyd now? She tried not to care. She didn't want him hurt, but she knew she'd never be safe if he was free. Surely, they wouldn't let him go?

She wondered again what exactly the penalty was for using a fake passport. What if it *was* only a fine? But attempted murder, surely– My God! He really tried to kill me! He would have, and Christine would think–

But what if the police in Ft. Lauderdale didn't believe her? She started to hope that he *had* killed Nan. It didn't make sense, except for Nan's being a bride, but if he was guilty of murder, she wouldn't have to worry, and Christine– But Enrico– There was something. At the auction? Pill was powerful. Arms won't move. Should have asked...

In her dream, Marty pushed blobs of cold shiny dough from a spoon to an enormous cookie sheet. As soon as she slid the last one from her spoon, she started to even them out, taking a little pinch from this one and tapping it onto that. Suddenly, one moved beneath her fingers. Drawing back in horror, she saw them all start to shimmer and quiver. Then they began to wriggle blatantly, and for the first time, she noticed that each blob had two little front claws that they raised and lowered like tiny railroad crossing gates.

A boning knife lay beside the cookie sheet, and the only way to make the blobs stop, she realized, was to cut off their claws. Choking back squeamishness, she gripped the knife handle with one hand and the blade tip with the other to affect a guillotine and approached one at the edge of the tray. It slid from under the blade on her first try, but she pinned and sliced it cleanly on her second.

Blood spurted in a geyser over the front of the white t-shirt she was wearing, and she dropped the knife and pulled the front of the jersey out and away from her body. She knew immediately, when she saw the beautiful pattern the blood had made on her t-shirt, that this was art blood.

Christine rushed in with a stack of canvases from Bethany then, and said that before the art blood creatures died, they had to get the blood art from each of them in order to save Olivia, who was now back at Christine's house hiding all of her jewelry in the folds of Christine's new towels.

22

Day Fifteen, Coming Into Home Port,

Ft. Lauderdale, Florida

A small noise from the mattress, not a squeak exactly, more like a tiny gasp, combined with a definite tug of the blanket and told her someone was in bed beside her. At first, Marty couldn't open her eyes. If she went back to sleep, they might go away. Maybe she was *still* asleep? She went over the dream she'd just left, the art blood dream. It made sense. Then she heard the breathing. Someone *was* here, inches away, just behind her back, and she was definitely awake. She remembered. Garrett. Had he gotten into her bed?

Quickly, she turned, opening her eyes—wide— scooting toward the edge of the mattress as she did so. A clump of orangey-red hair showed from the top of the covers and she jumped to her feet beside the bed.

Truce rolled over.

"Oh. Sorry. Did I scare you?"

Marty stood with her mouth open and Truce raised herself on her elbows.

"Calm down. It's okay. Only me. Sorry. Jeez."

"What are you doing here?"

"Babysitting ya'll."

Truce sat and situated the covers around her waist.

"They got Floyd. Garrett had to leave. He was afraid you'd wake up alone and be afraid. That damn loveseat is too short to sleep on. I didn't think you'd mind."

"Oh. No." Marty sat on the edge of the bed. That's okay. Thanks. They got Floyd?"

"Yeah. Garrett said he gave you a pill. You were dead out. I didn't think you'd wake up."

Marty shivered. Pulled a blanket up to her shoulders.

"That's okay. I'm still foggy. I was having a dream, I think I know..." She shook her head to clear it. "What happened with Floyd?"

"Garrett said he attacked you."

"He did. Oh my God."

Marty wrapped the blanket around her front and rocked a little, remembering the horror. Truce patted her shoulder.

"Up on Riviera. He tried to make me jump over the side. He had a gun, but he didn't. It was just a flashlight, but I thought..."

"That bastard! Lousy creep! You should have thrown him over!"

"I wish I could have, I would have."

"Jesus. How'd he get on? I thought they were sure he left at Ft. Lauderdale."

Marty explained about the fake name and recounted the attack.

"Wonder where they took him?" she added.

322

"That's the last thing you need to worry about." Truce sounded exasperated. "I told you, you need to look out for yourself."

"I'm worried that Christine…"

"Like I said. Christine has her own life now. It's not her fault her dad's a creep. And it's not yours either. I wish you'd *get* that."

"Well, I'm just thinking, you know, if her father is in jail…"

Truce glared. Then she yawned.

"You should go back to sleep. It's not even five. Want me to move back to the living room?"

"No. That's okay. You sleep awhile. I think I'll get some coffee. I feel drugged."

"Don't you leave this cabin!"

"Don't worry. You sleep. I'll just be on the balcony. Clear my head."

Truce looked a little uncertain, but she yawned again and snuggled down into the blankets."

Truce was snoring, the sun was just peeking over the horizon, and Marty's mind finally cleared as she rode her plastic balcony chair into Port Everglades at Ft. Lauderdale. Home port.

But not her home. She didn't know what would happen next, but she didn't want to leave the anonymity, or the possibilities, of the sea. If it could be arranged, she knew she would not be disembarking with the others.

That arrangement would be possible, she believed, but there was also other business. There was no telling what might happen to Floyd now. He might even find a way out of this.

Partly in an effort to take her mind off Floyd, and partly as a result of the strange dream, she'd decided that Bethany Pumphrey's being a "brilliant art conservator" figured in Nan's disappearance. She was certain.

Marty was going to see the captain. Floyd had been arrested, and God knew what lies he'd be telling by now. Her immediate job was to make sure he stayed arrested. The bite mark on her shoulder was proof. Visible. That, the false passport, and the Crafton police log would surely be evidence. And if he *had* killed Nan Brasheer...No, for Christine's sake she wouldn't hope that.

She knew she would be taken seriously this time, and she would not leave the captain's office until the police were summoned and had all the facts.

She peeked in on Truce, who was completely buried in the blankets now, scribbled a thank you note, and left the suite. Her tennis shoes beat an I-can-do-this rhythm along the deck. She didn't bother knocking when she reached Anthony's office, but shoved the mahogany door open and strode to the front of his desk. Tilting her head to show the mark, she described Floyd's attack, "for the record," as an attempt on her life.

Anthony stood and took Marty's hand.

"We have him. There has never been a passport issued for Raymond Venge. And look here, at his signature."

He produced a cruise document and Marty looked. She nodded.

"Yes. R. E. Venge. Revenge," the captain said.

"I can't tell you how sorry we are to have missed that."

"Well," Marty leaned a hip against the side of his desk, "I'm afraid that's not all you missed."

She proceeded to present her amazing accusation of Bethany and Joseph.

He didn't seem at all surprised.

"Avarice and lust," he smiled. Two of the big seven."

Marty followed his eyes to her right and blinked. Nan Brasheer was seated primly in the dark strawberry wing chair. Marty started toward her and sunk dumbly into its mate.

"We'll let our chef stew a bit longer in the brig with Mr. Arkus for now," Anthony continued, "and let the Ft. Lauderdale police bring him the news du jour."

"That being?" Marty directed herself to Nan, but the captain answered.

"That being that you are almost absolutely correct. The talented Bethany has been copying works from the Brasheer collection for years. At least twelve, with about that many paintings sold."

Anthony's beard bobbed rapidly as he continued.

"Her congressman thought she was only doing it to provide him with the style he was accustomed to, at her place."

Marty listened, but her eyes were drawn back to Nan.

"Did he know?"

Nan didn't answer, but gave Marty the defiant look most often seen by mothers of teenage girls.

"Richard was fine with Bethany's making copies for her place," Anthony said. But he had no idea his hard-earned art collection at home in Florida was being replaced with imitations like the ones in Bethany's collection in Virginia."

"Painting by painting," Marty said, nodding.

"Copies of copies. The real works of art, as you've deduced, sold for enough to keep Bethany in brushes and Joseph in island visits."

Nan cleared her throat. Her voice was melodic.

"Apparently this all started when Richard was married to his first wife."

She sounded like that explained it all and made it perfectly reasonable that her groom had continued his affair into his marriage to her.

Marty looked quickly at the captain.

"Two of everything," he muttered. Some men are like that."

He shrugged his big eyebrows, and he and Marty both looked toward Nan.

Nan smiled. Facing Marty, she tilted her head sympathetically, as though she didn't expect a woman with no Capitol Hill experience to grasp such high concept.

You got that right, Marty thought. She wanted to feel happy for Nan, happy that she was alive, but the woman disgusted her so, and the fact that Floyd had obviously not killed her... What was she thinking! Had she really wanted Christine's father to be a murderer?

"Mrs. Brasheer has faced quite a bit this week." Anthony turned to Marty. "As you thought, Enrico did tell her about the art scheme."

"On Orient Beach."

"Yes. He asked her to meet him at the Orient Beach restaurant for a business discussion about her husband. He told her the whole thing then, even pointed Joseph out. His motive was what you surmised, to induce Nan to leave her husband, thereby freeing Joseph."

"But Nan wasn't leaving," Marty interjected.

"Absolutely not. But she did want the art."

Nan made a closed-lip smile and reached to tuck her hair up behind one ear. Her silver hoop earring clinked against its matching bracelet. She looked bored.

"Of course."

Now Marty smiled and shook her head slightly.

"And Enrico couldn't help her with that."

"No. Enrico is not a criminal. He got caught up over his heart."

"And ended up over his head?"

Marty knew she was supposed to say that.

Anthony stroked his beard.

"And they made the latest exchange—a painting of three nudes wrestling a horse in the surf—at St. Thomas the day I saw them there."

Marty looked from Nan to the captain.

"It's the one we saw at their house. At the tea. Richard had the painting on this ship. Bethany dropped him off right at the dock."

Now Marty starred at Nan.

"You were by yourself with our tour. At Magens Bay. You were on the jitney and you shared our cab. Right?"

Nan didn't respond, and didn't meet her eyes.

"Did you see Richard there with Bethany? In the Jeep? Were you following them?"

This seemed to crack Nan's veneer of confidence.

"No. I mean, yes, I saw them. But I wasn't following."

Nan's words were flat, but Marty saw a sadness creep into her eyes.

"I thought he was on the scuba thingy."

She made an obvious attempt to smile and failed.

They were silent for a moment. Then Anthony spoke.

"Somehow, Joseph got onboard during our costume ball. Enrico probably helped him. And we can assume that Joseph or Enrico did put the gun charm on your daughter's necklace. Joseph knew that Olivia told Christine her story, so they probably thought it would implicate Olivia and keep the congressman quiet."

"That's exactly what it did do. It made him think Olivia was unbalanced. It made me think that."

"That's right. Actually, you had it all figured out."

"Well, no," Marty said. "That would require a dead Nan rather than a live one."

Just like Floyd's going to jail forever for murder would, she thought.

Beyond Nan's head, Marty saw Anthony's secretary open the outer office door and admit Richard Brasheer, who was apparently going to wait for his wife.

"A live Nan," she looked straight at Nan, who pat-covered a yawn, bracelet jangling, "would protect her lifestyle at all costs. And since so much of that depends on Richard's reputation," now Marty focused her gaze on Nan's silver-charmed wrist, "there'd be a real benefit to her in discrediting Olivia."

Marty rose and walked to Nan's chair. She grabbed Nan's braceleted wrist and jerked it up to the startled woman's face.

"You put the charm on Christine's necklace."

It was a cold statement. Marty dropped the jangling wrist and backed away.

Nan started an incredulous laugh, but just then, Richard stepped up behind her. He had been standing quietly just inside the captain's door.

"Nan?"

Her face crumpled when she heard her husband. She didn't turn to face him. Richard walked around the chair and crouched to hold both of Nan's hands.

"Is that right? Did you put the gun on her daughter's necklace?" He seemed to be addressing a small child.

She made a seething hiss. "Yes. That *is* right. That little bitch could ruin everything, and you're too stupid to know it. You're blind to it. Somebody has to protect you."

Marty stepped forward again. "Christine didn't–"

"Not Christine, that little bitch Olivia." Her voice rose. She faced her husband. "I saw you with her!"

Richard flung her hands down violently, stood and backed away. "She's my *daughter*."

"Daughter? You can't live like you live and have a *daughter*!" Nan was venomous. "The rest of it's bad enough. Then you think you can risk everything with this anti-stalking crap because of *her*!" She pounded her fists on the chair. "I'm supposed to hold my head up in Washington when everybody knows about Bethany. Well, fine. I knew that before. The big power thing. You *need* an extra woman. You *need* an extra everything. Fine. But you don't need a daughter, and you don't need to let some bastard child mess up our lives. You don't need to ruin our future for her. You don't need to push laws that nobody wants—that nobody with power—nobody like you—wants—" she was sobbing now, sputtering the words—"just for that bastard kid."

"That creep was stalking her. He tried to run her down with a car. He put a gun charm in her locker. He's a threat to her life." Richard was answering Nan, but directing himself to Anthony, and now he turned back to his wife.

"Power is just a tool you use to get what you want. I want things for my family. I want things for you. I want safety for Olivia."

"Safety for her while she tells everyone her sad story." Nan gestured toward Marty. "I heard them talking in the taxi."

Richard looked at Marty now. She started to explain, but Nan cut her off.

"Pete's no threat to Olivia. Annie's son put that charm in her locker. I paid him to do it."

"Who's Annie?" Marty was trying to follow. Richard ignored her, but Nan answered.

"Richard's housekeeper in D.C. Her son was in school with Olivia."

Anthony had gotten to his feet, and now Richard sat at the captain's desk and put his head in his hands.

"These gun charms. They go with that bracelet, don't they? It's the one your father gave you."

"He gave me the gun charm when I learned to shoot. I was fifteen, and I lost it—or thought I lost it. My mother got me another one so he wouldn't find out. Then we found the first one, so I had two."

"And you put one—had Annie's son put one—in Olivia's locker," Marty understood now, "because you hoped your husband would think his daughter was disturbed instead of thinking she was in trouble and needed his help."

"You have no idea what trouble this law is. There's virtually no support. It could ruin him. It could actually prevent reelection." Nan had drawn herself up, and she spoke with confidence in the rationality of her explanation.

Marty shook her head. "And you put the other charm on Christine's necklace for the same reason?" Nan nodded.

"But how? How did you get into our room? Our safe? How did you even know it was there?"

"Look," Nan actually smiled now, "it was just a whim. Of course I didn't invade your room! I would never do such a thing! I was in the beauty shop when you were showing the necklace off. It was on my bracelet that day." She leaned toward Marty conspiratorially. "I've been wearing this goddamn bracelet every day. You'd think he'd notice. But I knew he wouldn't. His head's in a tunnel."

"But where did you...?"

"You didn't even notice me; you were so thrilled about your daughter and her wedding. You were bragging! When you went to change out of your smock. I sat down right next to your bag. I just reached in and opened the box."

It was astonishing. Nan seemed to think Marty would be favorably impressed.

"They're good quality. Each charm has a little clasp." She held up her wrist for Marty to admire. "They slide right on." She smiled at Marty again. "I'm sorry you got caught up in our trouble."

Marty shook her head and smiled back. "I'm sorry somebody *didn't* throw you overboard."

Anthony spoke now. "Well, Enrico didn't throw her overboard. People don't *do* that on the *Mare Majestic*," he added, with a wry note. "And Joseph didn't either. But he did get her off the ship without turning a single head. Who would think that a pirate leaving a costume party with Jackie Kennedy was unusual? Who would know the knife wasn't plastic?"

Marty was confused again. "But why did Joseph take her off the ship? And where?"

"Enrico told him Nan knew about the stolen art, and Joseph realized what a foolish mistake Enrico had made by telling her." Anthony rubbed his beard. "Probably realized what a foolish mistake *he'd* made in telling Enrico. He took her over to St. Martin, and he and his fence friend parked her at a hotel, tried to scare her, brainwash her a bit. When that didn't work, he offered to cut her in," Anthony said. "She agreed so they would let her go."

"And they did," Marty said.

Now Anthony leaned back against his desk. "Well, not then. They apparently hadn't decided. Nan told them she needed sleep. She called for a ride while Joseph and his friend went downstairs to a bar to talk it over and decide whether they should trust her."

"Called for a ride? Oh, well, I suppose—"

"Yes. This is a lady with political connections. They get limos quickly. And flights to Ft. Lauderdale on an hour's notice."

Nan smiled serenely. Marty had an urge to spit in her face.

Anthony ignored her. "She went home—she said she went to count the paintings—and went to bed. Figured it wouldn't hurt Richard to worry awhile. She boarded this morning to tell him, and they came here together."

Anthony turned to the congressman. "Richard, why don't you take Nan down to your suite and rest while you wait for me. We're starting to disembark, and I need a few minutes with Marty."

But he continued talking. "Joseph got scared when he heard Nan was thought to be overboard. He didn't know

333

she hadn't returned to the ship, wasn't sure what Enrico might have done. He made up the story about Enrico mentioning it before she was missing."

"I see," Marty said. "Just in case."

"Right. He didn't want to be implicated in murder if Enrico had gone that far."

The congressman appeared to be in a daze. His wife led him out.

"I suppose he can write off any chance of reelection," Marty said.

"Maybe. Maybe not."

They sat quietly for a few minutes.

Marty sighed. "Well, I guess this clears up the gun charm."

"Hard to believe people," Anthony said.

"I know. It's a page one story. Political scandal and everything."

Concern flickered in Anthony's eyes. "You know, speaking of stories, your Blue Mountain Lodge story was great. Majestic would certainly welcome a person of your talent, not to mention detective skills, to handle port information. Our passengers are becoming more sophisticated travelers, and, frankly, the ports have become less appealing—thanks to ships like ours. Passengers are always looking for new sightseeing and activity ideas. They want native, out-of-the-way experiences. You write beautiful descriptions. Would you consider doing more brochures for us?"

"That's something I hoped to discuss," Marty said. "But first, what's going to happen to Floyd?"

"We'll meet with the Ft. Lauderdale police in about an hour. The passport issue will involve the FBI. Someone from one of those groups will remove him from the ship."

"But will they take him to jail? Lock him up?"

Anthony smiled sadly. "I'm not sure, but I doubt it. At least he will have a chance to post bail. Then, I'm sure there will be a hearing of some sort, maybe a jury trial. Depends."

"Will they call it attempted murder?" Marty looked straight into the captain's eyes. "That's what it really was."

"I believe you. But I'm not sure. Our security took statements from the people who were on the scene. I've read them. If Floyd is charged on that, it will be your word against his."

"So, you're saying he could get off with a fine or something, a suspended sentence?"

"I just don't know Marty. I really don't."

"Does the job come with room and board?"

"That depends." Anthony grinned with his whole face. His beard bobbed. "Do you like the Mediterranean? We reposition after this cruise and spend the summer there."

Marty pretended to consider carefully.

"What's the salary?"

"It's excellent. In addition to meals and lodging, I can give you a hundred dollars for each article. You'll probably do one or two a week."

"Sorry," she bluffed. "I can't do it for less than two-hundred dollars per. Otherwise, I'll have to consider returning to news."

She thought she saw a smirk, but Anthony put his hand over his mouth and nodded. "Okay. Two hundred for each article. Nine-month contract."

She smiled, thinking nine months should be just the right amount of time to give birth to a new life. "When do you leave?"

"Tonight."

"Good thing I didn't pack."

Marty took what seemed like a hundred pages of paperwork back to her suite to complete. Truce was dressed and preparing to leave.

"I'm so glad you made it back. I didn't want to go without seeing you, but they're kicking us off."

Marty hugged her. "Give me your address."

Truce pulled a card that advertised the "Donna Bed and Breakfast" from her purse, hugged Marty again and opened the door.

"Nan Brasheer is alive. I'll have to tell you the rest later. I'll write."

"Alive? What do you mean?" She closed the door. "How do you know? Did they find her?"

"I saw her. She was sitting in the captain's office! You have to go. I know. I will write. I'll tell you the whole thing."

Truce opened the door again. Then she stopped and hugged Marty again. "You better. You know… well, guess this sounds terrible, but I was kind of hoping your ex—"

"Had killed Nan. I know. Me too." Marty laughed now. "But I don't have to worry about him anymore, I'll be long gone."

"You hope. How long will he go to jail? I mean, he *will* go to jail, won't he? For attempted murder?"

Marty stopped laughing. "I don't know. We'll have to prove it."

"What do you mean, prove it? He did it!"

"I know."

The ship's warning horn sounded.

"Hey! You really better get out of here."

The cabin steward came in just as Truce, muttering about being better off with a vibrator that opens jars, left, and Marty tried to explain that she was joining the staff and wouldn't be leaving the ship. Most passengers were lined up to disembark and he had been waiting to have the housekeeper prepare her room for new folks to occupy in the afternoon. Marty remembered to tip him and wondered what the protocol would be now. Oh well, play it by ear. Coast.

"By the way," she said, pretending to search a nightstand drawer, "do you know Paras, the steward on Caribe Deck?"

"Yes, yes. I know him."

"Will he be repositioning with the ship?"

"No, his contract end this cruise. But if you have something for him…," he indicated the envelope she'd just handed him.

Marty winced. "No. I just wondered."

The steward, obviously confused, left.

She tried to ring Garrett, but he wasn't in his stateroom. Then she started filling out forms. When the task was finished, she was about to start writing about the parrotfish poop on Cozumel, but the steward knocked.

"Captain say you move."

"Oh." She was disappointed. "To where?"

"He didn't say. Only to pack you."

"I can pack me."

"No." The young man smiled. "Commodore Mascellino like you to rest, he say. I will pack well. You just take from safe."

"Oh, I know you will." Marty remembered how she had returned to her stateroom to find her jersey nightshirt folded on her pillow in the shape of a star. Not just a Paras talent.

"If you're moving me out, how will I know where to go?"

"Check with purser after five o'clock. Enjoy day!"

Marty took her jewelry, notebooks, and photographs from the safe and stuffed them, with her purse, into her blue beach bag. Then she looked around quickly for anything she might need for the day. She'd had too much sun on Cozumel, and swimming wouldn't be a good idea. There was nothing else she could think of, so she brushed her teeth and hair, left everything as it was, hoisted her laptop and beach bag, and said goodbye to the luxurious mini-suite that had been home for more than a week.

She'd probably end up in crew's quarters, or an inside cabin several decks down. She should have realized, should have negotiated that, but she didn't really care. She was crossing the Atlantic for the first time in her life to begin a Mediterranean itinerary. What was that saying about ships? Something that helped her find the courage to leave Floyd, to stop playing defense and start playing offense. That's right, she remembered, the harbor.

"A ship is safe in the harbor, but that's not what ships are built for."

Marty took her favorite chair on Promenade and settled back. She was on the water and unafraid. Passengers were disembarking and there'd be no need to make sure Floyd was among them. He'd be escorted off by the police; maybe even the FBI if passport forgery threw him into their bailiwick. Wherever they took him, he wouldn't be out in time for the repositioning cruise. And she intended to stand beside the gangway and watch every single passenger come aboard.

Why were people so crazy? Floyd, wanting to discredit her in their daughter's eyes, even willing to kill her, to avenge her escape from his control. Nan, wanting to discredit Olivia in her father's eyes. Enrico, wanting to make Richard look bad to Nan. Joseph was just a greedy creep. His goal in life must be finding clever ways to live without working. And Bethany! A good mother, probably. Not a likely art thief. But how could anybody have an affair with a married man for more than sixteen years? And how could she possibly take his finally divorcing his wife and then marrying someone other than her? Maybe she had a right to trick him with his selfish two-of-everything art.

But Bethany would surely pay. Art forgery was a big deal, and the fact that she had transferred the forged art on the high seas, so to speak, probably made it much bigger. Bethany, unlike Floyd, who had attempted murder, was extremely likely to spend a long time in jail. As was Joseph, for kidnapping and art theft, under the same conditions.

And where would that leave poor Olivia? With mother and stepfather in jail, a father who had to hide her, and a truly evil stepmother?

Enrico would at least lose his job as well as his love, and as accessory after the fact to art theft, might even join Joseph and Bethany behind bars.

The cruise line would suffer too; and Anthony, because it had all happened on his watch. Only Richard and Nan were likely to skate, although Richard's career might be harmed.

Richard and Nan were like Floyd. Floyd knew what he was doing. It would be her word against his, just like it had always been. Even if, by some miracle, he never bothered her again, he had, in a real sense, taken her life.

As crazy as he was, Floyd had cleverness enough to twist his knowledge of the law to make the system work for him. And Richard, a louse who had screwed up the lives of at least three women and a girl, had the means to manipulate the law itself.

Wouldn't that be nice? If your life isn't fair, you just pass a law to make it fair. Instead of being a martyr like Grandma Martha, you carve out your own life, make it what *you* need it to be, the way Grandma Mary did. You just make your own fairness and live with it. Your own justice.

She considered the possibility. It had never occurred to Marty before that she could create her own justice, but she saw it now, and she saw a way. Some truth would have to be sacrificed, yes, but wouldn't a greater truth be served? She was angry, but this was not a simple thirst for vengeance. The object of the game was survival. Floyd, not she, had arranged the pieces on the playing board, had left himself vulnerable to attack. It made sense and felt, well, *just*. She would do it unburdened by guilt.

It was now or never. Marty gathered her things, slung the bag over her shoulder, and walked resolutely back to the captain's office.

Epilogue

Garrett stood by the rail on Promenade, watching the steady stream of passengers disembark at Port Everglades, when Marty lugged her things, now including Mediterranean guidebooks from the captain's library, to her favorite wooden deck chair.

"Welcome aboard!"

She stacked the books neatly, moved to the rail, and took his extended hand. He placed his free hand over hers. His warmth reinforced her strength. They watched the last trickle of passengers bounce down the gangway. Truce and Donna spotted them. Donna waved and Truce blew a kiss.

"Now there's a lady who's finally learned how to vacation," Marty said. "Bet she'll be back next year."

Nan and Richard Brasheer attracted the attention of some reporters at the dock below, and Marty shook her head as she and Garrett watched the campaign resume.

Congressman Richard Brasheer was to take credit, with Majestic's Commodore Anthony Mascellino, for tracking down his own stolen art and catching the "thief"— Floyd Arkus, AKA Raymond E. Venge, lawyer turned computer salesman turned art forger, from Pittsburgh. Floyd's only possible defense would be that he had forged a passport and was traveling under a fake name in order to stalk and murder his ex-wife.

This kind of publicity would help insure the congressman's next election, and his important work on anti-stalking legislation could—and, as he'd assured Marty, *would*—continue. Nan's silver bracelet glinted in the sun as she turned to wave at everyone and no one.

"Enrico is packing. There'll be a big retirement sendoff for him at the Florida office." Garrett smiled and shook his head. "Too bad Anthony and I will be at sea and have to miss it."

"You got that right," Marty agreed, smirking. "Maybe they'll invite Joseph."

"Anthony's on the phone with Joseph and Bethany now. I suspect their cooperation will be gracious."

"Oh yes. No more money from the fake art, but no jail either. Sounds like a good deal to me."

"And don't forget, the anti-stalking work goes on."

"That's true." Now Marty smiled sincerely.

"Bethany and Olivia will be glad of that. And glad to know one stalker has been stopped. With their help."

"Nobody can be more glad than I am." Garrett squeezed Marty's arm. He leaned to kiss her mouth. She wrapped her arms around his waist. His hands slid up into her hair, and his lips down her neck. For a second, Marty thought the ship was underway. Her entire body pressed against him. "Tonight?" he asked.

"Oh, yes!" she gasped. Then felt panicked at what she was promising. This wasn't practice.

Anthony appeared at the top of the gangway. He shook hands with two men in dark suits. The FBI agents flanked Floyd, apparently handcuffed with a jacket draped over his wrists at waist front. Marty was surprised to feel so little remorse at this sight. Art theft. Art forgery. International crime. Crime on the high seas. Much stronger charges than passport forgery and the assault Floyd had described—modestly, sheepishly, macho-man-to-macho-man—to Anthony as "a love bite." Federal offences that could, would—put the man in that frame away for many years. Well, this was justice, and it might be a better reality for Christine to face than the truth.

"It's a great life," Marty said, wiping a tear she hoped would be her last, "if you don't weaken."

"Once around the ship?" Garrett offered his arm. "I promise we won't leave the deck."

They stopped on the other side and shielded their eyes to gaze into the bright Atlantic.

"I'm sorry," he said. "I didn't believe Enrico would, could, kill someone. But in the middle of that, I guess I didn't really believe how bad this thing with your ex was. I tend to think everything women say is exaggerated."

"Not your most endearing quality," Marty said.

"*You* are my most endearing quality."

He's good, she thought, but she couldn't help smiling.

"Maybe not tonight," she said quietly. But maybe someday."

She saw his rueful smile. Could tell he knew immediately what she was talking about.

"Fair enough."

Garrett walked her back, then left to attend to medical forms for transatlantic passengers. Marty settled herself in the deck chair and opened her laptop. She had decided how best to handle the situation with her daughter, but knew it wouldn't be perfect. Maybe justice never was.

Dear Christine,

Guess what? Not only is the missing-you-know-who alive and well, it turns out she was responsible for both charms! She may skate on this one, but justice, as they say, has been done. I'm sorry to be so cryptic. Please put your curiosity on hold, and don't ask me to explain further. This is not something I can discuss before we meet in person, but I needed to reassure you that your young friend is and will be safe, as are you.

I pray this finds you and Sam happily settling into your new home. What a wonderful couple you are! I anticipate a future filled with great joy for both of you.

For me as well. There is much I can't tell you yet, but will by next year. I hope to visit you and Sam in Raleigh for a few days then. In the meantime, I ask you to trust me completely, as I absolutely know I can trust you. Whatever you hear about, or from, your father, I swear to you, this justice is for the best.

I've been thinking lately about Grandma's responsibility for your Uncle Teddy. You are right about that. She was coping the best way she could, but of course, it wasn't my fault in any way, and they were wrong to let me feel that. I was wrong to imagine responsibility; I was only three. Honey, I hope you realize you were never responsible for anything bad in terms of your dad and me. Nothing! Not as unborn, infant, child, teen, or young adult. You aren't now, and you never will be. Please know that.

I plan to visit Grandma and Grandpa soon. I have a new job that should keep me busy, and lots of hope for the future. It's the job we discussed, but I'd rather not broadcast that. If anyone should ask, you can simply (and honestly) say that I'm writing in Europe this year. Meanwhile, Christine, you get out there, and be the mightiest apple tree that ever grew!

Love and God bless,

Mom

Hitting "send," Marty closed the computer and moved to the ship's rail. The line where sky met sea seemed a thousand miles away. Tomorrow will be May Day, she thought, smiling at memories of a little girl hooking homemade baskets of flowers over neighbors' front doorknobs, and soon we'll face a new millennium. She leaned forward from the high deck to look down at the undulating sea.

She was almost young, and midday sun made green sparkles on the water.

ACKNOWLEDGMENTS

Writing may be a solitary pursuit, but it sometimes takes the proverbial village to share it with the world. Years ago, an editorial assistant at Random House scribbled a note at the bottom of my first rejection: "This is much better than most of what we find in slush. Keep trying." Memory of that note made me pull this, my first manuscript, out of its digital drawer for one last revision this year.

Teakettle Junction Productions owner Jason Frye's editing and encouragement improved on that revision and shored up my courage.

Thanks to my writing friends: Jim Collins, prolific author of thrillers and a beautiful short story collection; lyrical short story writer Linda Thomas; and "keep writing" Lee Ewing; fellow renegades who broke from a large pack of Wilmington writers to form Cape Fear Fiction. Linda, Jim, and I have been beating each other's prose into submission ever since. Gratitude also, for the encouragements of recent members Chris Hague and Suzanne Grosser. Suzanne provided the title for this book. Thanks to Paula Ray, the most generous writer I've met, Washington Independent Writers, and splinter group (do you see a pattern here?) Reston Daytime Fiction, later Women Who Write. For years, Ruth Everhart, Judith Tabler, Susan Okula, and Sarah Snyder Plant gathered around my table, providing critique, drinking ice water from cartoon glasses, and refusing to give up. Sarah's plot twist idea made all the difference for my Marty.

Appreciation also goes to my more-creative-than-she-knows engineer daughter Kathy McClintic and movie-set-decorating son Bob Smith for their encouragement, and to stepson Dan Cross, back-up tech expert.

Much gratitude to my husband, IT guy, long-suffering reader, comforter, and supporter Dave Cross; to my father, Bob Damits, who thrilled and traumatized my childhood with selections such as "The Cremation of Sam Magee;" and to my cherished, late mother Sally Damits, who read to me daily "just one more time." She loved the books of Marcia Davenport and Pearl S. Buck, but I like to think she would have enjoyed "The Art of Escape" as well.

I owe the greatest debt though, to my daughter Sherry Butler Fabrizi and her Crafton Book Club, Elsa Norris and our Book Club in Northern Virginia, Jenny Widdowson in England, Min O'Burns in Reston, Diane White in Wilmington, and all of my book-loving family members and friends. These constant readers help me remember the most important element in this process.

ABOUT THE AUTHOR

Linda Cross lives with her husband Dave and a dog named Yankee in Wilmington, North Carolina. This is her first completed novel. For further information, write to risinghopepublishing@gmail.com

CPSIA information can be obtained at www.ICGtesting.com
Printed in the USA
LVOW12s1551110214

373261LV00001B/282/P

2/14 R